SHOT OF TEQUILA

a thriller

JA Konrath

I got a bottle of tequila, baby, who needs friends?

—Concrete Blonde

CHICAGO

1993

CHAPTER 1

Winter meant death in Chicago.

Death to the homeless, turned away from overcrowded shelters and forced to stuff their ragged clothes with day-old newspaper.

Death to the motorists, skidding on filthy, snow-covered highways into the paths of trucks and guard rails and head-crunching support posts.

Death to the elderly, slipping on sidewalks and shattering brittle bones, and to the poor, unable to pay both the food bill and the gas bill.

Death to Billy Chico.

Chico was a small-time hustler and big-time loser who liked to bet the ponies and hit women. He was more successful at the latter. On his more reflective days—and there weren't many—Chico figured he'd lost more than eighty thousand dollars in the ten or so years he'd been placing bets. He would have lost even more if the *puta* he married hadn't sent the Man after him for child support. Chico knew the kid wasn't really his. That child was bug-eyed, bare-assed ugly, and couldn't have had any of Chico's genes in his roly-poly body. Chico often compared himself to the ponies he loved to throw money after; sleek and muscled and hung, with a mane of gorgeous black and eyes that could stare through you, sister. A thoroughbred if there ever was.

Unfortunately, the thoroughbred just caught a bad tip, and couldn't cover the bet he'd made with his very connected bookie. Two thousand bucks worth of bad tip, baby, five weeks of factory wages. A debt he couldn't pay, especially since he had to fork out cash for rent, the bills, and child support for that skank and her ugly brat.

Chico, in a word, was powerfucked. And getting more PFed by the minute, because his marker was due and Marty the Maniac had definitely alerted his goons to begin collection proceedings.

Collection proceedings didn't involve friendly chit-chat over coffee. They involved hurt. Lots of hurt. And Chico was far too fine to have anything broken, scarred, burned, or severed.

So Billy Chico took his last sixty bucks, bought a piece from a runner with gang ties, and went out to rob Teddy's Liquors on 23rd and Cal.

It was cold, cold enough to freeze the juice that your brain floats in. Chico wore his trademark black leather jacket with the fringes hanging from the sleeves and he looked fly, even though it kept him warm for shit. The liquor store he picked was three blocks from his apartment; one with late-night hours and a constant flow of business. Not a corner store that just sold beer by the bottle, but a classy joint that had all that expensive wine and gift packs and overpriced whiskey in ceramic jugs shaped like Corvettes. Fancy shit like that. Chico figured on one of the busiest liquor days of the year—Super Bowl Sunday—the place would have at least two k in green. He might even come out a couple bucks ahead on the deal.

Billy Chico stopped at the front door, his skinny ass cheeks knocking together like two frozen oranges, an icy hand wrapped around the butt of the .32 in his jacket pocket. He hesitated. Having grown up on the streets, fear was something common to Chico, so fear wasn't what gave him pause. But staring at his reflection in the heavy glass door made him realize he'd forgotten to bring something to cover his face. The asshole in the store could identify him. Murder never occurred to Chico, because that was for psychos. He was too good-looking to do hard time. Prison scared him, almost more than that crazy bookie did.

Almost.

He considered turning back when he remembered the mesh hair net covering his wavy mane. With a nervous giggle he stretched it down over his face, staring out through fishnet.

In and out. Should be quick. He took a deep breath of cold city air and pushed the door open, rushing in with his weapon pointed.

"Gimme all the money! Now!"

The proprietor was an old white dude, skinny and small with tiny little Santa Claus glasses. He held up his hands and looked appropriately terrified.

"Move your ass, old man!"

Chico thrust the revolver into the prune's face, letting him see death through the half-inch hole in the barrel.

The old man stood stock-still, not moving an inch.

"What the hell is your problem, Grandpa? You deaf? I said get the goddamn money pronto or I'll shoot off your head!"

The old man remained where he was.

Chico stole a nervous glance at the door to see if any customers were coming in, then got closer to the old man, cocking his gun to show he wasn't playing around.

"I can't open the safe," the old man said.

"What?"

The old man pointed to the large sign sticking to the counter. Chico backed away and read the oversized words silently, even though his lips moved.

THE SAFE HAS A TIME LOCK AND CANNOT BE OPENED.

"What the fuck is a time lock?"

"Magnetic lock. Can only be opened in the morning at eight a.m." The old man swallowed. "You're welcome to wait around, if you want."

"Then gimme the cash register money!"

He pointed to another sign.

THE CASH REGISTER CONTAINS LESS THAN $50.

The .32 in Chico's hand felt heavy and foreign. His heart was beating in his throat. Even if he took the fifty, the gun cost him sixty, so he came out behind in the deal. What the hell should he do now? Leave and rob someone else? Or beat this old bastard senseless to see if he was lying?

The answer came to him in the shape of a champagne bottle. All Chico had to do was conk him on the head a few times with a magnum of *Totts,* then we'd see what was up with this time lock bullshit. Chico used his free hand to grab the handy bottle neck, holding the champagne like a club.

"You want to play rough, old man? I'll give you a punt-shaped head!"

A sound; the electronic bell attached to the front door, beeping when a customer left or came in. Billy Chico and the old man looked to see a short guy in a Blackhawks jacket enter.

"Get on the floor, corto!"

The short man gave Chico an even stare and stopped where he stood.

"On the goddamn floor or I'll blow your little head off!"

The man remained standing where he was. Weren't people afraid of guns anymore?

"Marty sent me to collect your debt, Billy," The short man had the low, steady voice of a talk radio jock.

"What the hell you think I'm trying to do here?" The sweat on Chico's body was a living thing, running over him in itchy waves.

The short man stood calmly, hands in his pockets.

"I'll wait. But you'd better hurry. You've been in here for a minute and forty-three seconds, and the owner there tripped his silent alarm right after you pulled your gun."

Chico began to shake like a withdrawing junkie.

"Give me the damn money, old man!"

"I can't. It's a time lock."

Chico threw the champagne at the old man, but it was lefty and he threw like a girl. The old man caught the bottle.

The short guy turned his ear to the front door, keeping both eyes on Chico. "Sirens coming this way."

"Shut up!"

Chico unconsciously pushed the hairnet up off his face and rubbed his forehead to think. No thoughts came, other than maybe gambling wasn't all it was cracked up to be.

"Better move your ass, Billy."

"I said shut up!"

The short man waited.

The old man behind the counter stared, probably memorizing Billy Chico's face.

Then Billy Chico made the biggest mistake of many big mistakes throughout his miserable little life. He began to swing his gun from the shop owner over to the short guy.

"Billy... don't."

Billy Chico hesitated. It was obvious he was leaving here empty handed. But he definitely wasn't going to leave with some broken fingers, or a busted arm or leg. He continued to bring the gun around, ready to shoot his way out of here if he had to.

"Drop it, Billy!"

The tone was so sudden, so commanding, that Billy Chico had to react. His brain offered three instantaneous choices: Drop the gun, wet his pants, or fire. Billy's finger began to pull the trigger.

He never got a chance to. In a blur the short guy whipped out two semi-automatic .45s from the pockets of his Starter jacket and fired sixteen shots into Billy Chico. His left hand put a controlled burst of eight into Billy's chest, and his right hand punched eight more into Billy's head and neck.

Billy Chico ended instantly. His heart never had a chance to stop beating, because it was carved out of his chest. His brain never had a chance to realize he was dead, because it got scrambled the same instant his heart was chewed away.

Chico's body jerked in electrical spasms and tangled itself in a cardboard display featuring several bikini-clad women holding beers. His body landed an instant before his gun clattered to the floor where he'd been previously standing.

The shop owner, who'd seen a few things in his day, wasn't sure whether to cheer or scream. The skinny man with the gun was scary, but it was a familiar kind of scary. In the almost three decades he'd been in business, he'd been robbed forty-six times, half of those within the last seven years as the neighborhood continued to decline. Junkies, gang members, ex-cons, and all shades of desperate men had walked into Teddy's Liquors looking to make a quick buck. The skinny guy wasn't an exception. He was part of a trend.

But this short guy with the two guns, this was something different. Something even scarier. When he killed the skinny man, his face had no expression. It didn't even look like he blinked. How can you shoot someone a dozen times and not even blink?

The old man forced a smile—something damn near impossible with his peripheral vision clogged red with spilled blood—and managed to sputter out, "Thanks, buddy."

The short man shook his head.

"I still have to collect his debt."

"But the safe is on a—"

The short guy placed the hot barrel of the .45 in front of his lips like a giant finger and said, "Shhh."

He pocketed the guns, and in three steps leapt the counter without touching it, jumping much higher than the old man thought possible. Within seconds he located the safe, in a cabinet under the cash register.

The sirens grew louder. The short guy stared at the safe for a long second.

"This isn't a time lock safe. This thing is older than I am."

The old man was too afraid to shrug, but he managed to sputter, "New safe costs a few thousand dollars. Sign was only $10.99."

"How about you give me the combination?"

The old man tried to swallow but he was all out of spit.

"The owner hasn't told it to me."

"Then how about give me your wallet?"

"My wallet?"

"Does that have a time lock too?"

The old man dug his wallet out with trembling hands and offered it up. The short guy avoided the money inside, instead removing the Driver's License.

"This is Teddy's Liquors, right?"

The old man nodded.

"Your name is Theodore. Is it worth having your fingers broken, Teddy, for a few thousand dollars that are insured anyway?"

The old man shook his head, knelt down, and opened the safe. He held up a money tray, head bowed, like an offering to the gods.

The sirens were much closer, screaming up the street.

The short guy quickly and efficiently counted two thousand dollars; the amount of Chico's debt. It went into his Starter jacket. The rest of the money from the tray went into an empty Jim Beam box that was lying behind the counter. He put another box inside the box with the money, so it looked like two stacked empty boxes.

"Hide this in back and then claim it all on your insurance. Busy night like tonight, they'll owe you at least five or six grand. Just don't let the police find it."

The old man nodded, getting it. He went from being terrified to strangely elated. The insurance company—those premium-hiking bloodsuckers—always demanded receipts and double-checked inventory to make sure his claims weren't inflated. This would be the very first time he was robbed and actually came out ahead of the game.

"Thanks," the old man said, realizing as soon as he did how strange it was.

"Remember to describe me correctly to the police. A very tall black man in a green jacket. I'd hate to have to come back here and find out you got my description wrong. Got it?"

The old man stared into the blue eyes of the short white guy. His stare wandered down to the man's hand, the back of which was covered with an extremely ornate tattoo of a Monarch butterfly, so realistic it appeared ready to take flight.

"No tattoos, either."

"Got it," the old man croaked.

"Take care, Teddy," the short guy said, and he slipped out the door into the night.

CHAPTER 2

The man named Tequila drove aimlessly through the city streets, car windows cranked down so the biting Chicago wind slapped at him on both sides. It tingled his scalp through his crew cut, and numbed his cheeks and ears. Tequila liked the very cold. He also liked the very hot, the heavy rain, and the few times a year when fog crept in from Lake Michigan and took over the shoreline.

Tequila wasn't into weather as much as he was into extremes.

Though his expression rarely ever changed from the blank, bored look he constantly wore, at the moment Tequila was pleased. He had gotten Marty's money, the weather was mean, and the remainder of the evening was open to him. Not even the Maniac, who sometimes endowed Tequila with supernatural abilities, would expect a collection this fast. Tequila could do what he wanted with the night, remaining on Marty's extremely anal time clock without anyone the wiser.

He pulled the white Chevy Caprice onto Lake Shore Drive, pushing the car up into the nineties as he buzzed southbound. The car looked like, and was constantly mistaken for, an unmarked Chicago police car, from the hand spotlight next to the side mirror down to the three antennae on the roof, all of them cosmetic. Tequila hadn't gotten a moving violation since buying the car three years ago.

The wind surged through the windows in freezing shrieks, drowning out the sound of the engine and the cars around him. He looked to his left and caught sight of the dead, frozen lake. He watched the light tower blink, halfway to Michigan, and wondered if the lake had frozen that far. He used to stare at that same lighthouse in his youth. Stare for hours, alone on an ugly stretch of shore far from the sunbathers and young lovers and joggers.

At 53rd Street he went over a short bump in the road that constituted a small bridge, and his chassis took air for the briefest of seconds and then bounced back to earth on reinforced shocks. Tequila got that tiny tingle in his stomach and groin and welcomed the sensation. He wondered if skydiving felt like that, multiplied a thousand fold. He'd try it someday, he decided. He'd made that decision dozens of times, driving over that bridge. On a whim a few months back, he'd even bought a parachute at an Army surplus store. He had no idea if it was operational or not, but the idea of owning one appealed to Tequila. It made someday a little closer.

At 57th he turned off LSD and passed the sprawling Museum of Science and Industry, which he visited once a week with Sally. She never seemed to tire of the coal exhibit, an informative ride in the museum that shuttled patrons through a fake mine on fake mining cars and showed examples of mining techniques that were probably thirty years out of date.

Tequila glanced at the digital clock on his dashboard and noted that Sally would be asleep by now. Her schedule was so regimented that she actually had preset times in the day to go to the bathroom. Tequila had once taken her to a movie on a weeknight, and she'd messed her pants during the flick because she'd missed her bathroom time. He'd since learned to heed her schedule.

From 57th he hung a left onto Michigan Avenue. The cold had driven everyone off the street. Usually there were dozens of bored black kids hanging out in front of the shops, drinking malt liquor from brown paper bags, waiting for something to happen. Something usually did, in the form of a shooting or an arrest or a fight. Nothing at all was happening with a wind chill of twenty below. The city, like the lake, was frozen.

Tequila found a parking space under a streetlight and set the car alarm on his keychain. He walked across the beaten asphalt toward the only sound on the block that competed with the howling wind.

When he opened the door the sound got louder. It came from a grizzled, ancient black man, singing an old blues song and accompanying himself on an even older piano. Tequila found a seat at the half empty bar and the fat black woman behind it set a rocks glass in front of him and filled it with three fingers of Applejack without being asked.

Tequila lifted the brandy and closed his eyes, letting his senses report. The air was cigarette smoky and stale, cut by the sharp scent of alcohol and apples under his nose. The room was hot, and the skin on his head and hands tingled as warm blood pumped into the cold flesh. The piano man, a kindly fossil named Bones, plunked away at an instrument missing at least five keys. It made his songs disjointed, and strangely, poignant.

Tequila put the Applejack to his lips and snarled. At the height of his snarl he emptied the contents down his throat. It burned from the tip of his tongue down to his ass, and he drew air in through his mouth to accentuate the tart aftertaste.

Bones ended his song short and went into *Dead Shrimp Blues*, a tune he always played when he noticed Tequila had come in. Tequila didn't particularly like the song, but years ago, the first time he came into the *Blues Note*, he tipped Bones a hundred dollar bill while Bones was playing this tune. It wasn't Tequila's appreciation of the music so much as his sharing the windfall from a multi-thousand dollar job. Though Tequila hadn't given him a cent since, Bones continued to play *Dead Shrimp Blues* whenever Tequila made an entrance.

Tequila opened his eyes and tilted his glass toward Bones, acknowledging him, and Bones ended the *Dead Shrimp Blues* and began *Come On In My Kitchen*, another old Robert Johnson tune.

Time passed.

Tequila drank another glass of Applejack and stared at the poorly mounted catfish hanging behind the bar in front of him. It was over a foot long, missing two fins, and resembled a gray boot with an unrealistic glass eye embedded near the heel. Tequila stared at it every time he came in. He reflected on why, and decided that he had his rituals just like Sally did.

Not once during the evening did he reflect on the man he'd killed.

After the third glass of brandy, Tequila left a twenty on the bar, nodded at the fat black woman who'd been serving him for years but whose name he'd never known, and got up to leave, *Dead Shrimp Blues* following him on the way out.

The night was a shock against his bare skin, and he welcomed it, the cold fighting the sleepy feeling the Applejack had induced. He stood for a moment, alone on the empty street, and took a deep lungful of dry, frigid air. Without telegraphing the move, he took two quick steps forward and slid on his belly over the top of an '85 Cadillac, tucking and rolling as he came down on the other side, landing on his feet facing the bar with a .45 in each hand. The entire motion was over in three seconds, and he hadn't made a sound louder than his footsteps on the sidewalk.

Satisfied that his reflexes showed no trace of the brandy, he judged himself sober and put the guns back in his pockets. Then he walked lightly to his car, disengaged the alarm, and drove home, thinking about sitting next to a lighthouse, fishing for catfish shaped like boots.

CHAPTER 3

Matisse scratched at a new tattoo on his massive right biceps, causing it to bleed. He had various tattoos decorating his torso, all smeared because he clawed at them during the healing process. This new one portrayed a young-looking mermaid with large bare breasts and a hook through her head.

The caption below it read *JAIL BAIT*. Matisse picked at it again, smearing her face.

"Kind of cold in here," Matisse said.

He looked to Leman for some sort of response. His fellow collector was cleaning his teeth with the edge of a Visa card, watching the television monitor in the corner of the room with obvious boredom. The monitor was hooked up to a camera outside the room's only door. Anyone approaching the room was captured on tape before entering.

The door itself was reinforced steel, and it operated by a security code which Marty changed weekly. All four walls were also reinforced, essentially making the room a large vault. At any normal time there was between twenty and two hundred thousand in the room, ready to be escorted by armed bodyguards to whichever laundering location Marty chose.

"You're ruining it." Leman gestured at the way Matisse was butchering his latest skin art.

"Itches."

Leman went back to picking his teeth. Matisse went back to scratching.

Marty wasn't due for another hour or so. Matisse liked Marty. He liked paling around with such an important man. The money was great, and Matisse went through it like water, keeping a penthouse apartment, buying two cars a year, impressing the chicks he met while bouncing at *Spill*. Impressive for a high school drop-out who couldn't make it as a mechanic. And Super Bowl week was the best week of the year. He'd get a huge bonus, get drunk with Marty and the guys, and Marty would set him up with some high class piece of ass to take home.

Marty himself never took a woman home, probably because he had a hard-on for money, not women.

Tequila never took one home either, but Tequila was strange. He scared Matisse, even though Matisse was easily twice his weight and a foot taller. When Matisse first signed on with Marty, he made the grave error of poking fun at Tequila's short stature. Tequila had broken Matisse's nose, ruptured an eardrum, and bruised his kidney before the other guys could pull him off.

Matisse pissed blood for a week. Neither of them ever brought the incident up again, and they'd worked fine together several dozen times, but Matisse was still wary of him.

Matisse liked Leman okay, because Leman was good to drink with and made a lot of jokes. He liked Terco, because Terco was just as big as he was and they'd work out together three times a week.

The last collector, Slake, scared Matisse as much as Tequila did. Maybe more. Slake was almost as tall as Matisse, but razor thin and mean as hell. It was the bad kind of mean, the kind where he liked seeing people hurt. Matisse once witnessed Slake use an electric sander on a ten-year-old boy's arm in front his parents to get a marker paid. Slake had been grinning the whole time, singing softly to himself. It was the single most horrifying thing Matisse had ever witnessed, and still haunted him years later. Only recently had he asked Slake what song he'd been singing that night.

"*Hello Again.* You gotta love that Neil Diamond."

Matisse shuddered at the memory and scratched his forehead, feeling a chill in his armpits.

"Are you cold?" Matisse asked Leman again. "Maybe the heat is broke."

"What the hell is *that?*"

Leman stood up and yanked his .32 from his shoulder holster. He was staring at the vid monitor. Matisse took a look himself, and saw two people standing outside the vault door. Both wore ski masks, black jackets, black jeans, and gloves. One carried a suitcase, and the other had a hand truck hauling what looked like a keg of beer.

"Who the hell are these guys?" Leman asked.

Matisse didn't know. The faces were hidden behind the masks. But one thing was clear; one of the men was very short.

"What are they doing?"

The accountants had stopped their counting and were also staring at the monitor. The short man outside the door opened up his suitcase, and assembled what looked like a machine gun.

"It's a drill," one of the accountants said.

His prediction proved correct when the short man attached a four inch drill bit to the base of the object.

"What's he gonna do with that?"

What the short man did was touch the drill bit to the door and begin boring a hole in it.

"This ain't good," Matisse shook his head. "This really ain't good."

Leman's eyebrows scrunched up. These guys were obviously trying to break in, but even if they did manage to get the door open, Leman and Matisse would shoot them dead. Neither of the intruders carried anything looking like heavy firepower, except for that keg of beer thing. How did they think they could rob the vault, unless...

Leman laughed. "They don't know we're in here."

"Huh?"

"Take a look, muscle-head. They aren't even armed. They don't know we're in here. They think they can just break in, take the money, and go."

"So what do we do?"

"We just wait on either side of the doorway, and when they get in, we take them out." Leman laughed again. "Stupid amateurs."

"Alive, right? We're not gonna kill them, are we, Leman?"

For someone so goddamn big who made a living breaking people's bones, Matisse could be a real pussy.

"Naw. We'll just bring them to Marty. He'll take care of it."

"Yeah. Good idea. Marty will know what to do with them."

Torture them and kill them, Leman thought. Not smart trying to steal from Marty the Maniac.

Leman didn't like his boss. He didn't like the endless stupid lectures. He didn't like the way Marty tried to pretend they were buddies, even while abusing them. The work was okay, but Marty insisted on a minimum sixty hour work week, and even demanded they punch a clock.

But the money was unbelievable. Sure, he was hourly, but Leman figured out that with bonuses, he averaged about thirty bucks an hour. That was eighteen hundred bucks a week, cash. A big step up from the six bills a week he was making as a member of Chicago's finest. Plus it was a lot less dangerous than breaking up gang fights or investigating shots fired at a housing project. In five years, Leman figured he could retire. Move out to the tropics and sip drinks out of coconuts while native girls blew him.

Five minutes later, the amateurs had managed to drill a hole through the door the width of a finger. Leman had everyone be quiet and move against the wall on either side of the doorway, where they wouldn't be seen when the burglars entered. Then he turned the monitor toward him so he could watch their progress.

But instead of trying to open the door, the burglars kicked a large wedge under it. Then the short one pushed a long tube through the hole he'd made.

"What's that?" Matisse asked.

Leman told him to shut up, watching as they hooked the other end of the tube up to a nozzle on the keg.

Leman frowned and said, "Gas."

"What?"

"Gas! I was wrong. They know we're in here. They're gassing us."

"What do we do?"

"Cover up the hose!"

Matisse backed away. "You cover up the hose!"

A faint hiss came from the tube, and Leman took a deep breath and plugged up the end of it with his thumb. The hissing continued. He stared at the tube and saw that the two feet of hose hanging into the room was perforated with hundreds of tiny holes.

"Help me seal up the tube! There are too many holes!"

Matisse and one of the accountants put their hands on the tube, trying to cover up all the holes. The other accountant sat in a corner and hugged his knees, trying to make himself very small, which was a trick he learned in Kindergarten.

"It's still coming through!" Leman said through clenched teeth.

"What do we do?" Matisse's eyes were wide with panic. Leman took out his pocket knife and tried sawing at the tube. The hose was made of some material that didn't cut.

"I'm feeling funny," one of the accountants said.

Leman noted that he was feeling strange too. Though he was trying to hold his breath and take in good air over his shoulder, some of the gas was obviously getting to him. He was lightheaded, and it would only get worse.

Leman looked around for the air vent. Maybe he could survive by breathing the air coming in. He saw it in the far corner of the room, near the ceiling. Though he hadn't noticed during the past two hours he'd been in the room, the vent had a piece of sheet metal covering it up, screwed into place.

Matisse saw it at the same time.

"I told you it was cold! They cut off our air!"

"Shut up!"

"We're going to die!"

"Shut up!"

Matisse threw up on the floor. Leman, becoming dizzy, held his .38 up to the point of the hose that met the door. He tried to angle it so he just shot the hose off. Then they could shove something in the hole and stop the gas. Or maybe he could even shoot at the burglars through the hole. The problem was the metal door. If his bullet hit the door it would ricochet around in the room. But if they were dead anyway...

The ex-cop fired. The bullet neatly severed the tube, almost flush with the door. Leman, vision blurring, shoved his finger in the hole.

"Stopped... it..." He smiled drunkenly.

Then his eyelids fluttered, and he jerked his hand back and began to wail. Blood ran in rivulets down his arm. The spinning drill bit appeared briefly through the hole, and was then removed and replaced by another two feet of tubing.

The hissing began again.

Before everything went black, Leman heard someone order a drink.

No, it wasn't a drink. It was someone's name.

Someone, very clearly and loudly, said, "Tequila."

CHAPTER 4

"Tall, over six feet. Wearing a green jacket."

"Eyes? Hair?"

"I told you he was a black man, you think he was blond and blue-eyed?"

Liquor store owner and recent armed robbery victim Theodore Binkowski rolled his eyes. His on-the-scene interrogator, Detective Jacqueline Daniels, glanced behind Binkowski at the bloody remains being carted off by three men wearing disposable plastic parkas. The city's job was to remove the body. It would be up to Binkowski to take care of all the blood, which had showered half of his shop.

Daniels worked Homicide out of the 26th District. She was an average-sized woman with shoulder length brown hair, brown eyes, and a no bullshit expression that made her look older than her early thirties.

"Did he have glasses?" Daniels asked, turning back to Binkowski. Her tone was somewhere between bored and condescending. "Was he cross-eyed, bug-eyed, squinty, bloodshot? Was his hair long, short, nappy, wavy, in a drip bag, did he have Afro-puffs..."

"Afro-puffs? That sounds like a cereal."

"Answer the question, Mr. Binkowski."

This from Detective Herb Benedict, Jack's partner. He'd been walking the crime scene and had wandered back over. His gaunt face spoke of an aversion to eating regularly, and the jacket he wore drooped across his bony shoulders as if they were a wire coat hanger.

"Brown eyes. Short black hair, close to the scalp."

"What color jacket?" Benedict asked.

"Green."

"Leather? Nylon? A hoodie?"

Binkowski blinked. "Leather."

"Not too many green leather jackets around," Jack said. "Especially on guys over six feet. What kind of shoes?"

"Tennis shoes."

"Must have had big feet, being so tall. Anyone else in the store with you at the time of the robbery?"

"I told you already."

"Right. Just the tall black guy in the green leather jacket who waltzed in, blew away a robber, and disappeared into the night with all of your money. Quite a coincidence, two guys trying to rob you the same night at the same time."

Binkowski shrugged and offered a blank stare.

"We're going to ask you to come to the station, make a full statement. I'd also like you to work with a police artist, see if we can work-up a picture of this guy. And please explain to me why I'm getting the impression that you're trying to protect a man who robbed you. Did he threaten you in some way? Say he'd be back?"

Binkowski went sullen. "He saved my life."

Jack took a step forward, getting in the shop owner's face.

"And he also shot a man dead, Mr. Binkowski. What about the next time he walks into a store and blows someone away? Maybe a woman or a kid this time. Maybe your wife and kids, Mr. Binkowski. You think about that when you're giving your statement. Think about it real hard. And also think about the *obstruction of justice* and *accessory after the fact* charges I'll throw at you if I find out the perp wasn't a tall black man in gym shoes, but a short white guy in cowboy boots."

Binkowski paled. His mouth opened and closed several times, silently, like a goldfish who managed to leap out of the bowl and suddenly figured out it was a bad idea.

Jack turned on her heels and walked out of the liquor store and into the freezing night. She knew that Binkowski was lying. She knew because she'd been questioning witnesses for almost ten years. Binkowski's description stank. Plus there was no way in hell two people tried to rob the same store at the same time.

There was also the matter of a size 7 boot print found in a spatter of blood in front of the register. A print that didn't match Binkowski, or the corpse, and certainly not anyone over six feet.

Jack sucked cold air into her lungs. Maybe Binkowski had shot the robber himself, hid his money, and was waiting to claim it all on his insurance. The insurance scam had been around ever since insurance was invented.

But a search of the store and the block failed to turn up the weapon, the cash, or gloves; the techies had done a swab of Binkowski's hands and had come up negative. The shop owner hadn't fired a gun. But he could still be in league with whoever had.

From the wounds on the body, and the blood patterns decorating the shop, Daniels guessed the killer was a professional, and a damn good one. She'd done some competition shooting, but firing that quickly and precisely—with both hands at once—wasn't something that happened by accident. Fourteen brass casings had been found, but Jack didn't hold out any hope they'd get a print off of them.

Daniels breathed out, watching it steam around her head. She'd know more tomorrow when all the reports were in. But already she had a strong instinctive feeling. In Daniels's career she'd been involved with several high-profile murder cases. The worst were the repeat killers; the ones who did it over and over again. She'd had many such cases, a few of which almost killed her. This one stank the same way. There would be more bodies before the shooter was found.

She watched the body being hauled into the back of a meat wagon, the blood on the black bag turning shiny as it froze. The wallet on the deceased held ID in the name of Billy Chico. Chico, according to the computer, had a rap sheet going back to the womb. Never did hard time, but with a file filled with assault, battery, attempted rape, car theft, and various other infractions, it didn't take a strong imagination to figure he'd graduate to armed robbery. But that was the part of the equation they already had.

Jack took as much of the cold as she could stand, and then went back into the shop. The smell of violent death mixing with the indoor heat made her nauseous. Benedict was talking to one of the Crime Scene Team guys, and Binkowski had his coat on and was waiting to be escorted to the station. Jack popped some peppermint gum into her mouth to help combat the blood stench and wandered over to her partner.

"You figure he's lying?" Benedict asked her, out of Binkowski's earshot.

"Like a throw rug."

"If the perp was a tall black guy in a green leather jacket, I'll eat my hat."

"You don't have a hat."

Benedict smiled. "Not since Bush was elected. It didn't go down easy either."

"So what's his game? Think he's running a scam?"

"Maybe. We'll see how much his insurance claim is. Couldn't be more than a few grand. Do you kill someone for that little?"

"People get killed for el tokens." Which was an actual case of theirs a few months back.

"But why did anyone have to die? If he wanted to cheat the insurance company, all he had to do was hide his money, conk himself on the head, and say he was robbed."

Jack nodded. "Binkowski's hiding something."

"Are you saying we should take him back to the station ourselves and grill him?"

"Until he's well-done."

"You want to be the bad cop?"

Jack smiled. "Let's both be bad cops."

CHAPTER 5

Tequila drove up to his parking garage and honked the horn. After a delay of a few seconds, the garage door opened and the attendant, who'd been sleeping in the booth, gave Tequila a courteous nod as he drove past.

For the eighteen hundred bucks a month it cost to rent here the attendant shouldn't sleep on duty. Tequila considered calling the Building Association about it, but decided to let it go. Tequila wasn't the type to rat on anyone, even somebody whose salary he helped pay.

He parked in his usual spot, next to the lobby doors, and set his car alarm after getting out. It was supposed to be a security garage, but then it was also supposed to have an attendant who was awake to let people in and out. Tequila didn't believe in luck, but he did believe in odds. He stacked the odds in his favor whenever he could.

He walked into his lobby and was greeted with a smile by Frank the doorman, who was quick to ring for Tequila's elevator.

"Good evening, Mr. Abernathy."

Tequila nodded and stepped into the lift, all chrome and mirrors and carpet. He pressed the button for the thirtieth floor and stared at the doorman's smile until the doors closed.

The building was under ten years old, featuring state-of-the-art elevators, and twelve seconds later Tequila was on his floor. The hallway had been done in cream, with expensive plush carpeting and lattice pattern wallpaper. Works of art adorned the walls between apartment doors, and a black Drexel coffee table stood in the corner where the hallway turned, with a large silk arrangement in an iron vase perched upon it.

Tequila followed the hallway through the bend and to the first door on his left. He checked the knob, pleased to find it locked. China was almost religious about security, but Tequila still checked it every time. A habit from when he and Sally used to live in a much different apartment building, before he worked for Marty.

He unlocked the door and announced himself as he always did.

"It's me, China."

China poked her large black head out of the kitchen and smiled at Tequila.

"How was work, Mr. Abernathy?"

"Fine. And you?"

"Sally wet the bed again. She don't like falling asleep when you ain't home. I changed her, and put on fresh sheets. She sleepin' now."

"Thank you, China."

Tequila hung his coat up in the closet and walked into the kitchen, taking the apple juice from the refrigerator. He poured himself a glass while the overweight care-giver watched.

"It's getting late," Tequila said after downing the juice. "You can stay the night if you'd like."

"I just might do that, Mr. Abernathy."

China pulled herself up from the confines of the kitchen chair and walked out of the kitchen with precise, petite steps, wool slippers already on her feet. Whenever Tequila worked late, it was a given that China would stay over. But she always waited until asked. He'd tried more than once to hire her as a live-in, but China insisted on her independence.

"Got to be able to do what I want to," she said time and again.

Yet for the last four years, her sole job was taking care of Sally. She had no family that Tequila knew of, and the one time he followed her home—a small bit of surveillance to make sure he knew what kind of person she was before he hired her for Sal—he found she lived alone in a tiny apartment that bordered on squalid on Chicago's far west side. Nothing the slightest bit homey, or even pleasant, about the place. But at least once a week she would trek back to that apartment, even though almost all of her clothing, her possessions, and even her pet goldfish was here.

Freedom is an important thing, noted Tequila, even if it was only symbolic.

Tequila went to the fridge and poured himself another glass of apple juice, emptying the bottle. He put the cap back on and placed the bottle in the plastic recycle bin under the sink. Then he hit the release button and tugged his guns from his shoulder holsters, setting them on the kitchen table.

In a cabinet next to the dishwasher Tequila removed a metal box the size of a portable television. He unlocked the box with a key on his keychain and flipped the top open. His keychain only held four keys. One for the box, one for the car, one for the apartment, and one for *Spill*. Also on the ring, next to his car alarm remote, was a small Swiss Army knife and a yellow metal smiley face Tequila had gotten from Sally as a birthday present. It hadn't been his birthday, but he accepted it as if it was. Sally gave him birthday presents many times a year.

Tequila removed several metal trays from the box until he got to the one he wanted. In the partitioned slots of the tray were gun oil, a wire brush, a chamois, and several long metal tubes with threaded ends.

He picked up the first of his .45s, a custom-made pistol that incorporated parts from several gun manufacturers. It had, among other things, Novak night sights, stippled grips, a beveled magazine well for speed reloading, a wide competition trigger, a lowered ejection port, a ramp and throat job for the use of hollow-point bullets, and a contoured hammer. The gun had also been dehorned, a process that involved beveling every sharp edge so it didn't snag clothing or holsters.

Stripping the weapon, Tequila cleaned and oiled every moving part with attention bordering on intimacy. When the last traces of its recent usage had been polished away, he replaced the barrel with a new one from his metal tray. The barrel on any weapon was its signature. The rifling—the twisted grooves inside the tube that made the bullet spin—marked that bullet in a particular way, as unique as a fingerprint. Replacing the barrel was like having an entirely new, and consequently clean, weapon. The old barrel went into the recycle bin under the sink, to be disposed of the next time he went out.

Tequila reassembled the pistol, and then repeated the procedure with its twin. China came into the kitchen during the process to bid her goodnight.

"I'll just sleep in the guest bedroom."

Tequila nodded, concentrating on his work. China'd been sleeping in the guest bedroom for four years.

Completing the task, Tequila made sure both safeties were on and then put the guns back into their holsters. The holsters were a piece of work in themselves; a criss-cross leather rig custom-made to perfectly fit the .45s. It weighed almost three times as much as a normal dual holster set-up, and under casual inspection the holsters appeared to be too long for the guns. That was because each contained a ceramic magnet and a battery. Wires ran from the batteries through the leather webbing and to a hidden button in the center of the outfit. When pressed, the button engaged, juicing the magnets and holding the guns in their holsters with more than three hundred pounds of pressure. Depressing the button allowed the guns to slip out easily.

It was a safety feature that not only prevented his guns from being taken from him, but was also necessary with Sally in the house. She was under strict orders not to touch his guns, but strict orders only worked with people who understood them.

Tequila put the tray back into his box and locked it. Then he washed out his juice glass, dried it with a hand towel, and replaced it in the cabinet. He brought his rig—the guns safely magnetized in their holsters—with him into his bedroom.

The bedroom was different from the rest of the apartment in that it completely lacked any decoration. The walls were bare. The furniture consisted of a bed, a dresser, and a small valet stand next to the bed. The decorator charged by the room, and a ridiculous amount at that. So Sally had a nice environment, Tequila paid that ridiculous amount, but he stopped when it came to his personal living space. The minimalism of the room suited him fine. He shut the door behind him.

The alcohol had almost worn completely off, and Tequila decided on a quick work-out before retiring. He placed his holsters on the valet next to his bed and stripped the shirt off of his developed upper body. Then he took off his cowboy boots and the white athletic socks he wore under them. The boots went into his closet and the socks and shirt went into his hamper. Still wearing pants, Tequila dropped down to the floor and did three hundred push-ups. His chest and arms burning, he stood on his hands and walked on them over to the wall near the bedroom door. Feet against the wall, he did fifty vertical push-ups, his crew cut kissing the floor every time he lowered himself down.

His thoughts when exercising were always the same, even though it had been almost ten years since he'd competed. It was a mantra for Tequila when he worked out. With every strained breath he softly chanted it. A single word. Once syllable. Three letters.

Win.

He never stopped to reflect that the word no longer held any meaning for him.

Pushing off from the wall into a back bend, Tequila held the bridge momentarily to stretch out his spine, and then shifted his weight and pulled up to his feet. His breathing was hard but controlled. He considered doing some squats, but decided to jog tomorrow instead. He was supposed to be at work at nine o'clock. If he woke up at seven he could get in a few miles beforehand.

He stretched his arms over his head, flexing his fingers, when he heard the cry.

"Kill-ya!"

It had come from Sally's room. Tequila went to his dresser and took out a towel from the top drawer, using it to wipe the sweat from his face and upper body.

"Kill-ya!"

Hanging the towel over his shoulders, Tequila opened the bedroom door and walked down the hall to his sister's bedroom. China was already bedside, trying to shush Sally down.

"Kill-ya!"

"I'm right here, Sally."

She smiled at him, her tongue protruding from her mouth. Her chubby cheeks and almond eyes shone in pure joy.

"You gotta get to sleep, Miss Sally," China chided. "You got school tomorrow."

"I want to show Kill-ya my pit-chur."

"You can show him tomorrow dear."

"It's okay, China," Tequila said. "What picture, Sally?"

"I made a pit-chur of you."

She reached behind her, under her pink pillow, and removed a crinkled piece of notebook paper covered with crayon scribbling, holding it out to Tequila with triumph.

Tequila took the paper from his big sister, staring at it hard. It was done in green and blue, and if he squinted and looked at it sideways, it slightly resembled a stick figure, except for the three arms.

"It's you, Kill-ya!"

"I can see that. It's like looking into a mirror. Thank you, Sal."

"It's good?"

"Very good."

"Good as a girl who don't have Down Sin-dome?"

"As good as any girl who doesn't have Down Syndrome, Sally. I'm going to hang it on the refrigerator right now."

Sally beamed, clapping her chubby, curved hands together.

"I love you, Kill-ya!"

"Love you too, Sally. Now it's bedtime. You have school tomorrow."

"Night-night, Kill-ya!"

"Night-night, Sally."

Tequila nodded goodnight to China, who was already tucking Sally into bed. He walked back down the hall and went into the kitchen, hanging the picture up on the refrigerator with a magnet. He stared at it again.

The expression on the stick-figure's face was blank. The mouth a simple straight line. The eyes two blue dots. Six strands of hair stood up from the head like embedded arrows. Other than the third arm, it was probably the best picture Sally had ever drawn. And she'd drawn hundreds over the past thirty years.

Tequila's first memory of his sister was from infancy. He'd been six or seven months old, and Sally, four years his senior, was trying to help him walk. She would hold his hands up over his head and walk behind him, keeping him on his feet when he started to fall.

She called him Kill-ya because she couldn't pronounce Tequila. She probably could now, but there was no real need to correct her. To Sally, he had always been Kill-ya, and always would be.

Tequila walked back to his bedroom, closing the door behind him. He lay down in his bed and locked his fingers behind his head. During the day, Tequila maintained focus on whatever job was at hand, his self-discipline almost military strict. But at night, just before sleep, his focus slipped, and Tequila's mind would wander. Like he did most other nights, he closed his eyes and thought about the past.

CHAPTER 6

"Shoulda killed the little retard at birth," their father would often say about Sally. Sometimes to her directly. Tequila had begun defending his sister from their dad when he was around six years old.

"Don't call her that," he'd reply, his face as serious as any Kindergartener's could be.

"And what you gonna do about it, *Kill-ya*?" his father would mock. "You're a runt even for a six-year-old. You don't talk back to me till you're man enough to back that shit up."

And then Tequila would get swatted across the room with a hard slap. Sometimes, if the old man was drunk or in a particularly bad mood, he'd get whipped with the belt.

But the beatings didn't stop Tequila from talking back. Every time the old man called Sally a retard, Tequila would tell him to stop. He also took Sally's punishments as well. The old man didn't care if Sally was mentally handicapped. If she crayoned the wall, he beat the shit out of her. Tequila couldn't take that. Sally screamed for hours after a beating, which usually prompted more beatings because she wouldn't be quiet.

So Tequila claimed responsibility for every mishap that happened in the household.

The name-calling, and the abuse, continued up through his teenage years. By then they had taken their toll. Tequila had no friends in high school. He was too cold, too introverted. He did mediocre in classes, scoring well on tests but rarely completing homework because he spent most of his free time with Sally. He also got into a lot of fights, defending himself when bullies picked on him because of his height. On the fourth trip to the principal's office, Tequila was threatened with expulsion unless he calmed down. The principal suggested he focus all of that energy on something constructive rather than destructive. He all but ordered Tequila to join a sport.

Tequila enrolled in gymnastics because it was the only sport open to him with his small size. He excelled immediately, coming in third on floor exercise at Nationals at the age of fifteen. But it was at a sacrifice. His training meant time away from home, which meant no one to care for Sally except for whatever floozy their father had living with them at the time. And whoever the floozy was, she didn't care a bit about Sally, which meant Sally would get into trouble without Tequila being there to take her punishment. Often Sally would wet the bed, and then try to hide her dirty clothes somewhere in the house. When the old man found them, he'd have a fit.

"That's why your bitch mother left. Because she couldn't handle looking after no retard and no preemie."

"Stop calling her a retard," Tequila warned. "Maybe if you sent her to school she could take better care of herself."

But their father, even though he earned enough as a factory foreman, refused to send Sally to school.

"Why should I pay to try and teach that dumb bitch retard something she'll just forget anyway?"

"Then I'll get a job and send her myself."

"You little faggot. How you gonna get a job when you spend all your time in the gym, playing on the mats with all your tights-wearing, dick-sucking, homo buddies?"

Tequila got a job during the weekends, sweeping floors. He saved his money, and eventually was able to send Sally to a special school twice a week.

But the old man refused to let her go.

"I said she ain't going, so she ain't. Use your money to buy a pair of those lift shoes, so you ain't so goddamn short."

When Tequila turned eighteen, his father called Sally a retard for the last time. Puberty had come, and though he didn't sprout up tall, all of his years working out and practicing gymnastics had turned Tequila's body into a rock. Tequila liked making his muscles bigger, almost as much as he liked working the rings or the high bar. And he was getting noticed for it. Colleges began actively recruiting him. Even professional gymnastic coaches came calling, scouting for the Olympics. Tequila, for the first time in his whole life, was finally being appreciated by someone other than Sally.

"You're too stupid for college, and you won't make no money on the Olympic team. It's non-profit, dummy. You should quit that crummy janitor job and come work for me at the plant. We can start you on the line making $6.35 an hour. Maybe if you do that I'll think about sending your retard sister to school."

"I'd rather eat shit than work for you," Tequila told his father. "And if you call Sally a retard one more time I'm going to kick your fat ass."

His father did a double-take. He'd been talked back to by Tequila before, but never insulted and threatened.

"All those trophies gave you a big head, you little prick. That will be the day when you kick my ass. And your retard sister can..."

That turned out to be the day. Tequila hit him hard enough to dislocate his father's jaw. He shouldn't have gotten up off the floor, but Ben Abernathy was a pig-headed man. He went for his son, anger masking pain. Tequila ducked his father's punch and gave the man ten broken ribs, a busted nose, a fractured pelvis, and a concussion before he finally stayed down. Then he dragged his father into the street and left him unconscious in an alley.

Ben Abernathy was discovered by a jogger. He was rushed to the hospital, but died en route. Of a heart attack, which may or may not have been a result of his fight with Tequila. When Tequila was given the news he felt nothing. No guilt. No resentment. No elation. The fact that he might have been the one that killed him didn't bother Tequila a bit.

Tequila hadn't expressed any emotion over anything since childhood; happy, sad, or anything in between. He laughed occasionally, if something was funny, but true joy always eluded him, even when he won gymnastics championships. Tequila had fought so long to control his emotions that sometimes he wondered if he had any left.

He sold his father's house, and with the money sent Sally to a live-in institution for the mentally handicapped. It was in Nebraska, and he'd looked at a dozen schools before finally deciding on this one. Its reputation was excellent, and its staff seemed to genuinely care.

He signed her up for two years, visiting every weekend that he could. Then he went off to pursue Olympic gold.

Two years later he picked up Sally with two bronze medals and a silver medal to his name. With the money he had left over from the sale of his father's house, Tequila rented an apartment and hired a weekly care-giver. Then he got a job teaching gymnastics at a local YMCA.

A case of mistaken identity changed his life.

The apartment Tequila and Sally had been living in was in a bad neighborhood, all they could afford. After four years without visitors, Tequila was awoken one night by someone banging on the door. He got up to investigate just as the door burst inward.

Standing in the doorway were two large, burly men. They wore tailored suits and each boasted enough facial scars for an entire football team.

"We want the money, Jackson," one of them said to Tequila.

"Then go find him. I'm not Jackson."

The thugs snickered. They had never seen the man Jackson they'd been sent to collect from. But they were told that this was his apartment, and that

Jackson was a short man. A very short man.

"Not Jackson, huh? Who are you then? One of Santa's little helpers?"

The thugs snickered again.

"My name is Abernathy. Tequila Abernathy. You guys have the wrong apartment."

"Sure we do, Mr. Tequila. Couldn't you think of a better name than that, Jackson?"

"Marty sent us," said the other one. "We want the three gees, or we have to break your legs for you."

The thugs stepped into the apartment. Tequila considered his options. The building was seedy enough that no one would have bothered calling the police when the men broke in, out of fear of getting involved. But if Tequila could prove to these guys that he wasn't Jackson, he might be able to avoid an incident.

"My wallet is on the kitchen table," he told them. "It has my ID in it. I'm not Jackson."

"It better have three grand in it," the thug on the right said. He walked past Tequila and entered the kitchen, picking the wallet up from the counter.

"Seven lousy bucks." He frowned. "I hope you have more hidden around this dump, Mr. Jackson."

"Look at my Driver's License. My name isn't Jackson."

"Sure it ain't." The thug pocketed the wallet without looking at it. "Now where's the money?"

"Kill-ya!"

Both hoods spun at the sound of Sally's voice.

"You got a bitch in here, Jackson?"

"My sister. She has Down Syndrome."

"You mean she's one of those mongoloid freaks? How is she gonna kill us? Does the retard have a gun?"

"Don't call her a retard," Tequila said.

"Or what? You'll throw us out?"

"I'm going to throw you out anyway. But if you call her a retard again I'll break your legs first."

"Louie, you go take care of the retard. I'm gonna kick this little shit's—"

Tequila took two quick steps and scissor kicked the big man in the face. The thug fell hard, and Tequila rolled to his feet a heartbeat later and threw a quick jab into his partner's soft belly. The partner doubled over, and Tequila snapped an elbow up into his chin and knocked him onto his ass.

The first guy sat up, shaking his head.

"You little—"

Tequila didn't let him finish. He did a handspring and landed directly on the man's knees, breaking them both. The man screamed in horror. Tequila silenced him with a chop to the throat.

The other thug rolled drunkenly onto all fours, and Tequila focused all of his energy into his right hand and power-fisted the man in the side of the head, knocking him out as well.

It was all over in less than fifteen seconds. Tequila searched the men, taking their ID, their guns, and his own wallet back.

"Kill-ya!"

"Hold on, Sally!"

Using their ties, he knotted their hands behind their backs and then used their belts to bind their feet. Then he called the police.

When the cops came the thugs were still out. An ambulance had to haul them away.

The next morning Tequila got a phone call.

"You the guy that beat up my two men?"

"Yes. Not only were they slow, they were stupid. They had the wrong guy."

"I know. Sorry about that. A misunderstanding. Is it true you're a midget?"

"I'm five-five."

"And you did that to my two best guys bare-handed? You into karate or something?"

"Or something."

Tequila had been taking classes in karate, judo, and boxing at the YMCA over the last few years, and found he was equally adept at the fighting arts as he was at gymnastics.

"No shit. Can you shoot a gun?"

"I've never tried. Who is this?"

"Name's Marty. Marty Martelli. You know, I could use a guy good with his fists. I've got a shortage now, since you put two of my people in the hospital."

"I said I've never shot a gun."

"You can learn. I pay my men seven hundred a week, plus percentages. Meet me over at Joe's Pool Hall over on Fullerton if you're interested. I'll be there until six."

"How do I know you won't try to kill me?"

"Buddy, I wanted to kill you, you'd be dead already."

And Marty hung up.

After the care-giver showed up for the day, Tequila called in sick at the Y and went over to Jimmy's.

The place was a grimy little hole in the wall, boasting only six pool tables, all badly in need of repair. But it was full of people. Bad people. Seedy people. Gang-bangers and ex-cons and low-life Italians with nicknames like "The Knife" and "The Weasel." They all turned and eyed Tequila when he entered, several of them snickering.

"I'm looking for Marty," Tequila asked the man closest to him.

The man motioned with his head over to the rear of the room. Tequila wove his way through the crowd, enduring several height cracks and giggles. In the back of the room, seated on the only chair in the place, was a pudgy, mustached man sporting thinning black hair slicked back over his scalp with some kind of oil. Around his neck were several heavy gold chains, and on his fat pinky perched a two carat diamond ring. He wore an expensive silk suit, open at the collar. His eyes were two cold black marbles, and they regarded Tequila impassively.

"You Marty?"

Two men flanking Marty's chair reached into their jackets. Marty raised a hand to stop them.

"You that guy I just called?" Marty asked.

"The name is Tequila."

Several of Marty's entourage laughed.

"Well, Tequila, if you're as talented as I've been led to believe, you'd be quite valuable to me. I've got a surplus of meanness in my little army, but a severe shortage of actual skill."

"And what is it that you do?" Tequila asked.

More laughter.

"I like to think of myself as an odds maker."

"You're a bookie."

"A very well-connected bookie."

"And you want to hire me as a collection agent."

Marty grinned. "Correct. If you think you can do the job."

The large man on Marty's right butted into the dialog.

"Come on, Mr. Martelli. This little shrimp couldn't collect forty cents for a toll."

"Do you think you can take him, Vincent?"

"No problem, Mr. Martelli. I'd squash him like a bug."

"I'll make you a deal, Tequila," Marty told him. "If you can knock Vincent down in less than sixty seconds, I'll hire you."

"At the rate we discussed?"

"Yes."

Tequila thought it over. That was four times as much as he made at the YMCA. It would mean a new apartment for him and Sally, around the clock care, maybe even a car. Tequila didn't see any downside.

"Fine."

Vincent stepped forward, shrugging off his jacket. He was a big man, with the over-developed chest and arms of a weightlifter. Everyone formed into a small circle, surrounding them.

Tequila looked for vulnerable spots on the man, but even his neck was thick and corded with muscle.

So he went for the one spot that he knew wasn't muscular.

Tequila did a hand spring, landed on his knees before Vincent's feet, and drove all of his weight into a fist aimed at the weightlifter's balls.

He connected and Vincent screamed falsetto, swinging a big arm to swat Tequila away. Tequila rolled to the side, made his feet, and jumped up and twisted in the air, spin-kicking Vincent in the side of the head.

Vincent went down and didn't get up.

The entire pool hall went silent.

Tequila, who hadn't even broken a sweat, turned and faced Marty.

"How long was that?" Marty asked one of his goons.

"Six seconds."

"I got five seconds," said another.

Marty grinned, offering Tequila his hand.

"You're hired. You start tomorrow. Be here at ten a.m. And let me have your Driver's License."

"Why?"

"Can't learn to shoot a gun without having a gun permit, right?"

Tequila handed over his license. The next day he had his Firearm Owner ID and began his five years of employment under Marty the Maniac.

Which ended that night as Tequila slept.

CHAPTER 7

Marty Martelli was not your typical bookie. He didn't have a head for numbers or point spreads or odds. He didn't follow sports much. In fact, he hated gambling, except for an occasional game of poker with the people he paid to be his friends.

But Marty was exceptionally good at ordering people around. Not leading; a leader was someone who took charge and inspired hope and confidence. Marty had about as much charisma as a bowl of vomit. But he got things done. Partly out of fear. Partly out of a natural ability to delegate authority to the persons most suited to complete particular tasks.

Marty surrounded himself with talent in every field. He had three of the best accountants in the world, all constantly checking each other's work. He had ins with all the important odds-makers and Mafioso. He had a dozen beat cops, a sergeant, two police captains, two Mayor's aids, four aldermen, the assistant superintendent, and a judge, all happy to help out with any little problem he had. If they couldn't help, even with all the money he gave them, Marty retained two very famous lawyers who could do everything but turn water into wine. And even that, with the right jury, was possible.

But the employees that Marty liked the best, the ones he identified with most, were the debt collectors.

Marty the Maniac worked his way up through the Chicago book system in the 1950s, as a leg-breaker. His plump sixty-plus-year-old frame was once muscular, and the scars on his face told tales of more fights than professional sparring partners.

"Fear, not pain, is the ultimate goal," he constantly told his underlings. "Pain fades. But fear continuously builds. Collecting a difficult debt means making the debtor anxious to pay. I want him to be bending over backwards in his eagerness to give me what he owes. Broken bones heal. Paranoia grows like weeds."

Marty's collectors were experts in scaring the living hell out of people. Most of the time, their mere presence had people scrambling for their checkbooks. Stronger personalities, such as criminals, or celebrities, or once even a House of Representatives politico, had to be convinced that paying off their debts was a good idea. This was simply a matter of finding out what they feared most. A tough guy with children could have them taken away for a while. A Congressman with claustrophobia could be locked in a coffin and buried for a few hours. A hot shot movie actor with a big libido could have his favorite body part shaved by a shaky man with a straight razor.

All of Marty's clients eventually paid, with very few of them being seriously hurt.

"Another reason not to seriously hurt a client," Marty was fond of saying over and over, "is that next time they want to bet, they'll go someplace else. Scaring off your business isn't good business."

Marty had five collectors, who served as his bodyguards and poker buddies when they weren't out getting his cash. Two of them, a bull-necked bodybuilder named Matisse and an ex-cop named Leman, had been on the clock at *Spill*—a trendy dance bar that Marty owned—where they'd been guarding the Super Bowl take.

They hadn't done their job, and were presently sleeping on the floor of his vault.

Marty lashed out with his right foot, kicking the unconscious Matisse in the head. Unfortunately for him, his four hundred dollar custom Italian shoes weren't made for kicking, and Marty the Maniac jammed his big toe. This propelled his rage into a spit-flying flurry, and after switching feet he stomped on the bodybuilder's back, heel first, over and over, trying to drive his foot through the worthless, muscle-bound idiot and into the floor. He succeeded only in winding himself.

Marty drew in air through his mouth, loudly and in great gulps. He tried to wipe his sweating forehead with a silk sleeve, and found that silk absorbed sweat for shit. His gaze shifted once again to the stainless steel table, the table that should have had over one million dollars stacked on it. It didn't. The only thing on the table was one dollar and thirty-two cents in change— the robber's idea of a joke.

"Get me the tape!" he screamed at Terco.

Terco jerked back as if hit, his canned-tan face pinching and his massive chest jutting out defensively.

"The tape?"

"The videotape! I want to see what happened! I want to see who these incompetent bastards let steal my money!"

"The videotape. Sure, Marty."

Terco lumbered off. Marty limped over to the prone Leman, watching his collector's chest rise and fall with each breath. Like Matisse and the two accountants, Leman was knocked out. Marty's hackles rose again at the injustice of it. Not only was he out his Super Bowl cash, but the idiots he had protecting it weren't even injured in the robbery. For what he paid them, they should have defended that money with their lives. Instead they were all snoring like babies. Babies with sleep apnea.

"Asshole!" Marty screamed, stomping on Leman's chest and cracking two ribs. Leman groaned. Marty stomped three more times and again had to stop to catch his breath.

"You should kill them both."

Marty turned to glare at Slake, who offered Marty the wicked-looking switchblade he'd been using to clean his nails.

"You aren't the boss, Slake." Marty pushed the knife aside and got in Slake's face. "You're a grunt. If I say fetch, you fetch. If I say roll over, you better turn a fucking cartwheel. And don't you forget it."

"If you had let me guard the money like I said, this wouldn't have happened." Slake said it quietly, meeting his boss's fierce glare with apparent disinterest.

Marty drew the .38 snub nosed revolver he always kept in his waistband and jammed it under Slake's chin. Staring into Slake's empty eyes, Marty seriously considered killing him right there. Slake had been smarting-off a lot lately, and too many of his recent collections involved fatalities, something Marty couldn't abide. A dead gambler can't lose any more money.

Slake apparently recognized the intent in his employer's eyes, because his face morphed into something almost apologetic. He also threw in a touch of fear. Marty wasn't sure that Slake could actually feel fear, but he recognized the effort at subservience.

"I will forget you said that, my friend," Marty hissed, "because I've got enough shit to do here without having to clean your brains off of the ceiling."

Slake gave Marty a tiny, placating smile. Marty jammed the gun back into his pants and ran his non-absorbent sleeve over his forehead again. Slake was history as soon as this was over. He'd use him to help get his money back, and then he was out on his skinny little ass.

Leman groaned. The two men turned to see the ex-cop blink his eyes and try to lift up the hand that had all the blood on it.

"Who took my money, you shit!" Marty bellowed, flying onto Leman like a bug and grabbing two handfuls of shirt. "Who took it?"

"Water," Leman croaked.

Marty shook him harder. "I said who took my money!"

"Water. Please. My chest."

Marty spit in the man's face. "There's your water, you son of a bitch.

You're lucky I don't hang you from a flag pole by your colon. Who took it?"

Leman's eyelids fluttered, and Marty slapped him across the face. "Who?"

"Tequila."

"Tequila?"

"Yeah."

Marty released Leman's shirt, his mind absorbing the news. Tequila was his golden boy. Always did what he was told. Never screwed up. He hadn't had one single problem with Tequila since hiring him in that pool hall years ago.

But that in itself made him suspicious. Tequila never took the whores Marty offered. Or the drugs. He never talked back. Hell, he never talked at all. If anyone had a hidden agenda, it would be Tequila. You never knew what that son of a bitch was thinking.

"Get Tequila," he ordered Slake. "Bring his ass over here now."

"You really think he went home after robbing you blind?" Slake asked.

"I don't know what to think!" Marty's forehead veins stuck out like worms. "If he's not at home, find the little bastard! Do it!"

Slake shrugged and folded up his switchblade, exchanging it in his jacket pocket for a silver cigarette case. He opened the case and pulled out a French cigarette with thin fingers, then he strolled, unhurried, out of the room.

"Are you sure it was Tequila?" Marty nudged Leman.

"Huh?"

He gave the ex-cop a harsh slap. "Are you sure it was Tequila?"

"Heard someone say his name before I passed out. Plus we saw him on the vid monitor. Short guy with muscles."

"That son of a bitch."

Marty turned and faced the metal table. Gripping the edge, he upended it with a violent shove. The table flipped over, a metallic bang echoing throughout the vault, the coins on top tinkling and jingling on the hard wood floor.

If it was Tequila, he would know there was no place in the world he could hide. Marty was connected with all the Outfit families. He could put out a contract on that little shit's head and it would be filled within four hours, even if Tequila was hiding in a mud hut in Bombay, India.

So the question was: Would Tequila run? Or play innocent?

"Got the tape, Marty."

It was Terco, returning from the control room. He waved a VHS tape in the air and smiled widely.

"Get that stupid look off of your face before I kick it off."

Terco's grin dropped, and the two-hundred and sixty pound ex-professional weightlifter seemed ready to burst into tears. He blinked it away and set his massive jaw, looking like a punished puppy. Steroids might make you huge, but they did nothing for your emotional state.

"Call up Dr. Rankowski, tell him to come here and check these assholes out," Marty ordered, taking the tape from Terco and storming out of the room.

He brought the tape to his office, where he found Slake sitting in his chair behind his desk, smoking one of those awful Frog cigarettes and looking smug.

"Get your ass out of my chair. You find Tequila?"

"Called him at home," Slake said, slowly rising. "He's on his way over."

So the bastard didn't run.

"You tell him I was hit?"

"I just said you wanted to see him. An emergency."

Marty lashed out with a heavy right hand and slapped Slake in the face, knocking the cigarette across the room.

"Why didn't you go there and escort him personally, you stupid dink? If he doesn't show up, I'll do to you what I was gonna do to him."

"He'll show," whispered Slake, his dead eyes seeming to burn with hatred. "And if you ever hit me again..."

Marty shoved Slake back into the chair so violently he almost toppled him.

"You want to threaten me, you son of a bitch? You don't have the balls. You never had any balls, Slake. In fact, that's how I know you ain't the one that robbed me. Whoever robbed me has balls the size of toasters. You got little Tootsie Roll nuts."

Slake stared back, saying nothing.

"See? A real man, he'd defend the size of his cojones. Now get the fuck out of my chair."

The thin man removed himself from Marty's leather office chair and walked slowly around the desk.

"I talked to you, remember?" Slake said, a tremor in his voice.

"What?"

"I called to you while the vault was being robbed. Wrong number, remember?"

"Why do I give a shit?" Marty growled, fussing with the VCR. "You ain't a suspect, Tiny Balls."

He put the tape on visual rewind and got to the part where two masked individuals were walking out of the vault room with four suitcases obviously filled with money. He pressed play and let the segment run.

"Pause it," Slake said.

Marty paused it, too absorbed to realize that Slake had just given him an order.

"Right there. The short guy in the mask. Look at the back of his right hand."

The tape was black and white, and the pause flickered the image like a candle, but a tattoo of a butterfly could clearly be seen on the man's hand.

"Monarch tattoo. Like Tequila's."

"I'm gonna skin that son of a bitch and floss with his arteries," Marty whispered. Then he drew his .38 and emptied the cylinder into the television from almost point blank range.

CHAPTER 8

"A butterfly tattoo?"

"I swear. One of those orange and black ones."

"A Monarch butterfly?"

"Yeah. A Monarch butterfly."

Daniels wiped the sweat off her brow. The interrogation room was kept intentionally hot because some psychiatrist bozo wrote some paper about the effects of heat and stress and facilitating confessions. The shrink should have taken into account the stress levels of the cops doing the interrogation, who were just as uncomfortable and irritated as the suspects.

"So let me get this straight," she said. "The robber wasn't a tall black man in a green leather jacket and gym shoes. He was a short, blond, blue-eyed white guy with cowboy boots and a tattoo of a Monarch butterfly on his right hand?"

"Yes."

"And you didn't tell us this before because he threatened to kill you?"

Teddy Binkowski nodded like he had a spring in his neck. "Exactly. You didn't see it, Detective. He shot that guy twenty times in less than two seconds. It was terrifying."

Benedict got in the shop owner's face. "I think he's lying."

Jack agreed. "So do I. I think what we have to do is search his store again. Carefully this time. Break open every bottle of booze and every can of beer, to try and find out what he's hiding."

"I swear I'm telling the truth!"

"Call the boys still at the store, Herb. Have them use sledgehammers if necessary. But take that place apart."

Benedict turned to leave the interrogation room and Binkowski stood up.

"You can't do that!"

"Sit down, Mr. Binkowski." Jack put a firm hand on his shoulder and directed him back onto the metal chair bolted to the floor. "And yes we can. Your store was the scene of a homicide, and we're within our power to perform a thorough search of the crime scene."

"I want my lawyer."

"You aren't being charged with anything, Mr. Binkowski. You're the victim here, not the accused. What's a lawyer going to do for you?"

Binkowski's face twisted in panic. "Please! Don't! Don't destroy my store! I was lying. I admit I was lying."

Benedict stopped with his hand on the knob.

"About this guy with the butterfly tattoo?" Jack asked.

"No. He was real. But I wasn't protecting him because I was afraid for my life."

"Why then, Mr. Binkowski?"

"Because he didn't take all of my money. He only took two thousand dollars, and the rest he left behind."

Jack wasn't buying. "Herb, go call the squad. We're going to play Elliot Ness and bust open some booze."

"I swear it! He knew the guy he shot. Called him Billy. I think he was collecting a debt from him."

"A debt of two grand?"

"Yeah. Then Billy turned his gun on this guy, but he shot him first. The little guy didn't even have his guns drawn yet, but he shot Billy before Billy could even swing his gun around." Binkowski greened like a string bean. "It was the most horrible thing I've ever seen, and I've worked retail for over twenty years."

Jack studied the man's face.

"And after killing Billy, this man forced you to open the safe and give him two thousand dollars?"

"Yes. And he put the rest in a box for me to hide so I could claim it all on my insurance."

"Run through the whole thing, from the top."

Binkowski did, painting a much clearer picture then the vague one he'd given an hour earlier. Clearer, yes, but still highly suspect in Jack's mind.

"So this guy shot Billy Chico, in self-defense, and only took two thousand dollars instead of the entire contents, which were how much?"

"About five grand."

"So where's the other three grand?"

"In a box of Courvoisier Grand Reserve on my cognac shelf."

Jack nodded at Benedict, who then went to go check on it.

"Don't destroy my store!"

"We won't if you're telling the truth, Mr. Binkowski."

"I am. I swear."

Daniels looked deep into his pleading eyes and had the feeling she'd finally heard the truth. He'd been holding on to the lie in an effort to make a couple more thousand dollars from the insurance company, and that made some sense. But that was the only part of the story that did.

"Mr. Binkowski, we're going to have you work with a police artist, see if you can put together a picture of this guy. How tall did you say he was again?"

"Under five-six."

It would be a simple maneuver to program the computer to bring up the files of all short white males with tattoos. How many could there be? They'd have a name within an hour or two. Unless he didn't have a record, which was unlikely with the cold-blooded way he had killed Chico.

Benedict re-entered the interrogation room and gave Jack a nod, indicating they'd found the money.

"Okay, Mr. Binkowski. Thank you for your cooperation. Someone will be with you shortly to take you to our sketch artist."

"What about my money?"

"You're money is safe, Mr. Binkowski. But if I were you, I'd make an extra hard effort to remember every detail about this guy. It would be a shame if your insurance company were to learn you were trying to scam them."

Binkowski nodded, his frown as long as the night.

Jack walked briskly over to Benedict and led the way down the hall on the third floor of the 26th Precinct. It was coming up on one in the morning, but the activity in the building was loud enough to force the volume of their conversation higher than normal speaking level.

"So you think it was a private debt, or that this Butterfly guy was collecting for someone connected?" Herb asked.

"Someone connected. He's got to be well paid, or at least well paid enough that he wasn't tempted to take all of Binkowski's money. Just what was owed. What kind of killer would turn his back on a free two grand?"

"He was making sure Binkowski wouldn't ID him, banking on his greed."

"That could be part of it. But there's something else here. What do you think about this self-defense angle?"

"Chico had a gun on him. Could be self-defense. If he was really collecting a debt, what good would killing him do? He'd wait for Chico to finish, like Binkowski said. Except Chico didn't finish. Instead he panicked, turned the gun at Butterfly, and Butterfly shot him."

"Maybe."

They hung a left at the end of the hall and Benedict led them into the stairwell. Unlike the rest of the building, the stairwell wasn't heated, and the temperature was a good twenty degrees cooler. Because of this anomaly, lining the edges of the stair on every floor were brown paper bags and lunch boxes, left there by night patrol cops who wanted to keep their sandwiches and soda cold. Benedict and Daniels took the stairs down, ignoring the bags.

"Doesn't a threat work better than a bribe?" Daniels asked, still pondering why Butterfly hadn't taken all the money, just a part of it.

"Sometimes. Sometimes a bribe works better because then the person incriminates himself, and is then on your side."

"You ever been tempted?"

"Who hasn't? Christ, remember that time in Vice, when we raided that drug house? More money on the table than I made in ten years."

"You take any?"

"I've thought about that night many times. I was the one who found the stash. I could have filled my pockets without anyone else knowing."

"Why didn't you?"

"I guess," Benedict said, opening the door for Jack when they reached the first floor, "because I'm an honorable man. It wasn't my money. I was sworn by my duty not to steal. What would you have done?"

"Same thing. Did you find drugs on that raid too?"

"Yeah. I ripped off two keys of Mexican brown."

Daniels laughed.

"Stuffed them down a pants leg," Herb said. "How do you think I bought a house while still so young?"

"You mortgaged the hell out of it."

"Damn right. Come to think of it, I should have stole some of that damn money."

They walked side-by-side to Jack's office, and Jack plopped down in the ratty swivel chair behind her desk. She rolled over to the table where the computer perched, the screen saver a picture of Homer from *The Simpsons*.

Punching a few keys, Jack accessed the data entry screen and fed in information on the killer with the Monarch butterfly tattoo. She programmed in three searches; one for white males under five seven, another for individuals with tattoos, and the last one incorporating both.

"So why didn't Butterfly just kill Binkowski?" Herb asked. "Why risk leaving a witness alive? He'd already killed one guy. Why not kill two and take all the money?"

"That's the million dollar question."

The dot matrix printer, big as a Studebaker and damn near as old, began to slowly spit out search results.

"How's things at home?" Herb asked.

Jack's face pinched. Last month, after a particularly mean-spirited fight with her husband, Jack had been off her game and Herb caught her on it. In a moment of weakness she'd confessed to some marital problems, which Herb apparently thought was okay to talk about at any given time.

The thing was, unlike practically every other cop in the District—all sharing Y chromosomes and waiting to pounce on the female detective if she made the slightest mistake—Herb didn't seem to be using the information as a lever or a bludgeon. He seemed genuinely concerned.

Jack had no real friends, either on the Job or on the outside: Her eighty hour work weeks were already causing a big strain on her marriage, and there was zero time left over for herself. It was a high price to pay to be taken seriously in this old boys' network, and because of that Jack didn't really have anyone to talk about her problems with.

Herb engaged in the normal station camaraderie that Jack was excluded from because of her sex, but he didn't seem to have a chauvinistic bone in his skinny body. He was, in fact, the perfect partner.

But could she trust him?

"The usual," Jack said. She figured she could skimp on the details, downplay the seriousness. "He's worried he's going to get the call to ID my body at the hospital."

"That's crazy. I'm your partner. I'd be the one who IDed you."

Jack saw the humor but didn't smile.

"It's not easy being a cop's wife, Jack. Or husband. You have to be stronger than the cop you're supporting. Bernice is much stronger than I am. I'd go nuts if I knew she was on the street, constantly in danger of getting killed. I couldn't handle it."

"Maybe Bernice should talk to Alan."

"I can ask her, if you'd like."

Jack pictured Alan getting a call from Herb's wife, how her husband would scream that she was airing their dirty laundry.

"Probably not a good idea. It wouldn't go well."

Herb opened his mouth to say something supportive, but Jack cut him off.

"Computer says seven hundred and forty probables in the first search alone. Why don't you go home, Herb?"

"You should too."

"I will," Jack lied.

"See you tomorrow, Jack. Or later today anyway."

The skinny cop left the office, and Jack Daniels leaned back in the leather swivel chair and stared at the ceiling, listening to the printer whir.

She'd stay there tonight. Start going through the list. The prospect of going to her apartment, to Alan, was depressing, and she knew that no sleep awaited her there. If she were lucky, she'd catch a wink or two at the desk.

Daniels only slept when total exhaustion overcame her. When she tried to sleep, tried to go to bed the normal way, her mind refused to shut off and kept her awake with guilt.

Jack breathed guilt like most people breathed air.

She yawned, picturing the bloodbath in the liquor store earlier that night.

"Are you somewhere in here, my man?" She stared at the printout, which was already three pages long. "And will you do it again?"

Jack removed the notepad from her jacket pocket and scribbled the word PRIORS, as a mental note for her to check for similar murders once Ballistics came up with a make on the slugs and the casings they had found. It would be interesting to see if others had been killed in such a style. Jack was reluctant to do this, because a search of that scope would mean Federal involvement since it crossed borders, and bringing the FBI into an investigation was like sitting on a screw driver—screwing yourself. Still, it was important to see if the MO had been documented before.

Because Jack was sure she would see the same MO again. And soon.

CHAPTER 9

When the phone rang, Tequila knew it was work. No one else called in the middle of the night. No one else called, period. Tequila had no friends, of the female gender or otherwise. His only family was his sister, and she was asleep in her room. He'd tried dozens of times to teach her their phone number, but Sally didn't understand numbers. The only number he'd managed to drill into her head was 911, if there were ever an emergency.

He guessed it was around one in the morning from how rested he felt, and a quick glance at his digital clock confirmed his guess.

This all flashed through his mind during the first ring. He picked the phone up before it rang again.

"Yes."

"Tequila, this is Slake. You better get down to *Spill* right away. Marty wants you. It's an emergency."

Tequila hung up and held his chin, jerking his head to the left in order to crack his neck. It didn't crack, because he hadn't been asleep long enough for the calcium deposits to build up. He dressed in the dark, finding his chinos, shirt, and socks in the drawers where they always were. Instead of putting on his boots he chose a pair of black Reeboks, lacing them so tight they felt like an extra layer skin. Then he slipped into his gun rig and slipped out of the bedroom, walking down the hall and knocking once on China's door.

"Mr. Abernathy?"

"I have to go out, China. Please keep an eye on Sally."

"No problem, Mr. Abernathy."

China had no qualms about him leaving in the middle of the night, any more than she had qualms about the guns she always saw Tequila with. She had no idea what Tequila did for a living, and didn't much care either. Which was more than could be said about the previous care-giver. When Tequila had brought home his first gun, after being taught to shoot by Marty shortly after his hire, she panicked and fled. When screening replacements, he told applicants he was a bodyguard and showed them his carry permit. Almost as a rule, women who cared for the mentally challenged had an abhorrence to firearms. Until he found China. She didn't seem bothered by anything.

He pocketed the incriminating .45 barrels that he'd taken out of his guns and left in the recycle bin. Then he grabbed his coat from the hall closet and locked the door behind him when he left. As he walked to the elevator he let his mind dwell on what Marty considered an emergency. Marty was an over-reactive type, and several times Tequila had been summoned at odd hours to help track down the latest bimbo in Marty's life, who had taken off with his car, or some cash, or once his gold chain—the one Marty got from some top dog in the mob hierarchy.

Marty was also prone to summon Tequila during the wee hours because one of the other guys was sick and couldn't play bodyguard, or because Marty just caught a line on some big debtor whom they hadn't been able to find.

Tequila didn't think it was any of those, though. Tonight was Super Bowl night. It probably had something to do with that.

Like most around-the-clock employees, Marty's collectors rotated work details on holidays. That way none of them had to work two Christmases, or New Year's Eves, or Thanksgivings, in a row. Super Bowl Sunday was considered a holiday as well, and Tequila had worked last year's, making him exempt this time around. He should have gotten the night completely off, but Marty had gotten a fix on Billy Chico, and sent his only available collector to track him down. It wasn't a paid holiday like it should have been, but it beat sitting in that steel vault for six hours while Marty's accountants counted the day's take fifteen times each.

Tequila reached the lobby and took the door to the parking garage. Frank the doorman gave him a friendly nod as he walked past. He disengaged the car alarm with the device on his key ring, which also opened the doors. The yellow metal smiley face keychain he'd gotten from Sally seemed to wink at him as he started the car. Her birthday was coming up in a few weeks. He'd have to think of something nice to get her.

Once again he had to honk at the watchman, who didn't open the garage door because he'd been sleeping. Tequila decided he wouldn't let it slide this time. He'd complain to the association and get the man fired. What if there were some kind of emergency, especially with Sally?

He drove out into the night, opening his windows and letting the frigid atmosphere slap at him. *Spill* was only ten blocks away, and he parked in the alley around back. He buried the gun barrels in the bottom of a nearby Dumpster, making sure the prints were wiped off first, and placed some boxes over them.

The club was located on the first and second floor of a ten story office building, which Marty owned. When Marty had toyed with the idea of opening a dance bar, he'd been able to get this entire building for less than what it would have cost to build a club from scratch. The remaining floors he rented out to a few legitimate businesses, and kept the rest for himself.

Tequila went around to the front of the building, where a line of people waited to get in, freezing in their miniskirts and dago tees. Looking good was more important than keeping warm at a trendy club like *Spill*. Tequila walked past the line and nodded at the doorman, who was scrutinizing a young blonde girl's ID with a penlight. It should have been Terco or Slake at the door, as Leman and Matisse were on money guard duty tonight, but instead it was O'Neal, one of the bartenders. Terco and Slake had probably been pulled away to deal with whatever the emergency was.

O'Neal gave Tequila a mean face for cutting in line until he noticed who it was, and then the mean became a curt nod and he let the smaller man pass.

The interior of *Spill* was similar to other clubs of its type. Dark, except for the flashing lights on the dance floors, cramped to capacity with people, smoky, and louder than hell. Tequila pushed his way through the crowd of twenty-something partiers and to the back bar by the DJ booth. He used his access key to open the door marked PRIVATE. The door locked automatically behind him, and Tequila walked down a short hall and then up a staircase to Marty's office, mercifully soundproofed from the rest of the club.

Marty the Maniac was in his office alone, something Tequila hadn't expected. He appeared to be hunched over some kind of contract, and he motioned for Tequila to come in without looking up at him. Tequila, without knowing exactly why, felt slightly on edge. He entered the office but didn't sit, waiting for Marty to say something. As he always did, Tequila took in his surroundings and noticed two unusual things. The first was that Marty's television, usually on a stand by the wall, was missing. The second was that whatever Marty had in front of him, he wasn't reading it. Only pretending to.

Marty appeared to reach the end of his reading, and then pushed it aside on his desk and sat back in his chair, meeting Tequila's stare. He looked extremely calm. Too calm for Marty. Tequila's apprehension kicked up a notch.

"Where's the money?"

Tequila assumed he meant the collection from Billy Chico. Maybe that's what Marty was upset over. The fact that Tequila had killed Chico, and that it might lead back to him somehow.

"I've got it on me," Tequila said.

Marty smiled, but the smile was as dead as his eyes.

"Funny, Tequila. Very funny. Aren't you wondering how I knew it was you?"

Tequila didn't understand the question. He waited for more.

"You forgot about the videotape. I've got the whole thing on tape. Got a great shot of your tattoo."

Tequila replayed the words in his head, trying to make sense out of them. He was missing something here.

"What are you talking about?" he finally asked.

"What am I talking about?" Marty chuckled. "I'll tell you what I'm talking about. I want my Super Bowl money, you stupid little shit!"

All of Tequila warning bells rang at once. He sensed quick movement coming behind him and swung around, connecting a right cross into the face of a charging Terco. Terco's head snapped back as if on hinges, and he fell to his knees.

Then Matisse came at him, leaping over Terco. Tequila pivoted left and snap-kicked him in the ribs. The larger man grunted, reflexively dropping his cocked fist to his chest to stop the hurt. Tequila spun around fast and used the momentum to smack the back of his left hand into Matisse's nose. It burst like a rotten tomato, and Matisse howled as if part canine.

"Freeze!"

Tequila heard the gun cock and back-flipped onto Marty's desk. While still in the air he hit the release button on his shoulder rig and jammed both hands into his holsters, coming out with two .45s as he landed on his feet. One was pointed at Marty and the other aimed at Leman, who was now standing behind the beaten Terco and Matisse and aiming a shotgun at Tequila's noggin.

"Don't kill him!" Marty cried.

"You lousy, piece of shit thief," Leman spat.

Tequila kept his sights rock steady, fighting against the adrenaline surging through his veins.

"This is a big misunderstanding, whatever it is." He kept his voice even, tried to control his breathing. "Drop the gun, Leman, or I'll shoot your finger off so you can't pull the trigger. You know I can."

Leman swallowed, tensing up. They'd gone shooting together once, at a gun club in the suburbs. Using his .45, Tequila had put three full clips, twenty-one rounds, into a controlled space the size of a quarter from forty yards away. Then he put twenty-one more rounds through the same hole with his left hand.

"No, Tequila, I think you'll be the one dropping the guns."

It was Slake, coming from behind him. Tequila glanced backwards and saw the evil son of a bitch peeking out of the closet, a 9mm trained on the small of his back.

Tequila weighed his options. He'd obviously been accused, and already convicted, of doing something he hadn't done. The obvious guess was that someone had taken Marty's Super Bowl stash, and everyone thought it was him. He could either try to convince them otherwise, or try to kill everyone here.

He figured the odds for each choice were about the same, and neither of them very good.

"Drop the gun, Tequila," Slake cooed.

Marty shook with rage. "Drop it, you shit!"

Matisse and Terco slowly gained their footing, making the situation worse. If Tequila jumped to the side and shot Leman while in motion, he might have enough time to draw a bead on Slake before Slake popped a cap in his head. He'd have to drop Slake with one shot, because Terco and Matisse would then draw on him, and Marty sure as hell had some heat on his person as well.

The deciding factor was Slake. If it had been any of the others in the closet, Tequila would have gone for self-preservation and shot his way out of there. But he knew Slake. Slake had hated Tequila since they'd first met. Part of it was jealousy. Slake had never been in Marty's favor, while Tequila always seemed to be. But mostly, it was because deep down inside, Slake was a rotten human being. Tequila sensed that Slake would dearly love to put a few bullets into him, and his eagerness to do so meant Tequila wouldn't have the advantage his quickness normally gave him.

"I'll lose the guns," Tequila said, calm as a sunset, "if someone tells me what's going on."

"You stole my money!" Marty screamed, his red balloon of a face threatening to pop.

"I didn't steal any money. I don't know what you're talking about."

"If you're innocent," Slake said, in a voice barely above a whisper, "then you don't have anything to worry about."

Tequila stared hard at Slake. He saw little sparks of what looked like flame in the thin man's eyes. He also noticed that Slake was slowly, every so slowly, pulling the trigger on his nine millimeter.

"Fine," Tequila said, turning to Marty. "But I'm being straight with you. I didn't steal any money. I've worked for you for five years Marty, and I haven't wronged you once. Whatever reason you think I did, it's incorrect. I'm innocent here, Marty. And I'm putting away my guns to show good faith."

Tequila could feel the heat from Marty's stare, all of the anger still boiling on the surface of his face.

"One more thing, Marty. Slake's about to shoot me. If he kills me, you won't know what I know."

Marty turned his angry gaze to the closet.

"Slake, you asshole, if you shoot him so help me I'll gut you with a fork and string tennis rackets with you."

Tequila saw the tension go out of Slake's hand, the trigger returning back to its normal position. Moving slowly, testing the waters, Tequila lowered the gun aimed at Marty and holstered it. Then he gave Leman his full attention.

"I'm sure Marty would gut you as well, Leman, if you decide to take it upon yourself to end my life."

"Drop it," Marty ordered the ex-cop.

Leman made a sour face, and then stuck the pistol in his pants. Tequila reciprocated by holstering his other .45. He hopped off the desk, his eyes locked onto Marty's.

"Now tell me what you think I did."

"I can do better than that. I can show you. Matisse!"

Matisse was pinching his bloody nose, an action that had consumed his full concentration for the last few minutes. He seemed to snap awake when his name was called.

"Yeah, Marty?"

"Go find me another TV. Hurry up."

Matisse nodded and lumbered off.

"Okay, Tequila. I'm going to give you the benefit of several hundred doubts. Earlier today, two men drilled a hole in the steel door of my counting room and gassed Matisse, Leman, and my two number crunchers. We've got it all on tape. One of those men was short and muscular, and had a butterfly tattoo on his right hand. It was an inside job. All of my men have been accounted for during the time of the robbery. And Leman, right before he went out, heard one of the burglars call your name. What does all of that add up to?"

"It sounds like someone set me up."

"So where were you during the robbery?"

"I was tracking down Billy Chico, as you told me. I found him robbing a liquor store on Devon, and he drew on me. You'll read about it in the morning papers."

"What do you mean, as I told you? I didn't send you after Chico. It was your day off."

"You called me around six."

"Are you saying that I don't fucking know when I call you and when I don't?"

Tequila tensed another notch. He replayed the phone call again in his brain. It was Marty's voice, telling him to go collect the two grand marker from Chico. He'd even given Tequila Chico's description and his new address, the apartment Tequila had trailed him from. But if it wasn't Marty who called him...

"If it wasn't you, it was someone claiming to be you."

"And you don't know my voice from some other schmuck pretending to be me?"

"It sounded like your voice."

Marty stared at him. Matisse entered the office lugging a twenty inch Zenith, which he'd gotten from the utility room where the video security cameras were wired up. He and Slake placed it in the nook where the previous TV used to reside before Marty had assassinated it. Slake hooked up the VCR while Matisse fiddled with the cord, trying to figure out which way the prongs fit into the electrical outlet. Slake finished first.

Without a word, Marty the Maniac hit the PLAY button on his remote control, and Tequila watched the robbery unfold. First the men approaching with the tank. Then the drilling. Then the hose. Then the opening of the door by punching in the correct access code. And finally, the exiting the vault with four suitcases full of cash. Matisse paused the frame on the clear still of the butterfly tattoo.

Tequila's mind swam. He realized that he'd chosen incorrectly. This tape damned him, damned him beyond a doubt, and he should have shot his way out when he had the chance.

"So tell me, my friend," Marty's voice edged with hostility, "that that isn't you."

"That's not me. I was at the liquor store. And after that, I was at a bar called the *Blues Note*. I'm being framed. The burglars wanted that tattoo to be seen, to blame me. If I robbed you I wouldn't have taken off the gloves."

"You made a mistake. You took them off in the vault to load the money, then forgot about them."

"I don't make mistakes, Marty."

"Oh, but you did, Tequila," Marty said, rising out of his chair. "You made the biggest mistake of all. You robbed ME!"

Tequila had cleared leather on both guns when Slake hit him with the tazer. He dropped the .45s in a spasm and fell backward as his entire body held rigid by the electric shock. The pain was magnificent, every nerve firing at once, every muscle contracting into knots.

His last conscious image was Slake's face, smeared with a grin so vicious he had appeared to be salivating, and then a fist to the side of the head.

CHAPTER 10

Tequila was out when Terco punched him, but Slake tazed him again just to make sure.

"Take him into the vault," Marty ordered. "Tie him up."

Terco and Matisse dragged Tequila off.

"Let me interrogate him, Marty," Slake smiled. "I'll get him to sing like Domingo."

Marty furrowed his brow. He didn't like the fact that Tequila had been so insistent on his innocence. Sure, all guilty men were liars. But Tequila either lied better than most, or else he was telling the truth. And if he was telling the truth, Marty was going to kill an irreplaceable employee. What he needed was more proof before he started the interrogation. Once the torture began, it didn't matter if Tequila were guilty or not. Marty would have to waste him. If he didn't, Tequila surely would return the favor.

"I'll do the interrogation. You go check his apartment, see if you can find the money."

"How about his car?"

"Yeah. Car too. And Terco, go check Tequila's alibi. The liquor store thing and that bar he mentioned, the *Blues Note*."

They scurried off and another troubling thought occurred to Marty. If Tequila didn't steal the money, who did? It had to be someone close to him. Someone who knew the routine, who had access to the vault.

One of the other collectors? Or maybe one of the accountants?

Marty thought of something he was always preaching to his employees. "Paranoia grows like weeds."

It was certainly growing in Marty. He tried to shrug it off, but it clung like a tight sweater.

"You want me to get your toolbox, Marty?" Leman asked. He'd been standing in the office, waiting for Marty to give him direction.

"Yeah. My toolbox."

Leman nodded and left.

Marty sat back in his chair, staring blankly at the paused image of a butterfly tattoo on his new television. That was Tequila. It had to be. He'd robbed Marty, and then hoped that his good record and his proclaiming innocence would be enough to avoid suspicion. And if the dumb son of a bitch hadn't taken his gloves off, maybe he would have gotten away with it.

"Dumb shit," Marty told the TV screen.

The Maniac clenched his fingers. By the end of the night he'd have his money back. Along with Tequila's accomplice. He didn't doubt it at all.

Slake appeared in the doorway, holding up a black sweater and a ski mask.

"These were in Tequila's trunk."

Marty grimaced at the stupidity of it all. Too stupid, maybe? It had crossed Marty's mind that Tequila might have been framed. With enough planning, anyone could have done it.

He didn't credit his entourage with enough brains to stuff a Cornish hen, but there was always the slim chance one of them recruited outside help.

But Marty knew from experience that the simplest answer, the obvious one, was usually the truth. He'd wait for Terco to report back on the liquor store and the *Blues Note*, and then he'd get the truth from the little shit himself.

In his day, Marty had been one of the most feared men in Chicago. He still was, but not in the same way as back then. Now days, people feared

Marty's power. Back in the sixties, they feared his rage.

There were seven unsolved murder cases in Chicago police files from those days. All had been linked by cause of death. Each of the victims had been systematically beaten to death. Almost every bone in their bodies had been broken, crushed, shattered, or fractured. Autopsy reports showed the use of hammers, pliers, wrenches, and even a vice. The work of a maniac, thought police. And they suspected a certain maniac up-and-comer named Marty Martelli.

Marty had been questioned for five of the murders, but had never been arrested. His friends had been too powerful, and he hadn't left any evidence behind. The Maniac was as careful as he was thorough. Not only had he escaped prosecution, but every one of those men had given up the information Marty had been trying to drag out of them.

Tequila would talk, all right. He'd talk until his lips fell off.

Or until Marty pulled them off.

"Go to his apartment, look for the money," Marty ordered Slake. "Bring Matisse with you. And I'll give you both a double bonus if you can find the other guy in the video."

Slake nodded and tossed the sweater and ski mask onto Marty's desk.

Marty's fingers twitched. He was itching to get his hands on Tequila, to use his toolbox on the little bastard.

Itching.

CHAPTER 11

Tequila awoke bound to a chair, the side of his head throbbing where Terco had hit him. He instantly registered several things at once: He was locked in the vault room, he'd been tied with clothesline, tightly and expertly, with his hands behind his back, his guns were missing but his holster rig was still on, and he could feel his keys in his front pocket.

A bad situation, but not a hopeless one. On his key ring was a Swiss Army knife.

Tequila began to flex and relax his chest muscles, shrugging and shaking his shoulders at intervals. The line that was wrapped around his body, securing his torso to the chair, slowly and inexorably undulated down his chest, until it rested, still tied, around his stomach. This gave Tequila enough room to bend forward.

Flexibility is just as important as strength in gymnastics, and Tequila was more flexible than most. His diminutive size working to his advantage, Tequila was able to touch his chin to his lap. With a combination of neck and hip motions, he gradually nudged his keys out of the pocket of his loose-fitting chinos. They jingled to the floor with more noise than he cared to make.

He straightened his back out to normal and stretched, trying to work out the soreness in his neck. Then he adjusted his position with his toes, took a deep breath, and rocked the chair onto its side. He hit the ground hard, and his head rang from the impact, making the vault appear to blur and spin.

After getting his bearings, Tequila felt around with his hands tied behind him, seeking out the keys. He'd predicted his fall correctly, and the keys were in his grasp within a few seconds of searching.

Sweating now, Tequila pictured the Swiss Army Knife in his mind and opened the longest blade from memory. Then, working his fingers like tiny pistons, he sawed back and forth at the rope binding his wrists.

The task required his total concentration. His fingers were strong, but the repetitive, restricted movement caused his hand to cramp up. Every so often his crippled fingers would spasm, and he'd dig the knife into his wrists. Sweat, and later blood, made the knife slippery, hard to hold. Tequila chanted his mantra silently in his head, as he did when working out, and willed the movement of the blade through the pain.

He had to cut through three knots, nicking himself dozens of times in the process, before the rope gave. Hands free, he made easy work of the rest of his restraints, and then looked around the vault. The door was the only entry point, and as expected it had been locked. Maybe with a battering ram and a few hours he'd be able to get it open. But he had neither. So he carried the chair over to the covered-up vent in the corner of the room.

The vent was about three feet wide and two feet high, and covering the grating was a sheet of metal, held in place with four screws. He worked out the screws using the Phillips head on his Swiss Army Knife, wondering why those idiots Leman and Matisse hadn't noticed that the damn vent was blocked off the whole time they'd been in there.

The final screw dropped to the floor and he removed the sheet metal. The grating was behind it, and four more screws removed that as well. Not stopping to think about it, Tequila hauled himself up to the vent and wriggled himself into the tight shaft.

Two things struck him as he wormed his way into the darkness. The first was the incredible heat. Marty had it cranked up to boiling, and he couldn't keep his hands in one place too long before they began to burn. But even more oppressive than the heat was the dust. It got in Tequila's eyes and mouth, and breathing was only possible after pulling his shirt up over his nose and mouth to filter out the airborne grit.

Tequila moved as quickly as he could in an almost completely horizontal position, dragging himself forward by his hands and elbows and adding a little propulsion with his toes. A tight, hot, filthy, uncomfortable, claustrophobic journey, but infinitely better than waiting for what the Maniac had in store for him.

Each sound he made was magnified, and banging a knee sounded like taking an aluminum bat to a tin garbage can. When he stopped to rest, the radiant heat of the metal seeped into his knees, palms, and elbows, threatening first degree burns.

Twice he had to smother his face into his shoulder to prevent coughing fits. Another time he couldn't stifle a sneeze quick enough and he heard it echo throughout the labyrinth of ducts, seemingly forever.

After four minutes of sweaty, painful crawling, his tunnel ended abruptly, meeting with a vertical shaft. Tequila squinted down into the darkness of the duct and was hit with a wave of heat that made his eyes dry and sticky. The furnace was down there.

So he went up.

He pulled his body into the larger vertical vent and held himself suspended by pressing his hands against the hot metal of the sides, very much like an iron cross on the rings. Spreading his legs, he turned sideways and placed his feet against the sides as well, thankful he had decided to wear gym shoes with rubber soles instead of his cowboy boots. Alternating his hand and foot holds, he made his way up the duct, mountain-climber style.

He was almost up to the next floor when he began to slide.

The sweat, conspiring with the blood seeping from his many wrist wounds, had soaked his palms and dripped down the walls of the vent. When his hands began to slip, he tried to hold his position with his splayed feet long enough to wipe his palms on his shirt. But all the dust, mixed with the blood and sweat, created a thin layer of greasy grime that his shoes couldn't get a purchase on. He slid another meter, and forced his hands and feet out with all of his might, willing his descent to stop.

Which was when the grip of his shoes gave out completely and he fell, straight down, toward the furnace.

Tequila was no stranger to falling. It happened often enough in practice. But falling in darkness unnerved him completely, and while his arms waved around frantically for something to grab, he unconsciously tensed his body, something one should never do in a fall.

His flailing hands banged and echoed against the metal ducts, and the heat licked up at Tequila like the beckoning flames of hell. He'd judged he'd fallen about thirty feet before instinct kicked in and he relaxed his body for impact. The only tense part of him were his ankles, held tight together with the toes pointed out, paratrooper-style.

Then he hit.

His ass smacked against his heels, a thunderbolt of pain surging up from his coccyx through his spine and snapping his jaw shut. But before he could even assess the damage to his body, Tequila was surrounded by a heat so intense it was like climbing into a hot oven.

He reflexively touched the floor and his hand sizzled on the grating covering the furnace. The massive machine somewhere beneath his feet was blowing up superheated air, powerfully and relentlessly heating the entire building.

Tequila got to his feet and patted out the fire that had started on his ass from his chinos touching the grating. He held his hands out to the sides of the duct to climb and seared them badly. Taking off his jacket, he tried to wrap that around his hands, but the heat got through just the same, making his ascension impossible.

He smelled something foul and knew it was the rubber melting off of his shoes.

Thinking quickly, he removed his gun rig from his chest and pressed the button to magnetize the holsters. Hopefully, the building was old enough that the duct work was steel instead of aluminum. He touched the holsters to the side of the vent and they stuck there.

Wasting no time, Tequila chinned himself up on his holsters, the powerful ceramic magnets holding his weight. Then he touched his feet against the walls and found that they gripped well, due to the sticky rubber that was melting on their bottoms. He hit the button on his rig again and touched it to the side of the vent up over his head before re-magnetizing them. Then he pulled himself up, and once more braced his body with his feet.

Slowly, inexorably, he got up high enough to where he could touch the vents with his bare hands without searing them. Then he wrapped the rig around his shoulders and doubled his efforts, muscles aching.

Tequila just passed the duct that led into the vault room when the bullets began to fly.

CHAPTER 12

Slake and Matisse rolled up to Tequila's apartment building in a 1979 Monte Carlo. It was a muscle car, dark silver with side engine vents that looked like gills. The vehicle resembled a shark, which was the reason Slake bought it. With his salary he could have had any car. But this one suited his personality.

They parked across the street and Slake reviewed their options. This was a security building, which meant that both entrances were monitored, and no one would be admitted without a resident's permission. The lobby was watched by a doorman. The garage was watched by an attendant.

Or at least, it should have been. In this case, the attendant was napping.

They walked up to the garage doors, and Slake gave Matisse a nod. Crouching by the door, Matisse took a firm grip on the handle at the bottom, straightened his back, and flexed his legs as if ready to attempt a deadlift.

The world record deadlift was almost nine hundred pounds, executed by a man weighing two hundred and seventy-five. Matisse weighed two-eighty, all of it muscle, most of it steroid-induced. The garage door weighed only eighty pounds, and the mechanical arm that opened and closed the door added four hundred pounds of pressure to the total.

Matisse vs. The Garage Door.

The Garage Door lost.

Slake was inside the garage, his knife in his hand, before the attendant had even opened an eye. He was already though the door to the security room when the attendant finally stirred, realizing something was wrong. The knife at his throat was the first clue.

"Caught you napping," cooed Slake, his stiletto tickling the man's Adam's apple..

"Take the keys." The attendant quavered, pointing to the rack of car keys hanging on numbered hooks behind him. Several tenants preferred valet parking to the do-it-yourself option, and the attendant, assuming the intruders were car thieves, had no hesitation in trading them all for his hide. "You want a Cadillac? Benz? Corvette? How about a Ferrari? Take all you want."

"How about a white Chevy Caprice Classic that looks like a cop car?"

"I don't have his keys." The attendant shrank. "He parks himself."

"What's his room number?"

"I don't know. I swear."

Slake looked at the Rolex on his wrist.

"You have exactly fifteen seconds to find out."

The attendant paled. He wasn't even fully awake yet. One minute he'd been having a dream about rubbing suntan lotion on Carmen Electra's butt, and now he was being threatened with death by some knife-wielding psycho who wanted information he didn't have. If only he hadn't been asleep, then he could have called the police before this wacko got in. He blamed Dr. Stubin, his chemistry professor. Mitch had been up the entire previous night studying for that asshole's midterm. This was all Stubin's fault.

Matisse came into the security office, having jerked the garage door back down after entering. Mitch flinched at the sight of the new man, whose appearance made his situation even worse.

Damn you, Dr. Stubin.

"Ten seconds," Slake said, eyes on his watch.

The attendant scooped up the phone in front of him and dialed the extension for the phone in the lobby.

Please, God, don't let Frank be in the john.

"This is Frank."

Thank you, Jesus. "Frank? Mitch. Who's that short guy, crew cut, drives the Caprice?"

"Five seconds." Slake tapped at Mitch's chin with the knife edge.

"Tequila Abernathy. Lives in 3014. Why?"

"Thirty-fourteen? Thanks Frank!"

The attendant smiled at Slake, his face a cross between hope and relief.

"Tell him his lights are on," Slake told him.

"His lights are on, Frank. I'll call him."

"Lights are on? He went out earlier tonight, hasn't come back yet."

"I guess he walked somewhere."

"That's strange."

"Tell him you have to go," ordered Slake.

"Gotta go, Frank. Have to piss."

The attendant hung-up and grinned weakly.

"What's the name of the day doorman?" Slake asked.

"Steve." Mitch was eager to please at this point.

"And are there any vacancies?"

"Uh, yeah. Some guy just moved out of, uh, twelve-ten. No. Twelve-twelve. That's open."

"Thank you."

The man's eyes got wide. "Did I do good?"

"Yes, Mitch. You did good."

Then Slake rammed his knife into Mitch's neck. He clamped his free hand across the attendant's mouth to block off the scream, and gave the knife a vicious twist.

The scream came out of the hole in Mitch's throat instead of his lips, but with the vocal chords severed and the blood running freely the bubbly sound he made was scarcely louder than a fart in the bathtub.

The killer withdrew his blade and set Mitch's head down on the desk, leaving him to die without ever knowing if he had passed his Chemistry mid-term or not. He hadn't. *That asshole Dr. Stubin.*

"Jesus, Slake, did you have to kill him?"

Slake wiped his knife blade off in the dead man's hair and grinned. "No, I didn't."

A shiver crept up Matisse's back and caused his shoulders to shake. Slake folded his knife and tucked it away, and wiped away his fingerprints on the door with his sleeve.

They went through the garage over to the lobby entrance. Walking in smoothly, appearing as if they belonged, Slake and Matisse headed straight for the elevator.

"Gentlemen?"

Frank the doorman raised an eyebrow at them. If they'd gotten through the garage, they were obviously tenants or friends of tenants. But Frank made it a point to recognize everyone—a necessary trait for someone who depended on tips to earn a living—and these two he didn't recognize.

"You must be Frank." Slake smiled widely. The smile didn't quite work on his harsh face. "The name's Collins, just moved into twelve-twelve. I hope you'll be as helpful as Steve was this morning. I chose this apartment for its privacy, and he seems like a man ready to protect mine."

Slake shook hands with Frank, offering him a palmed bill. Frank took it without glancing at the denomination.

"Privacy is something that should be protected, Mr. Collins." Frank grinned, snuck a look at the bill—a twenty—and grinned wider. "I'll certainly do my best."

Slake nodded, and Frank pressed the button to call their elevator. He eyed the pair peripherally. Big tippers aside, there was something about them that wasn't quite right. The big one looked nervous, and the thin one looked, well, sinister. And it was quite odd that neither the Building Association, nor Steve, had told him about any new tenants.

Frank wondered if maybe they were misrepresenting themselves. Not tenants at all, but burglars or criminals of some sort. He'd lose his job if he let anyone like that into the building. He wondered what to do about it. Call Mitch, ask him? No, Mitch said he was taking a leak. Besides, Frank's duty was to the tenants, and if these two were tenants, offending them would be inexcusable.

They all waited for the elevator with mounting tension. Matisse began to sweat, hoping Slake wouldn't kill anyone else. He hated working with Slake. Slake reminded him of that Nazi commander in that movie *Schindler's List*, the guy who shot prisoners from his balcony when he was bored.

"You know," Frank began. Matisse closed his eyes, knowing what was coming. "Steve didn't even mention to me that you moved in."

"Really?" Slake appeared uninterested.

"Yeah. Kind of an odd thing for my brother to do, don't you think?"

Matisse swallowed loud enough to create an echo.

"Brother?" Slake grinned. "Forgive me for asking, but is one of you adopted? Because the Steve I met this morning was white."

"I meant figuratively," Frank said quickly. "He's my brother because we got the same job. You know what I mean."

"Yes," Slake said. "I'm familiar with spade talk."

The elevator arrived with a ding. Matisse opened his eyes and took a breath.

"Be seeing you, Frank."

Frank nodded curtly, and Matisse and Slake entered the lift.

"Dumb nigger," Slake swore as the doors closed. "Testing to see if I'd met Steve this morning."

Slake jabbed the button for twelve.

"How'd you know he was white?" Matisse asked.

"I dropped Tequila off here once during the day, saw the guy. Total luck. I think when we're done, I'm going to waste that bastard. Curiosity kills the coon."

The elevator stopped at twelve.

"I thought he's on thirty."

"He is," spat Slake. "From here we walk."

They found the staircase and began their ascent.

In room 3014, China and Sally slept in innocence, unaware that death was on its way up.

CHAPTER 13

It was the silence that woke Jack Daniels up. She raised her head from her desk and stared over at the dot matrix printer next to the computer. It had finally stopped.

Daniels checked her watch. Creeping up on three in the morning.

"Faster than I thought." The sleep made her voice sound clogged. She suddenly remembered a brief snatch of the dream she'd been having before she awoke. Jack was a child, second or third grade, the only girl in class. All the boys were teasing her, flicking spitballs, pulling her hair. She went crying to her husband, who was the only adult in the room, and he smashed a spitball the size of a toaster oven into her face.

Didn't need to be Dr. Freud to figure that one out.

"Let's see what we've got." Jack pushed the dream and its images out of her mind. She swiveled over to the continuous print-out of paper that the printer had spit up all over the office floor. Lots of names in there. Lots of rap sheets. Lots of possibilities. Hopefully, in one of the lists, there was a short man with a butterfly tattoo on his hand.

Trying to be optimistic, she decided to look at the last search first. The one that listed all white males under five-seven with tattoos.

It was a list of eighty-six names, the shortest of the three. Jack scanned through it, looking for butterflies.

On name forty-six, she found one.

"Tequila Abernathy. Age 32. Height 5'6". Blond hair, blue eyes.

Arrested May 1990 for assault. Charges dropped. Case number 8867584. Tattoo of a Monarch butterfly on the back of his right hand."

Could this be the guy? Jack went to the computer terminal and pulled up the case number. As expected, she came up empty. Dropped cases weren't normally entered into the computer. The only way Jack could find out why the charges were dropped would be to manually pick up the hard copy down in the archives of the 12th Precinct, where Tequila had been arrested.

Either that, or she could call the arresting officer. Jack jotted down the officer's name and badge number. Then she picked up the phone and called the Desk Sergeant.

"Peters."

"Daniels. Has Binkowski left yet?"

"About two hours ago, Detective."

"He finish the composite with the sketch artist?"

"Yeah. Got a copy right here."

"Send one up."

She hung up the phone and pulled Tequila's file on the computer, including prints and mug shots. The precinct had two laser printers down in Records, and Jack sent the file to be printed down there.

"Tequila," Jack mused. "Who would name their kid Tequila?"

A uniform came in with the sketch and Jack scrutinized it. Binkowski's drawing looked tougher, and meaner, than the man in the mug shots. But there were a lot of similarities. A hell of a lot.

Jack looked at the clock again. Ten after three. It was late, but not too late to get a murderer off the streets. She doubted she could get a warrant with what they had, but if Binkowski IDed the mug shots, she could bring this Tequila in and hang the bastard.

Jack found Binkowski's home number on the incident report and punched the right numbers.

"Hello?" came the sleepy voice.

"Mr. Binkowski? Detective Daniels. I'd like to come over and have you look at some mug shots."

"What time is it?"

"Time to put this lunatic behind bars. I'll be over in half an hour."

Daniels hung up. Her fatigue was magically erased. Going over to the computer, she printed up four more random mug shots to show Binkowski along with Tequila's. Then she exited the office and went down to records, to pick up the color laser copies.

Maybe this bad feeling she had about this case was wrong. Maybe Tequila was their man, and they could bring him in before he killed again. As it happened in all types of work, sometimes cops just got lucky.

Unfortunately, this wasn't going to be one of those times.

CHAPTER 14

Terco had gone to the *Blues Note* first. He asked both the fat bartender and the old bag of bones on piano—a black man so old he probably farted dust—if a short muscular guy with a tattoo had been in there that night.

Both had said no.

Terco pushed a little. Giving the old man a slap. Throwing a bar stool. Breaking some glasses and scaring the hell out of the only two customers in the place.

They still denied seeing Tequila that night.

That was good enough for Terco. He used their phone to call a cop friend of his, someone out of the 12th on Marty's payroll. The cop had heard about the liquor store murder, and gave Terco the owner's address after looking it up.

Terco was there in twenty minutes.

It was a small house off of Addison. He parked in the alley in back and walked through the yard to the front door, the cold forcing him to blink so his eyelids didn't freeze. He knocked twice, and was pleasantly surprised when the door opened without him having to lie his way in.

"You Binkowski?" he asked, pushing inside and grabbing the old man by the loose skin hanging from his chicken neck. The dude was wearing a nightcap, for chrissakes, with a fluffy dingle ball on the end of it. He reminded Terco of the guy in that *Night Before Christmas* poem.

The old man's eyes bugged out and he nodded as well as he could with his neck being pinched.

"Tell me what the man looked like," Terco growled. "The one who robbed you tonight."

Binkowski's mind whirled. Was this a friend of the short man? Did he know that Binkowski had talked to the police?

"He... he was black." Binkowski blurted. "With a green jacket. Tall. Real tall."

"You telling the truth?" Terco snarled. "You sure it wasn't a short guy with a tattoo on his hand?"

Binkowski's lower lip quivered like an earthworm doing a rumba.

"I swear! Tall black guy! Green jacket!"

Terco dropped the man, apparently satisfied. Binkowski almost passed out from fear. He knew it wasn't over yet.

Detective Daniels had called and would be here any minute. In fact, that's who Binkowski assumed was at the door when he opened it. If this maniac was still here when the cop arrived, he'd put two and two together and figure that Binkowski had snitched. The situation couldn't get any worse.

"Get out of here!"

It just got worse.

Terco and Binkowski turned to face Binkowski's elderly wife, Marie, standing at the bottom of the staircase. She was shaking like an epileptic on a caffeine binge, and cradled in her arms was the family twelve-gauge.

"Marie! No!"

"You stupid bitch." Terco laughed, but it came out forced. Understandable, since a gun was pointing at him. "From there, you'll hit both me and the old man."

"I said get out!"

"Marie, please!" screamed Binkowski.

"Marie, please!" mimicked Terco. Then he regretted it. His hero, Sly Stallone, wouldn't tease an old woman. He'd say something cool. Terco tried to think of a cool line.

"I swear," Marie Binkowski said. "I'll shoot you if you don't leave."

"That gun will take your arm off, you dried up old lizard. Put it down or I'll come over there and shove it up your, uh, shove it in your shriveled, your wrinkled, uh…"

Shit. Another Stallone opportunity, lost to history.

Marie fired, peppering both her husband and the intruder across their chests.

Terco stumbled backwards, shocked. Sly never got shot. He looked down at the blood on his chest, wondering why he wasn't dead.

"What the hell?"

"Want some more, buddy?" Marie challenged. "I said go!"

Terco studied his chest more closely, and noted that his wounds were superficial. Looking at the floor he saw why. At his feet were dozens of white crystals. He picked one up and sniffed it.

"Rock salt? You loaded your shotgun with rock salt?"

"My wife's a pacifist," Binkowski wailed, clutching his bleeding nightshirt.

The pain hit Terco like a wave. The shock of the blast had worn off, and now he had a chest full of salty wounds, which hurt like a hundred bee stings.

"You mean she was a pacifist," remarked Terco, drawing his revolver and shooting the old bat in the head. Her husband cried out, so he gave him a pop in the dome as well. Served the butt nuggets right, shooting him with rock salt.

"Butt nuggets," he told them, and then shut the door behind him, careful to smear his prints.

Sly would have been proud.

On the way back to *Spill*, he began to whistle, unaware and unconcerned that in the car passing him in the oncoming lane was a Homicide Detective named   Jack   Daniels.

CHAPTER 15

Marty the Maniac tugged at the gold chains hanging around his fat neck. It was a nervous habit, brought about by his impatience with Terco. What was taking the bastard so long? In retrospect, he should have sent Leman to check Tequila's alibi. Steroids did things to the brain, and Terco was two injections away from Potatoville. The guy's head was so empty that when he had a thought there was an echo. It was surprising the man could still dress himself.

Marty glanced at his watch, seeing it was almost four. *Spill* would be closing soon, and normally at this time on Super Bowl Sunday Marty and the boys were either playing high stakes poker or whoring it up.

Lousy stinking bastard Tequila.

He'd talked to his accountants, and they'd confirmed it had been his biggest take ever. Marty was planning on going to Hawaii for two weeks on that money. Had the Presidential Suite at the Hilton in Honolulu already booked.

Hell, fuck Hawaii. He had bills to pay. Property tax for *Spill*. Pay-offs. Salaries. Gifts. Bonuses. He gave the local Outfit chapter a meaty cut every year for letting him operate in their territory. If he didn't come up with the scratch...

Marty fidgeted in his chair. He'd get his cash back. There wasn't any other way about it. And if he were somehow wrong about Tequila, he had no problems with sacrificing the rest of his goombahs, one by one, until someone talked. He'd get his money alright, even if he had to kill every goddamn employee with his own bare hands. That's the kind of boss he was.

Terco, finally, showed up at his office door. Marty resisted the urge to scream at him. Instead, with the infinite patience and kindness that all good leaders were endowed with, he waited for Terco to begin.

"I got shot with rock salt," Terco finally said, unnerved by Marty's silence.

"I don't give a shit, you walking hunk of Spam! Did his alibis check out?"

Terco flinched at the attack and became red in the face. When he didn't answer immediately, Marty bounced a stapler off the crown of his forehead.

"It didn't check out," Terco whimpered, covering his face. "Tequila was never at the bar, and that old bag of wind at the liquor store swore a tall black guy robbed him."

"You're sure?"

"Yeah. I scared them all enough."

There was a sneeze from somewhere in the room. Both Marty and Terco looked confused as to its origins. Then Marty pointed at his closet, and made a motion for Terco to check it out.

"Huh?"

"The closet," hissed Marty.

"Who's in the closet?"

"Check the goddamn closet!"

Terco shrugged his shoulders, and Marty threw a scotch tape dispenser at him. Then he pulled his .38 out of his waistband and checked the closet himself.

Empty.

Leman appeared in the doorway with Marty's toolbox. It had taken him that long to find because it was behind a fake wall in a moldy corner of the basement, expertly hidden because the tools inside were covered with enough forensic evidence to give Marty the death sentence seven times over.

"I saw a rat," Leman said. "Big as my head."

"Quiet." Marty snarled. "We heard a sneeze."

"Could be a rat. Rats sneeze."

"Shut your dumb-hole!"

The three of them listened in silence, and then a loud clanging sound came from the heating vents next to the closet.

Terco pointed. "The heater!"

"Rats in the heater!" Leman nodded.

"Has anyone bothered to check on Tequila?" Awareness crept up Marty's spine, ready to bloom into rage.

"I was getting your toolbox..."

"You sent me to check on his alibi..."

"Move it!"

The three of them fought through the doorway and Marty led them to the vault room. Punching in the access code, he yanked the handle open and saw the room...

Empty.

Leman pointed. "He's in the vent!"

"No shit, chuckle-head," Marty spat. "And you were a cop?"

Leman hid his anger from the jab, and removed the .32 from his holster. Without waiting to be asked, he climbed up on the chair and peered into the darkness.

"I don't see him."

"Looks like he cut the rope." Terco held up a severed length of clothesline.

Marty came up behind Terco and smacked the bigger man across the side of the face with his .38. Leman grimaced at the sight, unconsciously holding his sore ribs from Marty's assault earlier today. Sure, they made a lot of money. But maybe, next pay raise, they should also ask for full health coverage.

"This is how you do a proper frisk for knives, you dumb tub of amino acids. First, check the pockets."

Marty swiftly kicked the fallen Terco in both hips.

"Move down the legs," Marty continued, kicking all the way.

Leman winced. The foot to Terco's kidney made a thump that he could practically feel.

"Armpits!" Marty yelled.

Terco clenched his arms to his side.

"Lift your flabby arms!"

The flabby comment hurt as much as his master's assault. Terco raised his arms and Marty kicked the insides of them, also taking the opportunity to stomp on Terco's chest.

Leman heard something in the duct and aimed his weapon into the blackness, firing five times.

Marty body-tackled him, spittle flecking off his chin like a rabid dog.

"You stupid shit! You want to kill him, so I never find my money?"

Leman knew anything he could say wouldn't stop his boss's anger, so he tried very hard to look blank. Fortunately, Marty's eyes weren't focused on Leman. They were thinking about other things.

"We can smoke him out of the vents," Marty said.

"Good idea, Marty."

Marty got off of his collector and tugged at the gold dangling from his neck.

"We block off all exits except one," Marty went on, "then send some smoke through the heating system. What's something that smokes?"

"Leman smokes," Terco offered.

"Good idea, Terco. We'll send Leman into the furnace with a pack of *Kools*. That will flush Tequila out."

"How about the smoke machine on the dance floor at *Spill*?" Leman offered.

"No good. It only pumps out that people-friendly CO2 crap."

"Wet blankets." Leman said. "Throw them right into the furnace. Real wet, so they won't burn. A wet blanket smokes like a mother."

"Fine. Leman, fill up the furnace with wet blankets."

Leman frowned, not anxious to go into the basement again and confront the rat. It was a big goddamn rat. He thought about mentioning it, but the quicker route would just be to slap himself. So he lumbered off, silent.

"Terco, call up Slake and Matisse at Tequila's and tell them to get their asses over here. No, just tell Slake to come. Leave Matisse there, in case Tequila somehow gets away and goes home. Then get some plywood and start sealing off vents. Move it!"

Terco nodded, repeating the key words in his head so he didn't forget them. He'd been using that *Mega Memory* program to help improve his retention, the one that advertised on TV real late a night with the guy who memorized all the names of the studio audience. What was that guy's name again? Terco sucked his lower lip, trying to remember. Then he realized he was in danger of forgetting his instructions, so he went back to his repetition. Slake, Matisse, Plywood. Slake, Matisse, Plywood. He trudged off.

Marty uprighted the chair and stood on it, peering into the blackness of the vent.

"Tequila!" he screeched. His voice echoed through the ducts like a bouncing basketball. "I'm coming for you, Tequila! I'm coming for your ass!"

Marty listened for a reply.

There wasn't one.

CHAPTER 16

Matisse answered the phone without speaking. He had to cover up the mouthpiece to muffle the screams coming from the retard's bedroom.

"Slake?" asked the voice on the phone.

"No. Matisse."

"It's Terco. You guys find the money?"

"We didn't find shit."

Sobbing from the bedroom now as Slake appeared, zipping up his fly.

"That Tequila on the phone?" Slake grinned. "Tell him his retard sister isn't a virgin anymore."

"It's Terco." Matisse automatically handed over the phone. He'd *absolved*—a word he learned from watching that smart Alex Trebec on *Jeopardy*—himself from the responsibility of the evening. First the killing of the parking lot attendant. Then Slake slicing up that fat black woman after they'd tricked her into opening the door by saying they were the police. And now this. None of this was the reason they came. They came to find Marty's money. The money might have been here too, but Slake hadn't even bothered to look for it. He'd been too busy acting out the role of crazed psychopath.

Matisse stood back and gave him room, quietly absolving.

"Couldn't find the cash, Terco," Slake said. "Tequila's got it stashed someplace else. Marty get anything out of him yet?"

"He got away, crawled into the heating vents. We're gonna smoke him out. You've got to come back to *Spill*. Leave Matisse there in case Tequila escapes and goes home."

"Fine."

Slake hung-up and frowned. How could Tequila have gotten away?

"You've got to stay here," he told Matisse. "That little shit escaped. He may come back."

Matisse didn't like that at all. What if the cops showed up? What if a neighbor called to complain about the screaming? He didn't want to take the blame for Slake's little blood bath. Hell, it wouldn't be too long before someone discovered that parking lot attendant, and the place would be crawling with pigs. And what about that nosey doorman? He got a good look at both Slake and Matisse. Too many loose ends.

"What about the bodies?"

"I'll take care of the guy downstairs," Slake said, though he had no intention of doing so. "Why don't you take a knife to that fat coon bitch and flush her down the toilet a piece at a time? Shouldn't take more than two years."

"Seriously, Slake."

"Well, stop being serious." Slake got in the bigger man's face. "Go have a siesta with Tequila's beautiful little sister in there. I've already got her broken in."

"What about the doorman?"

"Let him find his own piece of ass."

Matisse picked up the phone and began to dial the number for *Spill*, but Slake hit the hang-up button and his switchblade magically appeared at Matisse's neck.

"Look here, big man. We're going to do what Marty says, and Marty wants you to stay. You'll probably get a call in the next hour or so. Wipe down everything here that we might have touched. I'll take care of the door man. Got it?"

Matisse didn't answer. Slake flicked his fingers and opened up a line of skin on Matisse's chin. The blood tickled as it ran down his neck.

"Fine," Matisse, said trying not to show the fear he was feeling. Watching Slake systematically cut up that black woman was even worse than the time he watched him skin that little kid's arm. Matisse was almost double Slake's weight and could probably rip his arms from his sockets, but the thin man still scared the hell out of him.

Slake grinned, and gave Matisse a tiny kiss on the cheek that revolted Matisse so much he had to fight not to flinch.

"Call you later, baby." Slake began walking towards the front door. "Before you leave, don't forget to kill the Mongoloid. Such a shame too. I think, given time, she would have become a real pro."

Slake left. Real class act, that Slake. Matisse had never been *adverse*—another *Jeopardy* word—to taking a piece of ass if he wanted it, but a retard? That was sick. And the only men Matisse had killed were in self-defense. Sure, he may have provoked the fights, but at least the men he fought had a chance. Slake had killed two people in less than fifteen minutes, and both were totally helpless.

Maybe he should talk to Marty about Slake, tell him he was over the edge. Yeah. That's what he'd do. Fuck Slake. Matisse picked up the phone and was about to punch some numbers when he heard tones coming from the receiver.

"What the hell?"

He dropped the phone and hurried to the retard's bedroom. She was gone. He found her in Tequila's room, kneeling by the phone, sobbing.

"You little bitch!" he screamed. With a big paw he swatted her away from the phone, knocking her sprawling across Tequila's bed. She curled up into a ball, hysterical.

"Mergency! Nine-one-one is mergency!"

"I'll give you an emergency, you dumb shit!"

He grabbed her by her hair and dragged her screaming into the hallway.

She kicked and tugged and managed to turn around and bite his hand. Her teeth sunk into his knuckles and gripped like a pneumatic press.

Matisse didn't mean to hit her as hard as he did. But he was angry, and in pain, and too damn strong for his own good. He brought his fist down on the back of her neck, right at the base of the head, in an effort to get her to let go.

Her spine snapped like dry kindling. She was dead before she hit the carpet.

"It's your fault, you stupid retard!" he yelled at the body. "You didn't have to bite me!"

Sally didn't answer, but her blank, staring eyes accused him.

Matisse cradled his injured paw in his good hand and looked at the damage. Blood was flowing freely, and he caught it before it dripped onto the carpet. The cops could get DNA—deoxygen newribo acid according to Alex Trebec—from blood. The last thing he wanted to do was leave them evidence.

He hurried to the bathroom and rinsed away the red, grimacing at the jagged edges of his wound. Didn't he once hear that human bites were dirtier than dog bites? He rubbed a bar of soap into the cut, concerned about infection. Maybe more than infection. Maybe, since a retard bit him, he would become retarded. He should probably go to the hospital, get an anti-retard shot. This situation was getting worse and worse.

Finding gauze in the medicine cabinet, he wrapped a makeshift bandage around his wound and secured it with white tape. The blood seeped through, so he wrapped another layer of gauze over the first. Then he looked at the bloody mess he had made in the sink and panicked, thinking about DNA evidence again.

Now he was just as guilty as Slake was. Murder One. No absolvinglution. And Illinois had the death penalty.

"Oh shit," he mumbled, suddenly overcome by self-pity. He didn't want to go to prison. He definitely didn't want to get gassed, or electrocuted, or whatever they did in this state.

Matisse went into the kitchen and found some *Liquid Plumr*, and he poured that all over the dead retard's face and mouth and then down her throat to destroy any of his blood she may have swallowed. Then he took a wet rag and began to wipe down everything, absolutely everything, that he or Slake might have touched.

"This isn't fair," he said to himself over and over. "Not fair, not fair at all."

The *Liquid Plumr* foamed bloody in Sally's dead mouth.

Matisse kept wiping.

CHAPTER 17

Tequila Abernathy heard Marty's threats echo around him as he continued his climb up the heating duct. He heard them, but didn't pay attention to them. Tequila's mind was totally focused on the task at hand, and that task was getting out of the damn vent.

The heat and the strain were taking their tolls. Twice Tequila had to stop his ascent for fear of passing out. Passing out meant a drop down to the furnace again. He was at least four stories up now, and if the fall didn't kill him, he had no doubts that the heat would.

The problem was that all of the ducts horizontally adjacent to this main one were too tiny. He could barely get his head into some of them, let alone his whole body. The vent running from the vault had apparently been some kind of fluke in its size, because Tequila hadn't found another as big to climb into, and he had to be at least halfway up the building.

He paused to rest again, making sure his feet had a firm grip on the walls before wiping the blood and sweat off of his hands and onto his shirt. That didn't help much anymore, because his shirt was equally drenched.

Wouldn't it be funny if the only way out of this duct was back through the vault room?

He began to climb again.

Though his eyes were by now accustomed to the dark, they still couldn't penetrate the all-encompassing blackness. That's why he was completely surprised when he reached the grating.

His right hand touched it on the side of the duct, and he almost lost his balance. Planting his feet, he moved his fingers around the edge, getting a feel for what it was.

It covered an opening almost three feet by two feet. Though Tequila couldn't see it, he sensed space beyond the barrier. He clicked his tongue quietly, and listened to the sound extend down this new duct. It probably led to some office, or maybe to one of the bathrooms that graced every floor. If Tequila could remove the grate, then he'd be able to move horizontally for a while instead of vertically. Even if it didn't lead anywhere, it would at least give him a space to lie down and rest for a bit.

He pulled on the grate but it didn't give. It was thick, like fence mesh, though with smaller holes. Tequila felt around for a release lever and came up empty. Then he tried feeling for screws, but his burned, tired hands lacked the sensitivity to find their holes.

Tequila stifled a cough. Then he had to stifle another immediately. Something was different. He opened his nostrils and took a tentative sniff of the air around him.

Smoke.

Coming from below.

The bastards were trying to smoke him out. Either that or the building was on fire.

Either way, he was in trouble.

Tequila tried to make the decision. Keep climbing? Or try to force the grate open?

He pressed his face against the grating and found he could breathe a little better from the clean air coming through it. Smoke rose, which meant it would follow him as he went higher. If he had any chance at all, this was it.

No longer worrying about noise, Tequila grabbed the grating with both hands and yanked as hard as he could.

It didn't budge, and his feet slipped, causing him to hold himself suspended by the fingers he had wedged into the grate. The wire bit into them like tiny teeth, and he flailed his feet around until he finally got another grip with them.

Okay, pulling didn't work. Maybe pushing would.

Tequila coughed again, a burning sensation beginning to fill his lungs. He climbed up the duct another twenty inches, until one foot was on the grating. He put his back against the duct wall opposite it, and put his other foot on the mesh as well. His hands holding onto his holster which he had magnetized to the duct wall, Tequila pushed against the grate with both feet.

He grunted with effort. Little flashes of color danced before his vision. His jaw clenched hard enough to crack marbles. He focused all of his energy into his legs, willing them through the barrier.

Then, suddenly, the grating burst inward.

Tequila's hands slipped off of his rig at the sudden loss of tension, and he began to fall. But his legs were now past the grating and into the new duct, and he splayed them out and managed to hang upside from the opening by his knees.

The smoke was thick as soup now, and Tequila wasted no time pulling himself up to the new opening. Before sliding into it he took his rig off the wall and pushed it ahead of him. Then he began to crawl through the duct on his belly.

The smoke followed. Tequila tied part of his soggy wet shirt around his mouth and nose in a futile effort to breathe better. After crawling ten yards down the curving duct he began to suffer the primary effects of smoke inhalation. He became disoriented. Light-headed from lack of oxygen. His throat and lungs burned as if on fire. Passing out was only minutes away when he finally reached the vent.

He pounded at the new barrier with his palms. On the third hit one of the screws snapped. The fourth hit snapped the other screw, and the vent fell down into a room.

Tequila pulled himself out after it, gulping in the clean air. The room was completely dark, but the cold tile floor and the echo of his coughing told him he was in a bathroom. He got to his feet, still shaky, and felt his way through the dark until he bumped into a sink.

The water was like honey in his throat. After drinking his fill he splashed it over his face and arms and body. He felt around for the liquid soap dispenser by the sink and rubbed the sweet smelling gunk into the cuts on his wrists. It hurt, but hurting meant he was still alive, and Tequila welcomed the pain.

He was just about ready to leave when the door burst inward and the lights came on.

Squinting against the sudden brightness, Tequila saw the looming form of Terco blocking the doorway.

"You look like shit," Terco told him.

Tequila forced his eyes wide open, trying to speed up their adjustment to the new degree of illumination. Terco drew his .38 and pointed it at the small man's head.

"Come on. Marty's got a few questions for you. I'm sure it will hurt."

"You need..." Tequila said. His voice sounded ripped from his throat. He hacked, spit on the floor, and tried again. "You need a gun to handle me? I always knew you were a wimp, Terco. Twice my size, and you need a chickenshit gun."

"Kiss my ass, shrimp. I don't need a gun to kick your little punk butt."

Tequila spat again.

"Sure you don't, Terco. You're a real tough guy. Roughing up kids trying to get in with fake IDs. Scaring sixty-year-old men with heart problems into paying their markers." Tequila coughed. "Are those muscles just for show, or can you use them for more than jerking off?"

"I'm a taekwondo black belt. I can break boards."

"Boards don't hit back."

Terco stuck the gun back into his shoulder holster. Then he planted his feet and held out his hands. He made his voice low, like Stallone.

"Come on, Tequila. Show me what you got."

Tequila showed him. Taking two quick steps forward, Tequila launched himself into the air in a flying kick aimed at Terco's mid-section. Terco tried to swat Tequila away, but at the last moment Tequila scissored his legs and drove his heel into the underside of Terco's chin.

Terco stumbled backward, biting off the tip of his own tongue. Tequila rolled gracefully to the floor and up to a standing position.

Terco advanced, keeping his center of gravity where it should be. He feinted a left and then spun around much quicker than a man that size should have been able to, lashing out with a right leg and kicking Tequila into the sink. Terco took a step forward, then executed the reverse kick again, connecting with Tequila's right shoulder and hurling him to the ground.

Tequila rolled up to his feet and wondered if he might have underestimated the weightlifter. That reverse kick was almost as fast as his own, and with the weight and the power behind it, Terco could literally kick Tequila to death.

Terco moved in, sensing victory.

"Board's don't fight back, huh Tequila? Neither do you."

Tequila noticed the slight pivot of Terco's hips, telegraphing that he was going to try another reverse kick.

Tequila ducked under it this time, feeling the wind as the big limb moved over his head. Still crouched, he sprang out at the man's vulnerable body, driving a fist into Terco's left kidney.

Terco doubled over. Tequila cracked the top of his head into Terco's jaw, then stuck out a leg and tripped him onto his ass.

Terco didn't even have time to open his eyes before Tequila executed a reverse kick, the same kind Terco had used on him except Tequila's was faster and cleaner. It connected with the muscle man's left ear and pitched him onto his side like a three hundred pound sack of manure.

"Should have stuck with boards," he told the unconscious figure.

Tequila took Terco's gun and then got out of there, exiting into a hallway. It was dark and deserted, and Tequila moved cautiously. Smoke was coming into the halls through the floor. Perhaps the building was on fire. That made the elevators a definite out. Instead he found a staircase. Now the question was whether to go down or up?

Tequila was sure that down meant Marty and his bodyguards, all armed. He chose to go up.

Fatigue was gnawing at him when he reached the access door to the roof. As he'd expected, it was locked. Shooting a lock open wasn't as simple as it was in the movies. Blowing off a door knob didn't do a thing to disengage any dead bolts or locking mechanisms. The way to do it was to aim at the door jamb where the dead bolt entered. Then there was a chance of shooting the bolt off, or at least weakening the jamb that held the bolt so the door could then be forced. Tequila wasted five of his six rounds before he was able to kick the door loose from the jamb.

The cold wind felt clean on his body, and the coolness in his lungs seem to rid them of the last vestiges of smoke. He headed south on the rooftop, where he knew the fire escape to be. Leaning over the side of the building he saw it there, a wrought iron framework of ladders bolted to the side of the building beginning a floor below him.

He also saw, about halfway down, someone waiting on the fire escape for him. It was Leman, and from his quick glance Tequila saw what appeared to be an automatic weapon occupying the ex-cop's arms.

One bullet from a revolver, even in Tequila's capable hands, didn't beat an unlimited supply of ammo that could be dispensed at twenty rounds a second.

Tequila considered the situation. He could go back down the staircase, but how did he know his gunfire hadn't already drawn attention? Someone could be coming up the stairs right now.

So the only solution was to find another way off the roof.

Tequila went around to the opposite end of the building and looked over the edge. No fire escape here. But he noticed that every office window had a concrete sill that extended out about six inches. Enough to stand on. But enough to land on from a distance of ten feet every floor?

Balance beam was women's competition, but in his youth Tequila had attempted some simple routines just to see if he was any good.

He wasn't. Flexibility and strength he had. Agility he had. Balance wasn't his strong suit. He could still remember the back flip he tried on the four inch beam. He'd missed his footing and landed squarely on the family jewels. It still hurt to think about it.

He went to the adjacent corner of the building, hoping for maybe a gutter or an antenna cable. It had no such contrivances. Neither did the side opposite that.

He was about to go back to the staircase when he heard voices.

"He's up there! Move your asses!"

They were coming.

So what would it be—Leman or the window sills?

A small grin formed on Tequila when he realized he'd made more decisions in the last two hours than he had during the whole rest of his life.

"The sills."

Tequila again went to the side of the building opposite the fire escape and looked down. He knew that if he tried to land on the sill with his feet, his momentum would knock him off balance and he'd be street pizza. He also knew that his fall would want to push him away from the building, when he wanted to stick close to it.

But what if, instead of trying to balance on the sill, he tried to grab it instead? He won a silver medal on the high bar. Catching and holding something while in the air was something he could do, and well.

He put the revolver into his shoulder rig. Then, easing himself over the side of the building, he hung from the roof. Looking down between his legs he saw his target; a concrete window sill sticking six inches out from the building, about ten feet below his hands. He tried to focus on that instead of the ground, which spoke of a pancake death a hundred feet below.

The voices spoke again, closer this time.

"He's on the roof!"

Tequila gave himself a slight push off from the building—so his feet wouldn't hit the sill and so he had a clear view of his target without his body in the way.

Then he let go.

The drop to the sill took less than three seconds, but during it Tequila entertained the thought that he might not be able to grab a slab of sharp concrete. Not with his burned hands. Not from this height. It was a far cry from a comfortable, powdered high bar.

But his hands found the cement outcropping, gripping it hard by the corners, and his feet braced to take the impact of the wall as he swung into it.

The sill held, and so did he, hanging there like a comedy sketch of a suicide attempt who had a change of heart a moment too late.

One down. Nine floors to go.

Without taking time to revel in his small victory, Tequila eyed the next ledge between his legs and again pushed off from the wall and dropped.

He caught the ledge, but his left hand scraped hard against the cold concrete corner of the sill, ripping roughly into the palm. Tequila hung there a moment, feeling his grip become slippery as the blood began to run. He considered chinning himself up and then breaking into the eighth floor window, but he worried that the sound of glass would be heard.

He sighted on the sill below him, and dropped another floor.

This time his injured left hand slipped, and for a crazy moment Tequila hung seven floors up by one hand, swinging wildly against the building. He regained his grip, but his stamina was nearly gone. And the cold, which he'd so welcomed when he first got on the roof, was numbing his muscles and freezing all of the sweat on his body. He knew he couldn't do this many more times, let alone six. He decided to climb in through this window and hope that Marty's goons were already higher up than that.

It turned out Marty's goons were higher up. They were on the roof, staring down at Tequila.

A gunshot rang out and Tequila felt the bullet whistle past his head. He fought off panic and tried not to flinch.

"You stupid shit! Don't kill him! If he dies, you die! Get your ass down to that window!"

Tequila chanced a glance upward as he hung by his hurting hands, and saw Marty grinning down at him.

"Hey, Tequila! Why don't you hang around for a while?"

Tequila quickly sighted the sill below him and dropped to it, causing Marty's breath to catch in his throat. As he fell, legs behind him, hands outstretched to grab the outcropping, he calculated that his drop was wrong. This window, for whatever architectural reason, was a foot over to the left.

Out of his reach.

Tequila had an experience he'd had many times before when he knew a trick was going wrong. An instant, panic surge of adrenaline that sent a shock through his system.

Twisting his body sideways, stretching out with his right hand, Tequila caught the corner of the sixth floor ledge. But he couldn't stop the momentum of his body and he swung—too far for him to keep his grip. So instead of stopping, he went with the swing and used it to propel him towards the next sill, one floor below him but one office window over.

He came at the fifth floor window sill on an angle, heading for it diagonally as he dropped. This time he had seen it coming and was able to adjust his body to the catch. He twisted back so he faced the building and caught the ledge firmly with two hands.

While the adrenaline was still pumping away, he sighted the floor below him and let go of the sill once more. The ledge looked as big as a tree trunk and he caught it without difficulty.

Then his hands began to give out.

He was still four floors up, a good forty feet. His grip was slipping fast, and he knew that attempting another window sill grab was impossible. Tequila had used up his reserves, and he hung there, unable to decide what to do next.

He knew the answer. Instead of grabbing with his hands, he'd have to try to land on his feet.

He sighted down below him again. The sill, which had jutted out enough to grip onto, didn't look like nearly enough space to stand on, let alone land on from ten feet up.

Actually, Tequila reminded himself, since he was hanging he could subtract the length of his body. The window sill was only four or so feet beneath his shoes.

That didn't comfort him much. Try landing on a six inch board jutting out from a wall from four feet above it. He knew that if he wasn't perfectly centered, he'd catch the ledge with his toes and then topple over backwards. The same would happen if he touched the wall at all during his drop. That would push him away from the building, and from the sill. It was either perfection, or eating sidewalk.

Tequila took a deep breath and eyed where he wanted to land his feet. He didn't have to let go of the ledge. His hands simply couldn't hold on any more.

He tried to float down rather than fall, willing his body against the side of the building without actually touching it.

His toes hit the sill and he cocked his knees out to either side, trying to absorb the impact in an awkward-looking squat.

The squat had its desired effect. He hugged the wall, knees at opposite angles, perched on the sill like an odd ballet dancer ready to perform a leap. Slowly, ever so slowly, he flexed his legs and brought his body up to a standing position.

Three floors above him Slake appeared at the window sill he'd hung from only moments ago.

"Tequila, you thieving shit! Guess what I did to your retard sister!"

Rage burned through Tequila like a drug.

"She was sweet, man. I wonder if all Mongoloids fuck that good. Or do you already know for yourself, little brother?"

The anger picked up where the adrenaline left off, and Tequila jumped on a diagonal to the window sill below him and to the left. Grabbing it with his right hand he held on for just long enough to swing from it, and then he swung away from the wall and dropped twenty feet, completing a double forward flip and a full axle before landing on the concrete below.

He hit feet first, but the height was too high and the ground too hard, and his ankles couldn't take the shock of the fall and he crunched hard onto his ass. He rolled backwards to offset some of the force, but everything went blurry when the rolling stopped.

He stared up at the night sky. There were no stars in the city. The smog swallowed them all. He wondered idly if he'd broken his spine.

Then the pain hit and he knew he hadn't. The pain was in his left ankle. He pulled it to his body, quickly and expertly feeling for damage.

It didn't seem bad. A hairline fracture maybe, or just a bad sprain.

He'd had worse. He'd competed with worse.

Tequila pulled himself to his feet, limping as fast as he could go, gun in his hand. He went around to the back of *Spill* and headed for his car.

Two floors above him, on the fire escape, Leman let out a yell.

"Hold it, Tequila!"

"Marty wants me alive!" Tequila yelled back. "You gonna wound me with an Uzi from thirty feet away?"

Leman's hesitation was enough for Tequila to plant his feet and aim, in a two-handed shooting stance, for Leman's head. He fired, hitting Leman in the shoulder and knocking him sprawling backward on the fire escape. As he dug out his car keys, Tequila idly wondered why he hadn't hit Leman in the head, where he'd been aiming.

The sights must have been off on the revolver. Then he pressed his car alarm button and climbed in, laying down ten feet of rubber as he peeled out of the alley.

He thought about Sally.

If Slake had so much as touched her...

He made the ten blocks to his apartment in under two minutes, fearing the worst.

CHAPTER 18

Jack Daniels hung up the phone. The warrants were on their way. She should have been feeling anticipation, the anxiousness that usually enveloped her when going off to arrest a suspect.

Instead she felt tired. Sick and tired and sad.

The crime scene was anything but smooth. The lab boys had barely gotten home from their late night work at Binkowski's liquor store before they had to come back and work some more on Binkowski himself. As a result their efficiency and alertness were noticeably lacking. One guy even tripped and fell down the stairs, landing on one of the bodies. And it was all captured lovingly on tape by the crime scene videographer. Maybe they could send the tape to *America's Funniest Home Videos*. Jack tried to find humor in the notion, but couldn't.

Two men in disposable plastic suits were scraping a lamp and part of a wall with tiny spoons, picking up Binkowski's brains and sealing them in individually labeled plastic bags. Another was using a wire brush on the staircase, picking pieces of Mrs. Binkowski up off of the shag carpeting.

The Homicide Detective couldn't help but blame herself. Why hadn't she seen this coming? Why didn't she post a watch on Binkowski, after the poor man spilled his guts in the interrogation room?

Because Jack hadn't predicted Tequila Abernathy correctly.

She broke the first rule—her own first rule—when involved in a homicide investigation.

Assume nothing.

Jack's assessment of Tequila had been wrong. She'd figured that since Tequila had let Binkowski live, he'd continue to let him live.

That wasn't the way to play ball with a psychopath. And this guy clearly qualified.

"We found a slug, Detective," said one of the ponchoed officers. With a pair of tweezers he held the misshapen ball of lead that he'd just dug out of the wall.

Jack scrutinized the slug. It didn't match those found at the liquor store. Too little, and its expansion wasn't the same. This one looked like it imploded in on itself, resembling a tiny, gray mushroom. The slugs found at the store were star-shaped.

Again her assumptions had been wrong. She figured Tequila was the type who'd stick with only one weapon. This was obviously the work of two different guns.

So far the only thing that Jack Daniels had predicted correctly was that there would be more bloodshed. She'd gotten that one right. In spades.

Detective Herb Benedict wandered into the house, looking appropriately ragged and sleep-deprived. He winced as he took in the scene around him. Jack couldn't be sure if he was wincing at the bloodshed, or at the plastic-suited officers stumbling around from lack of sleep.

"The good news is, we know who the guy is," Jack said. "I was on my way here for Binkowski to ID him, but he beat me to the punch. Name's Tequila Abernathy. Blond hair, blue eyes, five foot five, one hundred and thirty-five pounds. Tattoo of a Monarch butterfly covering the back of his right hand. He lives off of Lake Shore. I just talked to Judge Peterson, and Binkowski's testimony coupled with his recent demise was enough to get us warrants."

Herb yawned.

"I wouldn't have figured the perp for this," the thin man said. "Record?"

"Assault. Case thrown out."

"Why?"

"Don't know. Yet."

Herb stroked his mustache, extending the motion into rubbing his pointy chin.

"Why would he come back to kill Binkowski when he had the perfect chance to earlier, before the guy could ID him?"

"He's psychotic."

Benedict stifled another yawn. "No shit."

"That money part keeps bugging me too. For some reason, I read this guy all wrong. I pictured him to be, I don't know, more level-headed. He only robbed Binkowski of the money that Chico supposedly owed him, he didn't take it all. Why? Some misguided sense of right and wrong? And Binkowski said Tequila shot Chico in self-defense, that Chico pulled on him first. Does that mesh with someone who would kill two old people?"

"Maybe this was self-defense too." Herb pointed to the shotgun lying by the late Mrs. Binkowski's feet.

"Loaded with rock salt. Can you believe it?" Jack shrugged. "Lab boys found some blood on a few salt crystals by the front door. Maybe they can type it. Problem is, Binkowski's wife seemed to have also shot him. It will be tough to sort out all the blood."

"But your self-defense theory might work here too."

"Then why kill Binkowski as well? He had no weapon."

"He could ID him."

"Then why didn't he kill him at the liquor store? I don't know, Herb. I really screwed this up. I thought we were dealing with a hard-ass. Some mob collector who wants to be Clint Eastwood. But now it seems like this guy's totally off his nut. First he's playing Robin Hood, then he's killing innocents. My gut tells me it doesn't seem like the same guy. But my gut has been so wrong the last few hours..."

"Maybe Abernathy didn't kill these people. Maybe this is something else entirely."

"And what's the chance of that being the case?"

They were silent.

"Christ, I'm tired." Herb yawned. "Bernice made this horrible meat loaf. Tasted like one of my old shoes, but tougher. Feels like I've got a weasel in my stomach, trying to gnaw its way out."

"You ever been checked for an ulcer?"

"Huh? No. Why?"

"Every time you eat, you complain it hurts. Maybe you've got an ulcer."

"You think so?"

"That or a tapeworm. You're way too thin."

"I'm not thin. I'm wiry."

Jack changed directions. "You think Tequila will be good enough to be home when we stop by?"

"Doubt it. He's probably crossing the border as we speak. Or maybe he's waiting for us, ready to kill a few pigs."

"We'll wear full body armor, go in with the Special Response Team."

"Not me. The vest chafes. And that helmet doesn't match my shoes."

The partners were quiet as the body bags were brought in. For the first time, Jack noticed a picture on the wall of the Binkowski's with two young adults who were obviously their children. The deceased weren't the only victims. They hardly ever were.

"This would sure make a good headline," Herb said.

"What?"

"TEQUILA, CHASED BY JACK DANIELS."

Jack stared at him and frowned.

"Hell," Herb said. "I'd buy a copy."

"We'll swing by the armory, pick up our flak suits."

"There's another headline for you. TEQUILA SHOT."

"That could go the other way too."

Jack wondered if she would mind that terribly much. Being shot and killed. It was better than going senile or becoming riddled with cancer. In the line of duty was a good way for a cop to go.

She could almost hear her husband say *I told you so* at the funeral.

"You okay, Jack?"

Jack nodded. "Let's go get the bad guy."

CHAPTER 19

Marty the Maniac raged. It was a lucky thing that none of his collectors were around him at that moment, because in his anger he might have killed one or two.

Tequila, impossibly, had gotten away. Probably never to be seen again. Gotten away with Marty's money.

The Maniac howled, firing his gun up into the night on the roof of his building, emptying the chamber but still squeezing the trigger over and over until the clicking brought him back to the here and now.

He needed to regroup. Slake was somewhere on the fifth floor. Leman was shot, moaning on the fire escape, his value to Marty now questionable. That idiot Terco was off God knows where. And Matisse...

Matisse was at Tequila's apartment. If that's where the little shit was heading, there still may be a chance.

Marty hurried down the stairs as quickly as his chubby legs could carry him. When he reached his office he was panting harder than he had in years. Twice he misdialed, wasting valuable time and getting more frustrated by the second. When he finally punched in the correct phone number, he was treated with a busy signal. He tried it three more times with the same results.

"You stupid rectal sore!" he screamed at Matisse through the dead receiver. The dumb son of a bitch was probably on the line with 1-900-WANKOFF. Didn't he know to keep the lines cleared? Didn't he figure they'd try to call him?

And where was that screw-up, Slake? Where was anybody?

Marty hit the hang-up button and dialed another number. He paced his office while it rang.

"Yeah?"

"Put Fonti on."

"Who should I say is calling?"

"It's Martelli, you ignorant shit. Put your boss on now."

"Just a second."

The was a pause that lasted so long Marty was about to start screaming again.

"Marty?" a low, unrefined voice finally answered. "It's late. How are you doing?"

"Shitty, Fonti. Look, I need a favor. Remember that little guy Tequila, works for me? He's gone rogue, hit me for some money and shot up my guys. I need some men."

"Of course, Marty. My men are your men. How many do you need?"

Marty saw Tequila in his mind's eye, rappelling down the side of his building bare handed.

"Forty," Marty answered.

Fonti laughed. "You gotta be joking. This is a joke, right?"

"I need everyone you've got, Fonti. Everyone you can spare. And what's that guy's name? That guy you hire for wet work now and then?"

"Marty," Fonti warned, his voice lowering an octave. "This ain't a secure line."

"What's his name, Fonti? Royce! That's the crazy mother fucker. I want him too."

"You can't have him. And you can't have forty men. I don't even have that many on duty now, I'd have to pull guys out of bed."

Marty inhaled deeply, knowing that to get the help he needed, he'd have to spill all.

"He took the Super Bowl take, Fonti. Over a mil."

"Marty! How the fuck you let this happen?"

"I need those men, Fonti. If we get him before he goes to ground we could have this wrapped up by daylight. I think he's going home, to the Lindenburg Apartments on Lakeshore."

"I'll send some men."

"Thanks, Fonti. Don't kill him. I need him alive to talk."

"You've lost a lot of face here, Marty. A man should be in control of his employees. A general is only as effective as his soldiers are."

Terco walked into the office, his face swelled up like a bloatwurst and blood matting his hair.

"No shit," Marty said, and hung up.

"He blindsided me," Terco whimpered, unable to meet his master's eyes.

"You worthless waste of protein!" spat Marty. "You incompetent bag of gas! Why did your father waste the sperm on you?"

Marty raised his .38 and fired four times at Terco's chest, the hammer falling on empty chambers.

Terco, already drained from the fight with Tequila, felt the blood leave his head when Marty pulled the gun. He fainted, falling onto his face, and Marty went to find some bullets. He was searching his desk when Slake walked in, stepping over the unconscious Terco.

"Did you call Matisse, tell him Tequila was coming?" Slake asked.

"Line's busy."

Slake picked up the phone and tried for himself.

"Do you want me to go over there?" Slake replaced the receiver.

"It's being taken care of. Go grab that screw-up Leman off the fire escape. If he's too far gone, shoot him.

Slake smiled softly, enamored with the idea of taking Leman's life. Maybe he'd do it anyway, even if the fool only had a superficial wound.

Outside, approaching like a storm, a siren whistled.

"What the hell is that?"

Marty tore out of his office, running down the stairs and through the access door into *Spill*. Firemen were rushing in like salmon in a strong current.

"What the hell?" Marty demanded.

"Smoke is coming from your building, sir," said the nearest fire fighter. "You'll have to evacuate."

Marty took in his surroundings and noticed for the first time that it was smokier than usual. That asshole Leman. How many lousy wet blankets did he throw into the damn furnace?

"Kiss my hairy dago ass, fire boy. I ain't going nowhere. Everything's under control."

The fireman, a husky and very determined young man who'd dealt with dozens of disoriented victims, approached Marty with his hands in front of him, trying to appear non-threatening.

"I'm sorry, sir, but you'll have to leave the building."

Marty withdrew the .38 from the back of his waistband and pointed it at the fireman's head.

"I said go play with your hose someplace else, pole jockey. Or I'll ventilate your head."

The fireman backed off. Some people just didn't want to be rescued.

Terco appeared through the door behind Marty, rubbing his eyes and looking bewildered.

"Is there a fire?" Terco asked.

Marty slapped him hard enough to be heard in Indiana, and then went back up to his office to wait this little fiasco out. Never in his life did he want somebody as badly as he wanted Tequila. Every nerve in his body screamed for a chance to have that little shit in his hands. What should have been the celebration of the year had turned into the biggest failure of Marty's entire life.

Slake re-entered the office, disappointment inherent in his eyes.

"Leman's not on the fire escape. He probably wasn't hurt too badly."

Marty barely heard him. His entire being was focused on Tequila, and all the things he'd do to him when he had him in his grasp. He tried Matisse again, but the phone was still busy.

"You want me to go over there?" Slake asked again.

"How much do you know about Tequila?"

"Not too much. He never talks about himself. I didn't even know he had a sister until tonight. She's a retard, if you can believe it."

Marty's eyes flickered.

"She lives with him?"

"Yeah. Matisse is probably humping her Mongoloid ass right now."

"Go, as fast as you can. Bring her back here. If he lets the bitch live with him, she's probably important to him. Don't kill her, for God's sake."

Slake nodded and went off.

The sister.

Maybe this colossal ratty-assed clusterfuck would work out after all.

CHAPTER 20

Tequila parked on the street and came in through the lobby. At first, Frank the doorman didn't know who the bloody, filthy figure was, and almost went for the security phone. The familiar tattoo of a butterfly on the figure's hand stopped him.

"Mr. Abernathy? What happened? Should I call a doctor?"

"No. Has anyone come to see me, Frank?"

"No, sir. Are you sure...?"

"No one came here at all? Or asked about me?"

"Well, Mitch in the garage called me to say you left your headlights on. Were you mugged?"

Tequila ignored the question.

"Did any men show up that you didn't know? A tall thin guy who looks really mean?"

"Mr. Abernathy, what's going on?"

"Frank, goddammit, has anyone been here that you haven't recognized?"

"Yeah, a tall guy. Well, two guys, a tall one and a big one. Tall one said his name was Collins, just moved into 1212 this morning."

"Are they still here?"

"The tall guy left. The other guy, big and muscular looking, he's still here."

Tequila picked up the house phone, setting on a stand to his left, and dialed his phone number. Busy. He headed for the elevator, trying not to imagine what he'd find in his apartment. He imagined it anyway.

"Mr. Abernathy?"

Tequila pulled out his wallet and extracted five hundred dollars of the money he'd taken from that old man at the liquor store. He handed it to Frank.

"You never saw me, Frank. I haven't been in all day."

Frank's eyes bugged out comically at the cash he now held.

"Yes sir, Mr. Abernathy sir."

The elevator doors opened and Tequila hit 30. The ride, which normally seemed so quick, took an eternity. Tequila had no way of knowing who was waiting for him. Big muscular guy? Probably Matisse, since he'd just seen Terco back at *Spill*. But were there others? How many? What kind of weapons?

All Tequila had in the way of weapons was an empty revolver and his Swiss Army Knife. He idly wondered how many people he could drop with the corkscrew before they nailed him. The thought failed to amuse him. His hands were aching and his energy used up. If there was a big party waiting for him, Tequila knew he might not live another five minutes.

There was only one certainty he had, and he embraced it like a shield.

They wouldn't take him alive.

The thirtieth floor dinged, and Tequila stepped out, wary. He moved slowly down the hallway, staying close to the wall, listening for anything unusual. As he approached the corner, his eyes fixed onto the Drexel table with the flower arrangement. The silk and dried flowers were in a good-sized iron vase. Tequila hefted it and dumped the flowers out. The vase weighed close to ten pounds, and gripped by the base made a much better weapon than his corkscrew. He took it, limping silently to his doorway.

Sweat had broken out on Tequila's body again, covering him like ants. He held his breath, pressing it up to his apartment door, straining to hear.

There was a hum coming from inside. It took a moment for Tequila to place it.

A vacuum cleaner?

He placed his hand on the doorknob, checking to see if it was locked.

The knob turned. That meant big trouble. China never left it unlocked.

Tequila decided to go in slow, hoping the sound of the vacuum would mask his entrance. He gently opened the door, just wide enough to slip inside, locking the door behind him.

The living room was empty, the vacuuming sounds coming from one of the bedrooms. Tequila gripped the vase and moved towards the kitchen. He was going to trade the vase for a knife before exploring the rest of his place.

Tequila saw the blood before he saw the body.

China.

She was rolled onto her stomach, lying in a thick pool of red. Next to her head was a black, rubbery thing that defied identification until Tequila noticed the eyebrows on it.

It was China's face.

The vacuum cleaner shut off, and a moment later Matisse hurried past the kitchen through the hall entrance. He saw Tequila standing there and did a double-take.

The vase was in the air before Matisse could even see what it was. It hit him in the face, crushing his left cheekbone and spinning him around like a pinwheel, a swirl of blood streaking across the walls.

Tequila leapt China's dead body and sprung at the collapsing giant. He jumped onto his back, clamping an arm across Matisse's thick neck, trying to cut off the bodybuilder's air.

Matisse reached behind him, grabbing Tequila by the shirt. Without much effort, he displaced the small man and threw him down the hallway. Then he brought his hands to his face and moaned at all the blood. It was dripping everywhere.

"I'll never finish cleaning!" Matisse shrieked.

Tequila rolled with the throw and bumped up against something on the floor. At first he wasn't sure what it could be, but the realization came sickeningly quick.

Sally. Blood and drain cleaner streaming from her dead, open mouth. He looked lower, saw her ripped panties, the blood between her legs.

Time stopped. The image seared into his brain and he knew that no matter how long he lived, it would always be there when he closed his eyes.

His entire life changed in the space of a heartbeat.

Tequila roared. His roar drowned out Matisse's hysterics. It was a war cry, anger and agony and hate and sorrow, and it screamed for vengeance.

Matisse stopped his own wailing and looked over at Tequila, wondering how a human being could make such a sound. It was truly horrible, and it went on and on without pause.

Then it stopped.

The silence was even more horrible.

Tequila got to his feet, staring at Matisse like a malevolent demon. His eyes were filled with thirsting rage.

"You," Tequila whispered, pointing at the big man's chest. Something had changed inside Tequila. Or maybe something had awakened. His whole life had been spent denying emotion. Staying in control. He'd lived by responding logically to different stimuli, without offering anything of himself.

Now, finally, he had something to offer. Finally, Tequila felt an emotion, and the emotion burned in his heart like coal.

Hate. Tequila felt hate. It pumped through his veins and screeched in his ears and beckoned him to use his muscles to smash and punch and kill.

Matisse wet his pants. He fumbled for his gun as Tequila advanced. Drawing it from the holster, he barely had time to aim before it was abruptly kicked away, sailing across the room.

Tequila, supercharged with anger, hit Matisse with such a devastating right-cross that he broke the big man's jaw. He followed it up with rapid, rib-crushing hits to the body, working the killer like a heavy punching bag, driving him back against the wall and pinning him there with his flying fists.

Matisse couldn't defend himself. It was as if Tequila had five hands. And the man didn't tire, he just kept hitting and hitting and hitting.

When the tenth rib snapped, Matisse stopped trying to cover up and instead embraced Tequila with his powerful arms.

Tequila was crazed, and that scared the shit out of Matisse. But he was also half of Matisse's size, and if the bodybuilder had any sort of chance, it would be by using his strength and his weight.

Tequila struggled like a mad bull, but Matisse had spent thousands of hours in the gym, plus thousands of dollars on muscle enhancers. He got a good grip on Tequila and squeezed like hell, even though his broken ribs cried out in agony.

Tequila felt himself lifted off the ground. He was being crushed. The smaller man struggled and squirmed and kicked, but Matisse had a death hold on him.

Tequila's left shoulder popped out of its socket, and his mind registered the fact but he felt no pain. The hate in him was all encompassing, and didn't let any pain in.

Air, however, was another matter. Tequila was being so strongly constricted that he couldn't take a breath. Matisse's arms were stronger than Tequila's diaphragm, and Tequila was slowly suffocating. He kicked and twisted but Matisse still held him, and planned to until the tiny dangerous man was dead.

Tequila tried to butt his head against Matisse's chin but Matisse held his face away. Stars began to float around in Tequila's vision. He tried to blink them back, and his head filled with the image of Sally, the bloody gore dripping grotesquely from her mouth.

Tequila turned his head and sunk his teeth deep into Matisse's biceps. He bit as hard as he could, feeling his mouth well up with metallic blood, and then stringy muscle.

Matisse howled like a hurt puppy and tried to push Tequila away. He did, but Tequila took a chunk of Matisse's arm with him. He spit it out at the big man's feet and it lay between them like a skinned mouse.

The color drained from Matisse's face. He stared numbly at the large lump of flesh on the carpet, and then looked at the wound gushing blood between his fingers. The pain was amazing. A hundred times worse than a charley horse. His arm twitched spasmodically as his tendons contracted and pulled at the surrounding muscle tissue, unaware that the muscle was missing.

Tequila grinned at Matisse. His grin showed bloody teeth, and his eyes were so evil that Matisse swore he was staring at the face of the devil.

The devil spun around and reverse-kicked him in the head, sending him sprawling over a couch.

Matisse was face-down on the floor and trying desperately to crawl away when Tequila kicked him in his broken jaw, crunching his teeth together and cracking several. The big man twitched on the floor, and Tequila leapt up over him and came down knee-first on the back of Matisse's neck, snapping it like Matisse had snapped Sally's.

He knelt there on top of Matisse for almost a minute, breath ragged, blood dripping from his lips. Finally he noticed the pain in his shoulder. He glanced at it, judged it to be dislocated.

Tequila got off of Matisse's body and sat on the couch, feeling oddly detached from reality. Holding his wrist tightly between his knees, Tequila jerked his body backwards, trying to snap the arm back into the shoulder socket.

The shock of pain made him scream, but the arm popped back in. Suddenly, almost like being immersed in water, Tequila felt fatigue envelope him. He was tired. So very tired. He needed rest, and to get somewhere safe. He had to rest if he was to do what he wanted to do.

Moments earlier, Tequila had experienced his first real emotion in decades. With that emotion came a passionate goal.

He was going to kill everyone associated with his sister's murder.

First Slake. Then Marty. Then Marty's men. And then he was going to find out who started it all. He was going to find out who stole Marty's Super Bowl money. And he would kill them too.

Tequila got off the couch and went to his bedroom, careful not to look at Sally. He didn't see the point of funerals, or burying the dead. Whatever had made Sally special to him had left her body when she died, and he didn't regard the empty shell on the floor as his sister so he felt no need to venerate it. But that didn't stop it from being heart-wrenching to look at.

He didn't bother with clothes or keepsakes. All he took was cash, the twelve grand he had in the floor safe in his bedroom closet. He stuffed it into a gym bag and headed for the front door.

"Sorry, China," he said as he passed her body in the kitchen. He hadn't been particularly fond of the care-giver, but then he wasn't really fond of anyone. She'd been good to Sally, and it was wrong that she had to die like that.

As he passed through the kitchen his eyes caught the refrigerator. The picture Sally had given to him only hours before hung there sadly. He stared at his sister's drawing of himself, with the three arms and the stringy hair.

At first he thought he was throwing up, but the sensation was different. This release wasn't coming from his mouth.

It was coming from his eyes.

The man who hadn't shed a tear since grammar school was now finding it hard to catch his breath through the sobbing. He cried for Sally. He cried for everything she'd gone through in her poor, tragic life. He cried for the pain she felt at the hands of Slake and Matisse. He cried desperately for his big sister, who had needed him, who had loved him, who had held his tiny hands above his head when he was a baby, trying to teach him how to walk.

And after the tears for Sally had gone, he continued to sob. For himself this time. Because he'd never get to hear her voice again. Or see her smile. Or ride the coal car with her at the museum. Or listen to the sweet, sweet music of her laughter.

Fighting the twisting of his guts, Tequila reached out for the drawing and stuffed it into the bag with the money. Then he left the kitchen, left China, left Sally, left this entire section of his life behind forever.

He stepped through the front door and jumped back as fifteen cops in SRT gear came marching down the hall.

Tequila slammed the door behind him, locking it. He couldn't allow himself to get arrested. How could he avenge Sally's death behind bars?

But what else could he do? He didn't even have a gun in the house. Was he supposed to fend off that many armed policemen with some steak knives and the iron vase?

"I have an M-16 in here!" Tequila yelled. "With twenty mags of ammo! Plus enough C-4 to take out the whole building! Don't make me do it!"

Without waiting for their answer, Tequila ran into his bedroom. If he couldn't fight back, he had to run. And there was only one way to get out of a thirtieth floor apartment when the door wasn't an option.

He dug under his bed, pulling out the nylon package. Something he'd bought on a whim, months ago, because he'd always wanted to try it someday.

Well, someday was finally here.

Not even thinking if it worked or not, Tequila strapped the package to his back, buckling it around his shoulders and his legs.

Then he went to the large picture window in the living room, facing the Chicago skyline. The view was awesome, which was one of the reasons rent here was astronomical. He had a clear view of the John Hancock building, along with the dozens of sky scrapers that surrounded it. Further east, Lake Michigan loomed huge and impressive, from this height looking calm even in the fiercest winds.

"Tequila Abernathy! This is Detective Daniels of the Chicago Police Department! We have a warrant for your arrest! Don't be stupid, Tequila! You can't get away!"

"I've got three people in here!" Tequila yelled. "They're dead if you touch that door!"

Tequila picked up the twenty-inch television resting on the entertainment stand. After a quick sprint he threw it with all his might at the picture window. It was safety glass, and the TV bounced off and onto the floor. But a spider web of shattered fragments covered the entire surface of the pane, obscuring Tequila's eighteen hundred dollar a month view.

He hefted the fallen TV and again charged the picture window, hurling the fifty pound projectile with as much force as he could.

This time the television knocked the entire picture window out of its moorings, and both disappeared over the edge of the building, letting in an immediate blast of whistling, frigid wind.

Tequila looked out the new opening, thirty floors down, and felt his stomach lurch. The cars below were the size of bugs, even their color indistinguishable. Skydiving was one thing. You were so high up in an airplane that there wasn't any perspective, no frame of reference to show the mind how high you really were. Here, Tequila knew exactly how high he was, because he could see the ground, see the building, and see his television drop with such agonizing slowness that he wanted to puke.

He checked the buckles on his parachute one last time.

Behind him, the door burst inward.

"Freeze! Police!"

Tequila jumped.

His first reaction was shock that he actually did it, but that thought was wiped from his mind instantly as the ground rushed at him. Fast. It was coming so damn fast. Tequila squinted, tears streaking past his cheeks as the wind ripped at his eyelids.

He'd dropped ten stories in the time it took to take a breath.

His hand found the ripcord on his chest and yanked it, and he felt his entire body jerk to a stop as his parachute opened above him like a giant yellow flower.

Son of a bitch. It does feel like driving over a hill really fast.

Then the wind got him.

Normally, wind is a one way event. It blows relatively steadily, and air currents follow a singular direction. This did not hold true in a city with skyscrapers, like Chicago. Here, the wind gets chopped up by the buildings blocking its path. It swirls around them, goes off in different directions, forms complex, spinning, uneven patterns that are impossible to predict, let alone glide through.

Tequila's first trick was unique in the world of skydiving. A three-hundred-and-sixty-degree loop. The wind hit him from behind and then swirled upward, swinging Tequila forward like a pendulum. When he was upside down gravity took over and he began to fall onto his own collapsing parachute.

He tucked his knees in and spun to the side, as if performing a dismount from the high bar, trying to drop past his chute. If he landed on it he'd get wrapped up in the silk, plummet, and fall to his death. A question invaded his head, wondering if he would bounce if he hit the ground from this height.

His shoulder caught the underside of the parachute but he twisted away and plummeted past. Dragging his lines behind him, the parachute pulled into its upright position and again blossomed open.

But two of the lines had somehow tangled, and Tequila spun wildly, twisting them up even further. A sudden, powerful gust of air came from below, catching the chute and lifting it and Tequila upward. Tequila jerked his body sideways, righting the chute, but he then began to rock back and forth. On the third swing, he smacked hard into the side of his own apartment building, scaring the living hell out of a couple who had been watching *The Golden Girls* in their living room.

Stunned from the blow, Tequila could barely make out the ground beneath him, still ridiculously far away. He held onto the cords hanging at his sides, knowing their purpose was to somehow steer this thing, but he had no idea how they worked.

The wind kicked up again, this time from the west. Tequila rocketed away from the building and out over Lake Shore Drive, the traffic moving below him with dizzying speed.

He glanced ahead and saw he was headed out onto Lake Michigan. Landing in Lake Michigan, even only a hundred yards from shore, would kill him. He'd be hypothermic after only three minutes in the water. He couldn't go that way.

Tequila pulled on the left hand cord. Surprisingly, he turned left. He held the cord until he was facing the city again, once more heading towards his apartment building.

The wind didn't like him coming back though, and again gave him a taste. But this time, the hit came from above. His downward speed doubled, his parachute temporarily deflating. Under his feet, traffic was whizzing by at sixty miles an hour.

How ironic to jump out of a thirty story building only to get hit by a car.

He tugged hard on his left line, and the parachute swung him around like a sling. He continued to spiral, cutting over the highway, over the sidewalk, and onto the misleading safety of Oak Street beach.

It was like jumping into an empty swimming pool. He hit the ground on an angle, sort of skidding across it on his left side. He rolled with the fall, skinning the hell out of himself on the frozen sand. It felt, literally, like sliding naked over sandpaper. When Tequila finally stopped a good deal of his clothing had been scraped off, taking some skin with it.

But, son of a bitch, he was alive.

Then the wind gusted again, filling his parachute, tugging him backwards. Into highway traffic.

Tequila felt a momentary panic, so startled by the sudden movement he didn't know what was happening. The wind blew steadily, and his feet began to lift off of the ground. His parachute was only twenty yards away from the near lane, and if a car snagged it Tequila would get dragged.

He unbuckled his legs, feeling the harness drop away from his lower back. Then he reached up for the releases on his shoulders, but in his distress couldn't find them.

A bus, moving at seventy-two miles an hour, was coming up on the parachute.

Tequila's hand frantically searched for the buckle, tried to release it, couldn't.

The bus rocketed closer, the driver oblivious to the parachute in his peripheral vision.

Tequila's fingers dug into the buckles and unsnapped them, and he fell five feet to the sidewalk as his parachute was jerked away from him by the 2345 to Irving Park.

He landed, for the umpteenth time this evening, on his ass. His first thought was the bag of money, which was still wrapped around his waist.

His second thought was to vomit, which he did, voiding onto the concrete. Sirens, a lot of them, shrilled nearer, cutting through the freezing night.

Tequila got to his feet, half-limping, half-stumbling. He needed a place to hide.

And he had one in mind.

CHAPTER 21

"I'll eat my badge if he has people in there," Benedict said after hearing the threat through the closed door.

"He's bluffing," Jack agreed. But why? To stave off the inevitable? At first, when Tequila had yelled about an M16 and C-4 explosive, all of Jack's men cleared away. But now, it seemed as if the man behind the door was just trying to buy a little time.

Time for what? Daniels thought. He couldn't get away. Was he trying to fool us into believing he had hostages so he could make a ransom demand?

"Schultz, Jackson." Daniels motioned to the two men with the portable battering ram. It was a thick three foot tube of concrete with handles. Cops called it the Universal Key. With one or two swings it could open a meat locker.

Jack motioned for the men to ready the ram. Tequila was doing something in there, and Jack didn't want to give him the time to finish whatever it was.

"On three." Daniels held up one finger, then two...

On three they swung the ram, smack dead against the doorknob. The door burst inward, Schultz and Johnson hitting the floor, Jack and two others covering the doorway, guns pointed.

A short man with a backpack was standing by the window in the living room. No, not a window. A big hole in the side of the building.

"Freeze! Police!" she yelled.

The man jumped.

Everyone was quiet for a moment. Then Herb Benedict said, "Holy shit."

Jack checked around her and then entered the apartment in a crouch, her .38 on full cock and gripped in both hands. Her men streamed in behind her, some going left and some going right, all fully armored and ready for war.

Daniels only had eyes for one thing. The hole in the wall. The wind was rushing in with a savage strength, and Jack approached the edge with equal amounts of fascination and awe. Almost fearing to, she peeked over the edge, making out the descending yellow parachute as it floated out over the highway.

Vertigo began to kick in and Jack took a step back, bumping into Benedict and scaring the hell out of herself.

"So much for him not getting away," Jack said.

"That guy's got more guts than a slaughterhouse."

Officer Williams came over to report.

"We're clear, Detective. Three dead. One in the kitchen, one in the hall, one by the sofa here."

"Call the CST again. I'm sure they aren't asleep yet anyway. Then I want every available man down in the street, looking for this joker. Call the coast guard as well. He might be headed out to sea."

The three watched the diminishing parachute sail out over Lake Michigan. It was so absurd, so ridiculous, that Jack, without knowing it, cracked a tiny grin.

"Ever see anything like that before, Detective?" Williams asked.

"This is the third one this week," Daniels replied. "Where have you been hiding?"

Williams noted the sarcasm and hurried off. Jack radioed down to the surveillance team and gave them Tequila's whereabouts as he faded from her sight. She wouldn't be joining them. She had a crime scene here to work on.

Daniels often said that she didn't catch criminals, she just gathered the evidence to convict them. And surrounding her was evidence aplenty.

She and Benedict started with the body by the sofa. A big Caucasian, with a large laceration on his left arm. Jack couldn't determine cause of death, especially without turning him over, but she noticed the man's head was cocked at an odd angle.

"Broken neck?" Herb asked.

"Either that or he's extremely double-jointed."

Jack followed the blood drips, surprisingly easy because the carpet was light beige and the man had bled a lot. She followed it over the sofa, to the opposite wall. There was a small pool of blood there.

"He got wounded here, somehow fell over the sofa, and broke his neck," Benedict said.

"Think a man that big could break his neck just falling over a sofa?"

Jack went back to the body and touched the dead man's arm. Then she touched Herb's.

"This guy is still warm. Real warm. Couldn't have died more than five, ten minutes ago."

Jack took off her Kevlar vest, happy to be rid of its bulk. Fishing into her jacket pocket she came out with an evidence bag and some latex gloves. After snapping them on, she bent down and removed the lump of a wallet from the deceased's back pocket and opened it, finding his driver's license.

"Matisse Tomaglio. Heard of him?"

"A week back."

"You heard about him a week back?"

"I heard he had a weak back. See?"

Herb pointed at the man's twisted spine. Jack shot her partner a look.

"Sorry," he said, sheepish. "Over-tired."

Jack dropped the wallet in the bag and the bag into her pocket. She got up and walked over to the hallway to look at the second body. A woman, with the almond eyes and curved hands indicators of Down Syndrome. Her mouth was a bloody mess, and Jack couldn't guess what had happened there. But the blood between her legs and the ripped panties gave her an idea of what occurred before her death. She touched her neck and found her lukewarm, but still above room temperature.

"Jesus." She turned to Herb. "Go get the doorman up here. The one who tried to convince us Tequila wasn't home. Frank, I think his name was."

Benedict nodded and strolled off, happy to leave. It was getting awfully cold in there, with the window missing.

Jack went into the kitchen, but she didn't stay there long; it was too messy. Just enough to feel that her body was coolest of all.

She went next into the nearest bedroom. At first glance all the pink frills and stuffed animals made her think the room belonged to a young girl. Crayon drawings were proudly pinned to one wall. Children's books were stacked neatly in a bookcase by the bed.

But the closet was filled with adult female clothes and shoes, of a size that would fit the woman in the hallway. This was her room. Was she related to Tequila somehow? Jack took a look at the rumpled bed and saw the blood on the sheets. Had Tequila gone crazy and raped her?

She left the bedroom and went to the room next door down. It too was a bedroom. The furnishing was minimal but appealing, neither masculine nor feminine. A guest room, Jack guessed. The mattress on the bed showed a deep indentation, as if someone heavy had slept there often. There was a purse on the dresser, and Jack opened it and found a wallet.

She found ID in the name of China Johnston. She also found a card saying she was a licensed CNA. Jack checked the closet and found it full of clothing, all sized for a heftier woman. The corpse in the kitchen.

She went to the last bedroom. This one was completely devoid of any personalization. It looked to be an empty room, except for the bed and the dresser and some strange kind of stand next to the bed.

This was Tequila's room. This was the room of a sociopath. Someone who felt nothing. Aesthetics meant little to people of that type. Show them a beautiful swan, and they'd kill it as easy as pet it.

Something caught her eye on the bottom of the closet. Jack went to it and found a combination floor safe, yawning open. It was a good-sized safe, not very deep but wide. Filling it were papers. Hundreds, if not thousands, of neatly stacked papers. Jack reached in for a handful and turned on the closet light to see them better.

They were all drawings. Some in crayon, some in paint. Some on colored construction paper, some on loose-leaf. All were juvenile, and they matched the ones hanging on the wall in the first bedroom.

Jack flipped through them, fascinated. Had the Down Syndrome girl done all of these? Why did Tequila have them? In a safe of all places?

She looked through more. As she got to the bottom of the stack, the paper became brittle and yellowed. Finally, on one of the last pictures she grabbed, she saw writing for the first time.

It was a child's writing, and a child's picture, but more mature than the others. Done in pencil, on paper so faded it had to be almost thirty years old. The drawing was of two stick people holding hands, the taller one with long hair and a skirt, the shorter one in pants. A boy and a girl. Under the girl's name, written in Kindergarten hand, was SALLY 10. Under the boy's name was scrawled TEQUILA 6.

The realization gave Jack a slight surprise, and thoughts began to rush at her so quickly she needed to sit down and think.

Sally was Tequila's older sister. China must have been someone Tequila hired to take care of her. Matisse had come over, killed China, and raped and killed Sally, and then waited for Tequila to come home. When Tequila arrived, he got the better of Matisse and killed him first. Then he saw the cops coming and jumped out the window.

But why had Matisse done that? Was he after Tequila for something?

Had they known each other?

Jack suddenly wondered if it was Tequila who had killed the Binkowskis after all. Maybe it had been Matisse. Or someone else looking for Tequila. Someone who'd known where Tequila had been.

His boss?

Questions, there were a million questions. But Jack wasn't feeling sick and tired anymore. She was oddly invigorated. Maybe it hadn't been her fault the Binkowskis died. Maybe this was something big, some Outfit operation, that she'd stumbled onto accidentally.

Benedict came in, towing Frank the doorman.

Jack made her face look hard, shrugging on the role of tough cop.

Time to get a few of those million questions answered.

CHAPTER 22

Marty Martelli bit into his knuckles hard enough to draw blood. He didn't seem to notice, until it dripped down his shirt and tickled his flabby neck.

"Get me a freaking napkin," he said to Terco. Terco hurried off to find one. He was the only one of Marty's elite entourage still there at *Spill*. Matisse was at Tequila's, and Slake had gone to join him and get the sister. Leman had taken a cab back home and called from there, stoned on painkillers after pulling a Rambo and taking the bullet out of his shoulder himself. And Tequila...

No one had seen Tequila since he'd left *Spill*.

The phone rang, and Marty almost toppled over in his eagerness to answer it.

"Yeah?"

"It's Fonti. What the hell you trying to do, Marty? Get me nailed?"

"What do you mean?"

"I send ten guys over to Lake Shore Drive to take care of your little problem, and the place is swarming with pigs."

Marty's hopes sank. If Tequila was in custody, it would be a lot harder to get to him.

"They got him?"

"Not from what I hear. Seems your friend jumped off the thirtieth floor with a parachute. No one's found him yet."

"Dead?"

"I don't think so. The cops found the chute, but no Tequila."

Marty's thoughts seemed to mix around in his head and run out his ears.

"Any word on his sister?" he asked.

"I didn't know he had a sister. Found his car, though. Got two guys watching it."

"Pass the word to the network. Tell them to cruise bus and train stations, and the airports. And see if you can get a line on hotels and motels in the area. He's got to stay somewhere."

"Who's picking up the bill for this operation? Way I see it, you're broke."

Marty squeezed the receiver as if he were strangling the life out of a kitten. He needed Fonti's help, but he also knew he had to tread lightly. Power meant nothing without money. You couldn't buy soldiers or guns or the respect that came with it. The years of loyalty didn't matter. Yesterday didn't matter. What mattered was today, and today Marty was broke.

"Don't make me remind you I'm good for it," Marty said through clenched teeth. "You and I go back, Fonti. Back to the old days. We always helped each other. I didn't know you were keeping markers."

"I'll do what I can, Marty. The guy should turn up. What is he, Superman?"

"He's just a punk, Fonti. Just a sawed-off hard-ass little punk. Keep me posted."

Marty hung up, wondering if he really believed it to be true. The fact was, when Fonti told him Tequila had parachuted from his apartment, Marty wasn't surprised. He didn't ask for details. He could picture the little shit, doing just that. He'd always known Tequila was better than his other collectors. He just hadn't realized he was this good.

Idly, he wondered if Slake and Matisse were dead. No big loss. Dumb muscle was abundant in Chicago. But the real pros, the guys who got things done and demanded the respect normally reserved for made men, they were a rarity. Marty only knew of one such man like that, the man that Fonti retained named Royce.

He'd seen Royce at work once, years ago. Not from the outside either. From the inside, up close and personal.

Some bike gang had tried to hit a family operation. It was an after-hours club, with some gambling and some whores for members who liked a taste. A decent money maker, but hardly top mob dollar. It was operated by some wise guy named Dino, and he ran a pretty tight ship. Until the bike gang showed up.

They came in, twenty of them, armed to the teeth, and killed a few bodyguards. Not only did they clean out the place, but they took Dino hostage and wanted ransom for his wop ass too. As well as for the lives of the thirty or so members who'd been there that night.

Marty had been one of them, playing high stakes five card draw with some chronic losers, when the gang came in. One second he was bluffing a straight, the next he had five shotguns in his face. It was one of the only times, if not *the* only time, in the Maniac's life that he was actually afraid.

The mob had only one way of dealing with problems like this. It liquidated them. But there had been several of the higher-ups in there that night, along with a senator and two police captains. If they'd sent an army in after the gang, there would have been a bloodbath, and friendlies would have died.

So they didn't send an army. They just sent Royce.

Armed with two suppressed 9mms and a fillet knife, Royce had taken out the entire bike gang.

He wasn't a large man. About five foot nine, athletic build. But he knew about eighteen different martial arts, was an expert sharpshooter, knife-thrower, explosives expert, and a whole bunch of other dangerous shit. Former military, worked with one of those special ops teams that no one admitted actually existed.

Marty witnessed, in the blink of an eye, Royce shoot six men dead, break another's spine with a karate kick, and gut one more from crotch to sternum. Eight men killed in five seconds, and all of them in different parts of the room.

Before the hostages even had a chance to hit the floor, Royce had shot two more bikers and drawn the gunfire away from the crowd and over to an empty bedroom. The bikers, thinking they'd trapped him, shot the hell out of that room. They'd pumped enough lead into it to destroy the walls and make the building structure unsound. When the shooting finally stopped, three bikers went in to confirm the kill.

The three didn't return.

Three more went in, and also didn't return.

The four men left were terrified, and one of them had grabbed Marty, forcing a shotgun against his head and demanding Royce show himself.

Royce had blown the biker's head off from across the club. A distance of almost fifty yards. The other three ran upstairs, hoping to escape. Royce went after them.

He came down four minutes later. His fist was bloody, and at first Marty thought he'd been hurt. But it wasn't Royce's blood. Clenched in his fist were the three men's genitals.

That's who Marty needed right now. He needed Royce. He'd wipe his ass with Tequila, no problem. The only difficulty would be convincing Fonti that Marty had to have him. Fonti was odd when it came to Royce. He treated him like one would treat a rare, exotic jewel. You don't flash it around, only take it out on special occasions.

How could he convince Fonti that this occasion warranted it?

Terco skulked back in, holding a roll of paper towels. With his two front teeth missing, he looked even more dim-witted than before. Marty snatched out at the roll with such speed that Terco flinched.

The big man was near the end of his stamina. Marty had attacked him twice, Tequila had kicked the tar out of him, he'd gotten a chest full of rock salt, and every single inch of his body hurt. If he hadn't feared Marty so much, he would have quit then and there.

Marty recognized the beaten look in his man's face, and knew that a good leader would throw the guy a bone. Terco, with all his stupidity, was loyal, and loyalty was something that Marty might not have for very much longer.

"You look like shit. Go take a rest," Marty told him.

That was as big a bone as Terco would get.

The big man plodded off and Marty wrapped a paper towel around his knuckle. He watched the blood leak through, and wondered when he'd get the chance to make Tequila bleed.

Marty picked up the phone and dialed the familiar number.

"Yeah?"

"It's Marty. Put Fonti back on."

While he waited, Marty played with the wound on his knuckle, opening and closing it like a tiny mouth. When he opened it, the mouth dripped red.

"I thought we'd discussed everything we needed to," Fonti's low voice boomed, obviously irritated.

"I want Royce."

"You can't have him."

"It's worth a lot to me, Fonti. Above and beyond my tab."

"How much above and beyond?"

"Fifty grand. Yours. No splitting with the dons, no sharing with the soldiers. I'll take care of them, but the fifty is all for you, if I can use Royce."

There was a silence on the line. Fonti was rich, but not millionaire rich. Fifty grand was still a nice chunk of change.

"What if you don't recover the goods, Marty?"

"I'll make good, Fonti. I keep my promises."

"Fine. I'll send Royce. He'll expect to be compensated for his time as well."

"I know. Just get him here as fast as you can."

"He'll be there by noon."

Marty hung up. The tension that he'd been feeling since the robbery eased slightly for the first time all night. He rolled his shoulders and rubbed the back of his neck.

Royce would deal with Tequila.

He had to, because Marty didn't have enough money to pay all of his debts otherwise. And he'd just promised fifty grand to the biggest loan shark in the mid-west.

If Royce didn't catch Tequila, Marty knew who Royce's next assignment would be.

Marty shuddered at the thought, remembering the grin on Royce's face coming down those stairs, the three bloody lengths of flesh dangling from his hand.

But he was on Marty's side for now.

For now.

CHAPTER 23

Amazing the difference eight hours made.

Jack had put it together piece by piece, making the puzzle bigger as reports and information trickled in. Soon, all the bits conspired to make a pretty good picture of what the hell was going on.

Ballistics had shown that Billy Chico had been killed by bullets from two .45s, as Binkowski had said. Chico's ex-wife was interviewed, and besides being an abusive asshole, Chico was also a chronic gambler. She expressed great joy at Chico's demise, having taken a hundred thousand dollar life insurance policy on him when they'd still been married. Normally, that might have been a motive for murder, if the self-defense angle hadn't fit so well.

Binkowski and his wife had been killed by a .38. There were two blood types found on the rock salt that Mrs. Binkowski had shot from the twelve gauge. One was type 0, matching her husband's. The other was type B.

Matisse Tomaglio had type A blood. He also had a list of priors going back to his teens, mostly assault and battery, with a couple rapes mixed in to break up the monotony. His death was caused by a broken neck, due to a heavy blow from behind. The wounds on his body, including the broken ribs and jaw, were indicative that he'd been in a fight. The wound on his bicep was a human bite, but not a very large human. Either a woman or a small man had made the bite. Another bite had been found, dressed, on his hand. The teeth marks didn't match the wound on his shoulder, but did match Sally Abernathy.

China Johnston had died from loss of blood due to eighteen stab wounds and a partial skinning. The murder weapon was not recovered. It had been confirmed through her bank account and by the doorman Frank Michaels that she worked for Tequila taking care of his mentally challenged sister, Sally.

Sally Abernathy had been raped, and the semen was typed as 0. She'd been killed by a powerful blow to the neck, breaking her spine. Drain cleaner had been poured down her throat after death, probably in an effort to eliminate the blood she'd gotten in her teeth while biting Matisse. The apartment also showed evidence of being wiped down completely, and even vacuumed. Several bills were found in the kitchen drawer for Flynnbrook House, a very elite and expensive school for the mentally disabled. A call there confirmed Sally had been enrolled for over four years.

A gun was recovered from the floor in the kitchen. It was a .38, but not the murder weapon of the Binkowskis. The gun fit nicely into the leather holster on Matisse Tomaglio's shoulder.

Under the sink a large locked metal box was discovered. It contained gun cleaning equipment and extra barrels that would match a .45 semi-automatic, like the guns that killed Billy Chico. Two boxes of .45 ammo were also discovered. No parts or bullets for any other type of gun were in the apartment.

Also found, in a hallway closet in a box, was a collection of gymnastic trophies, along with three Olympic medals, two bronze and one silver. All won by Tequila Abernathy.

The parking attendant, a college student named Mitch Comsteen, was found dead in the garage, killed with a sharp instrument similar to the one that had ended China Johnston's life. Again, a search for the murder weapon failed to turn it up.

Frank the doorman spilled all, providing a fair description of Matisse Tomaglio and his thin companion, the man who claimed to be Mr. Collins. There was no record of a Mr. Collins moving into apartment 1212, or anywhere else in the building. The fake Mr. Collins had probably gotten enough information about the apartment complex from the late Mitch Comsteen to fool Frank into believing he lived there.

After getting in touch with the officer who arrested Tequila for assault in 1990, Jack found out why the charges had been dropped. Tequila had assaulted a patron while playing bouncer over at a dance club called *Spill* on Lincoln. The man had tried to get in with a gun, and Tequila disarmed him and then broke nearly every bone in the man's face. The man was hospitalized, and his wife told the cops what Tequila had done, neglecting to mention the gun part of it. Tequila had been picked up, and he refused to talk.

"The hardest son of a bitch I've ever seen," the arresting officer had told Jack. "I could have taken a blowtorch to his face, the sucker still wouldn't have made a peep."

It turned out Tequila didn't have to say a word in his own defense. He had barely been booked when the charges were mysteriously dropped.

Not so mysterious when one knew that *Spill* was owned by big-time Chicago bookie and racketeer Marty the Maniac Martelli. The same Marty Martelli who also had Matisse Tomaglio in his employ. And the same Marty Martelli who recently had a fire over at *Spill* last night. It had been a busy night for Marty and his gang.

Jack Daniels pieced it all together like so. Tequila, a past-his-prime Olympic gymnast, needs money to care for his mentally disabled sister. So he goes to work for Marty Martelli as a bouncer at his club. He proves himself over the years, and becomes a collector. Last night he trails Billy Chico to Binkowski's liquor store, to collect a marker. He finds Chico robbing the store in order to pay it. Chico draws on him, and Tequila kills him. He takes the two grand Chico owed on his marker, and lets Binkowski live, and keep a hunk of it, ensuring Binkowski would cover for him.

Then, somehow, Tequila had a falling out with his boss. Maybe he'd been holding out money on Martelli. Maybe he'd been nailing Marty's woman. Maybe he just got sick of working for the Outfit. Whatever the reason, Martelli goes after him. He sends Matisse and the thin man over to Tequila's apartment to wait for him. The thin man kills the parking lot attendant and China, rapes Sally, and then takes the murder weapon with him. Matisse may have also raped Sally, but hadn't ejaculated. The bite marks and the blow to the neck indicate he was the one that killed her. If it had been the thin man, he would have used the knife. He seemed to like that knife.

In the meantime, Marty sends someone to track down Tequila, and that guy gets a line on Binkowski. Maybe Tequila used Binkowski as an alibi to where he'd been that evening. Someone, maybe Matisse or the thin man, goes to question Binkowski, and kills him and his wife when the wife pulls a shotgun.

Tequila comes home, fights with and kills Matisse, biting him in the process. He then parachutes out the window before the cops arrive. Before he left, he emptied his floor safe. Probably of money, possibly Marty's money.

Daniels was pretty sure that's the way it went. The only thing she still wasn't sure about was the Binkowskis. She didn't know Tequila's blood type yet, so she couldn't be absolutely sure he hadn't been the one to kill them. But Jack didn't think he did. Tequila had somehow incurred the wrath of Marty the Maniac, and he was too busy running for his life to tie up loose ends.

So where does the investigation lead next?

First, find Tequila Abernathy and bring him in. Not only to get the whole story, but to protect him. Marty Martelli was so connected that it was rumored he owned police chiefs. Tequila wouldn't be able to hide for long.

Second, get a list of Martelli's employees, and try to nail the thin man and the guy with type B blood who killed the Binkowskis. It was doubtful that Marty would be helpful in this investigation, so Daniels was bringing in two men from the Organized Crime Unit who'd been putting a case together against Marty for the last three years. She was meeting with them this afternoon.

And finally, grab one, any one, of Marty's goons and find out what the hell happened at *Spill* last night. What did the fire have to do with it? Had Tequila been there? What had Tequila done? And most of all, had Marty ordered the deaths of the Binkowskis, Sally, China, and Mitch Comsteen the ill-fated parking lot attendant?

Daniels had known about the Maniac ever since she was little. Her mother had been a patrolwoman when those seven bodies were found, all mutilated and attributed to Marty Martelli. If they nailed him ordering executions, they had his ass.

Benedict walked into Jack's office, carrying a cardboard pizza box.

"Thought you might like a slice," he told his partner.

Jack smiled a thanks and reached into the box, finding exactly that. A single, lonely, greasy slice of pizza the size of a playing card.

"Hungry, weren't we?" Jack said.

"Saw the doc this morning, got some ulcer medicine. For the first time in ten years it doesn't hurt to eat."

"Careful. You might start gaining weight."

"Hurry up and take it, I want to lick the cardboard."

Jack took the slice and became irritated; it was delicious and there wasn't any more.

"Where do you think he'll go?" Herb asked. "Leave the state, or the whole country?"

"That's the thing. You saw what he did to Matisse. Broke most of his ribs. His face and jaw. Bit a chunk out of his arm. And then snapped his neck, just like Matisse had killed his sister."

"So he was angry."

"Real angry. I don't think he's going to run at all. Maybe he was going to at first, but since his sister died, I think his agenda has changed."

"You mean don't worry about checking the airports and the bus stations?"

"Exactly. I think he's going to stick around, and try to kill Martelli and whoever else was involved in Sally's death."

Benedict thought this over.

"One guy can't take on a big gun like Martelli by himself."

"You saw what he did to Matisse. Would you want to be Martelli right now?"

"Hell no. I still can't believe that parachute stunt. We should have put SRT on the roof with bungee cords."

Jack nodded. Seeing that yellow parachute sail out over a frozen Lake Michigan was something that would stick with her a long time. She knew she wouldn't have had the guts to do that. But then, she wasn't an accomplished skydiver either. Tequila must have been a pro. Maybe they had classes over at the YMCA. They'd done an employment check on Tequila, and before working for Marty he'd taught classes at the Y.

"Where'd you get the pizza, Herb?"

"Marino's down the street."

"Want to go in halfsies on another one?"

"Hell yes. Make it a large."

Jack picked up the phone.

"If he's not leaving town," Herb said, "he's got to be hiding somewhere. So the question is, where can a guy hide from the cops and the mob? Hotels are out. Not only the good ones, but the transient ones as well. People see things, people talk. He wouldn't go to any friends, because the mob would know his friends. We tried to find some family, but there aren't any other Abernathys in the area. So where is he?"

Jack wondered where she would go. Hell, she didn't need a place. She slept often enough at work.

Work.

Jack put the phone down after it only rang once.

"The YMCA. He used to work there, before Martelli."

"He's got to know we know that. Would he go back?"

Jack mulled it over, knowing Tequila probably wouldn't risk it, unless he was desperate.

"Maybe. Or maybe he'd do something else. What's a place that doesn't ask questions, is open to anyone 24 hours a day, and is so anonymous that few people even know it exists?"

"I don't know. Are you gonna order that pizza?"

"I'll give you another hint. They open up twice as many in the winter time."

A light came on behind Benedict's eyes.

"A homeless shelter. We've got a record-breaking freeze in the city. The shelters are all jammed with the homeless. All he'd need was a ratty coat and he could hide there all winter."

"Call the mayor's office, get a list of all the shelters in the area. I'll organize some search teams."

"How about the pizza?"

Jack picked up the phone again.

"We'll order it to go," she said.

CHAPTER 24

Tequila awoke smelling urine. He'd slept poorly. Twice, winos had attempted to steal his shoes, and once someone even tried to take his bag filled with money, which he'd been using as a pillow.

He'd dissuaded such action forcefully, each time breaking the would-be thief's nose. He would have broken their fingers to teach them to stop stealing, but they were homeless, and this was winter, and taking away their hands would be unnecessarily cruel. He was, after all, on their turf to begin with.

The shelter was located on Wabash, ten blocks from where he'd landed on Oak Street beach. To say it was crammed was an understatement. Normally the large main room, which had once been an art gallery back in the twenties, held ninety cots. It now was privy to twice that number, and as many as three people slept to a cot. The heat was being cranked, and a sweaty, cheap wine-vomit-piss stench seemed to float in the air like a tropical fog. The huddled, ragged bodies sprawled all over everything reminded Tequila of a rat's nest.

He'd checked in early this morning, figuring neither the police nor the mob would search for him here. Homeless shelters, like the homeless themselves, were invisible unless you made an effort to notice them. The supervising Salvation Army worker, exhausted and uncaring, had barely looked at Tequila when he'd entered. Shelters were usually run tighter, but with the recent life-threatening cold spell they'd been letting in anyone at all.

Tequila simply gave a false name, said he'd been kicked out of his apartment, and the man provided him with a worn grey cotton blanket that smelled of disinfectant and told him not to start any trouble.

Tequila sat up in his cot and stretched his muscles. He hurt. His twisted ankle seemed to bulge and ache with every heartbeat. The shoulder he'd dislocated was stiff and swollen. The skin on his palms was raw, and he had scrapes on both knees, both elbows, and his left hip. His muscles felt like boards, and he didn't feel rested in the least, even though he'd been there for almost seven hours.

He stretched, wincing at the kaleidoscope of pain that bloomed throughout his body. Then he began with his neck and methodically stretched every muscle group and flexed every joint. He worked his way down his back to his stomach and pelvis, and then did his shoulders, arms, elbows, wrists, hands, and fingers. Then he worked the stiffness from his hips, knees, legs, feet, and toes. By the time he had finished the warm-up his aches were bearable, and he'd gathered an audience of eight or nine street people, their faces curious rather than hostile.

"Were you some kinda athlete?" a filthy, bearded man in a stained overcoat asked.

Tequila ignored him. He didn't want to be remembered here, in case someone came around asking questions. Especially since he'd probably be back again. Until his job was finished, this was a good place to lay low. Maybe, if getting Marty took longer than he'd anticipated, he could answer an ad in the paper and rent an apartment for a month or two. But in the meantime he was going to bounce around Chicago's homeless shelters, and the fewer people who noticed him the better.

Tequila walked through the circle of street people, his bag in hand, his agenda posted up in his mind as if someone had tacked a list to the inside of his skull. First, find a bathroom and a shower. While this had been an alright place to spend the night, lice notwithstanding, he'd seen the washrooms on his arrival and they left a lot to be desired in the way of sanitary conditions.

He buttoned up his starter jacket and left the shelter.

His original idea was to hit the YMAC where he once worked, but it could be under surveillance by one or both of the factions he was trying to avoid. There was only one other place he knew where he could get a shower, and he'd risk being seen there. But he didn't have much in the way of choices.

It was eight blocks away, and the tears in his clothes made his walk even colder than it should have been. It was a dry cold, one that cracked skin and chapped ears and split lips. Pulling out his ID, he welcomed the heated lobby and hoped the attendant didn't look too closely at the dirt and blood caked all over his person.

She was flirting with some muscular program director and ran his membership card through the scanner without even glancing his way.

Tequila took the escalator up to the second floor of the fitness club and went to the men's locker room. His first order of business was to use the bathroom. Afterwards, he traded his card for a clean towel and a padlock, and then found an open locker and began to strip.

This was risky, because many of Marty's people liked to work out here. It had been Marty who'd gotten him the membership. Tequila just hoped that all of them would be with Marty right now during his time of crisis, rather than lurking around here someplace. If he could have gone without a shower, he would have, but in the daytime it was too obvious that the stains all over him were blood rather than dirt, and that might attract unwanted attention.

Snapping the padlock shut, Tequila walked naked with his towel and his lock key to the showers. Finding a solitary one in the corner, he turned it up to scorch and let the hot water revitalize him.

Dirt and blood swirled around his feet as he showered. He thought of the many times he'd taken showers here before, after workouts, and how life had seemed so different then. Or maybe not life so much, but his attitude towards life. Even though Tequila had always been a pretty tough bastard, he'd still known when Marty hired him years ago that Marty was one of the bad guys. He hadn't cared. The money was good, and Tequila was treated adequately. He figured that if something better ever came along, he'd take it, but for the time being it was fine.

Now Sally was dead, and it was probably Tequila's fault as much as Marty's. If you keep company with dogs, one day you'll eventually get bitten. Except he wasn't the one who suffered. It had been his poor, innocent sister.

He soaped the wounds on his body, stripping away the filthy scabs with his scrubbing. The reason he'd taken the job with Marty was because he thought it would benefit Sally. But if he'd really cared about his sister, shouldn't he have gotten a different job? One that allowed him to stay home with her, rather than having to hire China? What did Sally care about an $1800 a month apartment? Wouldn't she have wanted to spend more time with him instead?

Tequila knew that he'd not only killed his sister, but failed her as well. He wasn't any better than his old man after all. The sins of the father became the sins of the son.

He finished rinsing and began to dry off, the towel soon becoming pink with blood. Tequila didn't notice. He was too busy preoccupied with this new feeling he was experiencing. Guilt. He'd never questioned his actions before. He'd never deeply analyzed his motivations. And now, in the shower room at Remmy's Health Club, he was having a dual attack of the should-have-dones and could-have-beens.

Tequila walked slowly back to his locker, so into beating himself up that he didn't notice the massive form of Terco enter the locker room.

Terco's idea had been the same as Tequila's. He'd spent the night at *Spill,* and since Marty needed him on call and his home was half an hour away, Terco had come here to take a shower and change into the set of spare clothes that he always kept in his locker to wear after a workout.

The bodybuilder passed Tequila up without noticing him, absorbed in his own thoughts. He stopped six lockers down the same row and began to open his combination lock as Tequila got dressed.

The men noticed each other at the same time. Terco's attention was drawn by Tequila's familiar blond crew cut, and Tequila's reverie was broken when he noticed he was being stared at.

Both recoiled in shock and surprise. Tequila considered the .38 in his money bag, the one that he'd taken from Terco. It was empty, but he might be able to use it to threaten.

He didn't have a chance to try, because the big man was charging at him within an intstant.

Terco had no fear, even though Tequila had thoroughly trounced him their last meeting. All he could see was the smile on Marty's face when he brought Tequila in. Driven by the urge to please his master, he reached out to snatch Tequila's shirt.

Tequila dodged the move and brought his foot up into Terco's face. It had about as much effect as a slap, and Terco shrugged it off. Not only was Tequila barefoot, not having gotten around to putting on his shoes yet, but his ankle still hurt too much to be an effective weapon. He switched legs and kicked out with his good foot, but this put all his weight on the bad ankle. Even though he solidly connected with Terco's ribs, Tequila fell onto his ass.

Terco reeled slightly from the second kick, but then he was lashing out with his own foot at Tequila on the floor. He whacked Tequila hard in his dislocated shoulder and rolled him across the wet tile several yards away. The grunt Tequila emitted energized Terco, and the big man hurried after him.

Seeing stars, Tequila used the momentum of his roll to gain his footing, just in time to face the charging Terco. Since he couldn't use his feet too well, Tequila adopted a boxing stance and planted them far apart. As Terco neared, Tequila twisted his upper body and snapped a right cross at the big man's ear.

Terco got his arm up to block the punch, but Tequila followed it immediately with a left to the kidney, putting all of his weight and strength into the blow. The hit doubled Terco over, and Tequila jumped high into the air with his knee up, smacking it solidly into Terco's jaw.

Patches of light winked before Terco's eyes, and his knees buckled and wobbled. Tequila took careful aim and popped Terco in the bridge of the nose, trying to shatter the cartilage and force some into the brain to kill him.

He broke Terco's nose, but death didn't occur. The sight of his own blood seemed to energize the bodybuilder, and before Tequila could follow up the punch Terco lashed out with his long muscular legs and sent Tequila spinning over to the sinks.

Tequila bounced into an automatic hand dryer and hit the floor hard. He noted it smelled like foot sweat and urine while trying to stop the spinning in his head long enough to get up. He was on his knees when Terco reappeared, gore streaming from his nose in two flowing ribbons, plastering his T-shirt to his well-defined chest.

"This time I'm going to break your legs so you can't run away again."

Terco grinned. The blood ran over his smiling mouth and soaked his teeth. Tequila saw the familiar pivot of his opponent's hips, knowing he was going for that reverse kick he seemed so fond of.

The predictability of the move pleased Tequila. Terco might have been a black belt, but to Tequila he seemed more like a one trick pony. He probably relied more on size and strength than skill to win his bouts. The reverse kick seemed to be the only decent move in his oeuvre.

Tequila ducked the kick easily and got to his feet while Terco righted his stance.

"You couldn't hit me with that kick if I was tied up and asleep," Tequila taunted. He moved next to the hand blower as he spoke, hoping his body hid the metal object from Terco's sight.

"Oh yeah?" Terco hated the reply as soon as it left his lips. Stallone would have been ashamed too. But he still moved in, ready to kick the little man into the next century.

Tequila saw his hips pivot, then he dropped down under the automatic hand dryer.

He had to give Terco some credit, because his kick knocked the dryer clean off the wall. It had been bolted on solidly too, and caulked as well. But steel was still harder than flesh and bone, and Terco broke five bones in his foot hitting the blower.

The bodybuilder felt nothing at first but nausea, which told him what he'd done and warned him of the pain to come. He held the foot before him without resting it on the floor, as if he'd just stepped in dog crap and was looking for a place to scrape it off.

Tequila, on his knees, took the offering and lunged at the wounded foot, grabbing it in both hands and twisting it with his entire body.

Terco screamed, the pain hitting like a jackhammer. He crumpled to the ground and lashed out with his good foot, trying to kick Tequila off. The small man held firm, twisting and turning the broken foot until a few more bones snapped.

By now, the two had drawn the attention of the entire locker room. Two jocks, tan and buff and thinking their pecs made them invincible, conspired to pull Tequila away from the bigger guy.

One of them went to grab Tequila's right arm, and the other zeroed in on his left.

Tequila spun on them and knocked their noggins together with an audible clunk, *Three Stooges* style. The average man has never felt the sudden pain so often experienced in street fighting. Professionals knew how to overcome it, but amateur hard-asses who'd never been soundly thrashed couldn't handle much damage before throwing in the towel. Or in this case, throwing up, which was what the two Samaritans did. For good measure Tequila gave each of their prone forms a hard jab, breaking their noses.

Then he whirled back on Terco and was surprised to see the bodybuilder getting up. Taking two quick steps, Tequila launched himself at Terco, shoulder first, driving the big man backwards into the lockers. He grabbed Terco's shirt with one hand and used the other to rub the blood from Terco's nose into his eyes, temporarily blinding him. Then he grabbed both of Terco's ears and rammed his forehead into his broken nose. He did it one more, twice more, turning the cartilage into splintery pulp.

Terco lashed out with his hands, moaning. He managed to clip Tequila across the face, and Tequila sailed backward from the blow. Though a better fighter, Tequila was still only half of Terco's weight. The difference was most apparent when Tequila caught a hit. Even the slightest backhand, with all of Terco's heft behind it, was as deadly as a straight on punch from someone Tequila's own size. David couldn't have taken on Goliath without his sling shot, and Tequila had no such luxury.

Terco shook his head, trying to clear it. He was in incredible pain, but being a professional he was no stranger to it. He compartmentalized it into a section of his brain where he didn't have to deal with it right away. The prime directive here was subduing Tequila, and he would suffer a lot more before giving up. He stood up, favoring his good foot but nonetheless putting some weight on his broken one. Electric ripples of agony surged up through his body, and Terco eyed the man who had caused him that agony. He advanced.

Tequila found himself on the pissy floor again and wondered how it happened. He crawled to his hands and knees and felt the hot sting on his cheek where Terco had slapped him across the room. His ears rang, and he tried to focus on his hands and stop the double vision. Tequila blinked rapidly, shook his head, and felt his stomach begin to lurch.

Terco bent down to snatch the smaller man's jacket. Enough with the karate crap. Terco decided it was time to use his weight and his strength. He lifted Tequila up as if he were a small child and snugged him tight to his chest.

Tequila, for the second time in ten hours, was being squeezed to death. His arms were pinned to his sides and his face was pressed hard against the bodybuilder's bloody pecs. He tried to squirm but it was like being locked in a body-sized vise. Once again he couldn't breathe, and the lack of oxygen did nothing to help his nausea or double vision.

He tried to bite Terco, but his head was pressed too tightly into his chest. He tried to kick his legs, but Terco spread his own stance further apart so there was nothing to kick.

That was Terco's undoing. Spreading his legs, plus the fact that he was wearing sweat pants instead of tight jeans or spandex.

Tequila reached down and took a handful of balls. He squeezed with powerful hands that could crush soup cans.

Terco opened his arms like automatic doors, dropping Tequila and shoving him away. Tequila fell to his knees and followed up his squeezing attack with a left right combination to Terco's little guy.

Terco let out a high-pitched, keening whistle, and then both big Terco and little Terco collapsed face first onto the tile floor.

Tequila wanted to kill him. His rage was furious, and this asshole on the floor played a part in his sister's death. If he didn't kill him, Tequila knew that he'd have to at some later date anyway. But the problem was he had fifteen guys watching him, and he doubted they'd let him get away if he snapped an unconscious guy's neck.

"Call the cops," Tequila told the onlookers. "This guy just attacked me. Anyone see it?"

"I saw him rush you," one man said.

"I saw it too."

Tequila worked his way through the crowd and got back to his locker.

His money bag was still there, wonder of wonders. He quickly put on his socks and his shoes, followed by his holster rig and his starter jacket. Terco would have to wait for another day, he couldn't risk it now. Cold-blooded murder didn't bother Tequila, but cold-blooded murder in front of witnesses wouldn't bode well at the trial, if and when Tequila was finally caught.

Later, he promised Terco. He went to the sink and washed the blood from his face and hands. Then he continued walking and went through the showers and into the enclosed swimming pool.

"You can't come in here in street clothes," the life guard warned.

Tequila ignored him, and when the life guard strutted over, sticking out his big chest and holding up his hand like a cop at a crosswalk, Tequila broke his nose. His seventh nose of the day. Then he walked over to the emergency exit door and pushed it open. It sounded the fire alarm, which suited Tequila fine. The more confusion, the better. The door let out down a staircase and out into the alley, where the prodigal wind returned to smack his face with frost.

His next course of action was to get weapons. He was also thinking about getting some new clothing, but that could wait a day or two. Tequila's plan was to attack Slake first. That evil son of a bitch would be the next to die. Then he could concentrate on Marty and crew.

The easiest place to get a firearm was a pawn shop. He knew where one was, a few blocks away.

Using the gun permit that Marty had gotten for him, Tequila bought two .45s to fit into his holsters. He also bought a box of .45 ammo, and a box of ammo for his new back-up piece, Terco's .38. Bribing the pawn shop owner with a fifty, Tequila was also shown a collection of illegal knives and picked out a seven inch switchblade. Appropriately armed, he hit the streets to find a car.

Tequila knew his own car was being watched, so he figured to steal one. He stopped at the nearest pay parking lot, picked out a sporty black Trans

Am, and held one of his .45s to the attendant's temple until he handed over the keys. The man was eager to please, and Tequila hopped into the Pontiac and drove off. Add grand theft auto to his list of felonies.

Slake lived in a house in the northwest suburb of Palatine. Tequila had never been there, but he'd phoned Slake enough on Marty's behalf, and he simply called information to get a street address from the number. He took Congress Parkway to 90/94, and headed west.

An image of Sally, her mouth gaping blood and her eyes open in mute shock, wormed its way into Tequila's thoughts.

"Here I come," he said quietly to Slake. "Here I come."

CHAPTER 25

The man named Royce was smiling, and it was an ugly thing to see. As a child Royce's eye teeth—his upper canines—had grown in pointed, and they protruded grotesquely outward from the gums. It made him look like he had a double set of fangs, and he'd never bothered to get them fixed because he liked the reaction his smile caused in people. Like the reaction he was getting at that moment from Leman.

The ex-cop winced, and had to make a conscious effort not to look away. He was still shaking Royce's hand in greeting, and Royce was drinking in Leman's discomfort and refused to break the handshake.

"Good to meet you," Royce said. He had a hoarse, quiet voice, and a strong odor of garlic on his breath.

At least that proved he's not a vampire. Leman tried to gently tug his hand away, give a clue that the greeting was over, but Royce held on.

"Tequila did that?" asked Royce, indicating Leman's bandaged shoulder.

"Yeah. From about sixty feet. Bastard could have killed me."

"You were lucky it wasn't me. I would have."

Royce smiled again, and this time Leman pulled his hand away. This guy gave him the creeps. He turned and gave Marty a *what the hell?* look, wondering why the Maniac had to bring in this bozo. Weren't he, Terco, Slake, and Matisse enough?

"Mr. Royce is a specialist," Marty said by way of explanation. "He'll take care of Tequila for us."

"Do you really need outside help, Marty? I mean, between the four of us..."

"The three of you. Tequila killed Matisse last night."

Leman felt as if he'd been hit. Not that he liked Matisse that much, but the guy was okay. Only yesterday they'd been in the vault and watching the Super Bowl take being counted. And now...

"How?"

"Tequila beat him to death. So you can see we need more manpower."

"Besides," Royce added, "you aren't going to be much help with only one arm. I doubt you were much help with two."

Leman stung from the jab and felt his face go red. No creepy vampire son of a bitch was going to insult him like that and get away with it. He made a quick fist and threw a sucker punch at Royce's face.

Leman woke up staring at the ceiling, wondering what the hell happened. One eye was swelled shut, and there was something sharp pressing against his neck. He squinted and saw Royce holding a switchblade to his throat.

"Try that again," Royce suggested. "Try it whenever you like. But the next time, I'll cut off your nose."

He gave Leman a poke in the nose with the knife tip, just enough to draw blood. Leman yelped.

Marty grinned like a five-year-old on Christmas morning. One second, Leman had been throwing a punch at Royce. In a blur of instantaneous motion, Royce had ducked the punch, elbowed Leman in the eye, flipped him over, and knelt on his chest with the knife at his neck. It all happened so quickly that Marty thought that he'd missed it, even though he saw the whole thing.

"As I said, Mr. Royce is a professional. He'll take care of Tequila. You,

Slake, and Terco will be with me at all times, in case the little shit decides to try for me because that moron Matisse wasted his sister. Now get your ass off the floor."

Leman, still dizzy, refused the hand that Royce offered and painfully got to his feet. If he'd had use of both hands, he might have been tempted to go for the gun in his holster. Who did this asshole think he was anyway?

"Go ahead and reach for it," Royce grinned, sensing Leman's thoughts. "I won't kill you. I'll just shoot your knees off."

"Go to hell."

Royce's eyes went hard. There was a dark, flickering light behind them, and Leman could almost see the evil thoughts projected on the vampire's brain.

"I am hell."

And Leman, at that moment, believed him.

Slake entered the office, his expression neutral and his gait unhurried. He glanced briefly at Royce, dismissed him as a nobody, and signaled out Marty.

"Got two cops downstairs want to talk to you. Terco's in the hospital. Tequila kicked the shit out of him at Remmy's Health Club, then got away."

"They got a warrant?" Marty asked.

"No. Just want to talk to you, they said."

"Tell them to kiss off."

Slake nodded. His gaze fell on Royce.

"Who is he?" he asked.

"That's Mr. Royce. He's here to help."

"We don't need help."

"From what I've observed," Royce bared his fangs, "you guys would need help finding a turd in a toilet bowl."

"Nice teeth," Slake dead-panned. "I bet you were a bitch to breast feed."

Royce went dark, and Slake grinned at having ruffled his feathers. Then he turned and left, going downstairs to deal with the pigs.

"Who was that?" Royce asked Marty.

"That was Slake. So far he's the only man I've got who hasn't screwed up yet."

"He's got a big mouth. I might have to shut it for him."

"Whatever," Marty shrugged. "But wait until after we've nailed Tequila. I want that son of a bitch so bad my ass itches."

Royce pulled up a chair to Marty's desk, and brought his vulpine face close to Marty's fat one.

"And you will get him," Royce whispered. "Soon."

Leman stared at them, their eyes locked and grinning, and wondered for a freak moment if they were going to kiss.

"Want me to check on Terco?" he asked.

"Yeah. Go find out what the hell happened."

Leman nodded and turned to leave.

"One more thing," added Royce. "You telegraph your punches. You narrow your eyes. I saw it coming with plenty of time to move. Keep your eyes wide next time, you won't be so easy."

Leman blushed again, but filed away the suggestion. Next time he took a swing at Royce, he'd be sure not to telegraph the move. He went after Slake to find out which hospital Terco was at.

"That's another one I may have to put the hurt on," Royce said. "Nice bunch of guys you hired here."

"All that matters now," Marty said, ignoring the jab, "is that I've got the best."

Seeing that little display with Leman had convinced him. Tequila was no match for Royce.

No match at all.

CHAPTER 26

It was all coming together smoothly for Jack Daniels. She'd sent eight teams out with pictures of Tequila to the city's homeless shelters, and one of the teams had a hit within the first hour. Several witnesses confirmed Tequila had spent the night at the shelter on Wabash, checking in under the name *Mescal*. Cute. Jack had a team keeping the shelter under surveillance if Tequila returned.

Detectives Pierce and Rowan, the Organized Crime dicks that had been gathering information on Marty Martelli over the past several years, supplied Daniels with an extensive list of Marty's employees, complete with bios of the many who had police records. They even had a file on Tequila, with a list of several leg-breaking jobs he was suspected of. But as with all of the other assaults committed by members of Marty's gang, no charges were ever filed, or if they were filed, they were then dropped.

Marty's main men, according to Pierce and Rowan, were his collectors. They included Tequila, Matisse Tomaglio, an ex-cop named Jim Leman, an ex-professional bodybuilder named Sam Terco, and an ex-con named Hector Slake.

Slake was the most interesting to Daniels. His record was longer than the other men's records combined. This guy was a career asshole. Nine charges of assault and battery, six charges of aggravated sexual assault, two charges of attempted murder, and four charges of having sex with a minor before he finally served five years in Joliet for the rape and attempted murder of a fourteen-year-old-girl.

Even more interesting than his rap sheet was a small detail from his prison records. Hector Slake had type 0 blood, which put him in the lead for the role as the unknown thin man who murdered the parking lot attendant in Tequila's apartment building, along with murdering China Johnston and raping Sally Abernathy. The Identikit drawing that Frank Michaels the doorman had done bore more than a passing resemblance to Slake's mug shots. Jack was planning to swing by Frank's place and show him Slake's picture, to see if he could make him. If he did, they'd have enough to bring Hector Slake in for a line-up.

She and Benedict had been on their way to Frank's when they caught the squeal about the disturbance at the Remmy's Health Club. One of the perps was described as a short guy with a crew cut wearing a Blackhawks Starter jacket. A pretty good description of Tequila. They went to check it out, but the short man had gotten away after assaulting a life guard.

Flashing around Tequila's picture proved it had indeed been him in the fight. The other combatant was none other than Sam Terco, one of Marty's elite collectors. Terco was taken to Rush-Presbyterian Hospital, and that's where Jack and Herb had gone next.

Terco had played it tough at first, refusing to even open his mouth. But the dumb son of a bitch had been on probation for assault, and this incident, witnessed by over fifteen people, all of whom said Terco had started it, would get his probation revoked. Terco would do time.

He had been a wealth of information after that was brought to his attention. Terco admitted to attacking Tequila, but only because Tequila had stolen an undisclosed amount of money from respectable businessman Marty Martelli. Marty hadn't called the police because he'd caught Tequila in the act, and decided to give him a break. Tequila, however, had gotten away.

"Crawled through the heating vents like a rat," Terco had said. "We put wet blankets in the furnace to smoke him out."

Which explained the fire at *Spill* last night.

When Jack pressed Terco about how much was stolen, Terco hemmed and hawed. It had to be a lot to make them want Tequila so bad.

Changing tactics, Daniels brought up the Binkowskis.

At their mention, Terco became shifty, non-communicative, and betrayed himself as one of the worst liars Jack had ever seen.

Jack checked Terco's chart and found out he was blood type B. A match for the blood found on the salt crystals at the Binkowski's house. He also saw that Terco had multiple cuts and bruises on his chest, consistent with being shot with rock salt.

Terco demanded his lawyer, and Jack knew they had the bastard. A DNA test could match the blood on the salt crystals with his blood. Daniels treaded cautiously, talking to the State's Attorney, getting the proper warrants, and finally building a strong enough case against Terco to arrest the prick. She also got a warrant to toss Terco's place for the murder weapon, the .38. If they found it, Terco would be going away for a long time.

When two uniforms came to put Terco under police custody, Jack and Herb went to Frank Michaels's place to give him a look at Slake's picture.

Frank apparently wasn't home.

Daniels assigned two uniforms to watch Frank's apartment and call when they spotted him. Then she and Herb decided to go have a chat with Marty Martelli. Neither Jack nor Herb expected anything at all from the Maniac in terms of evidence, confession, or testimony, and they didn't want to intrude on the case being built by Detectives Rowan and Pierce. But one of Martelli's employees had been killed and three more were under suspicion of murder. That was cause enough for a little chat.

The first place they tried was *Spill*, Marty's club. It was a happy coincidence that Hector Slake was at the bar.

"Hi, Hector," Jack said, smiling broadly.

Slake looked at Jack and his partner and sneered. He'd been sitting alone, drinking a club soda and thinking things through.

"What can I do for you today, officers? We don't open until four."

"Just want a word with the boss. Is Marty around?"

"No, he's not."

"Why don't you check?"

"Because I'm sure."

"Too bad. He might like to know we just talked to Sam Terco over at Rush-Presbyterian. Seems a guy named Tequila Abernathy busted Terco up at Remmy's Health Club."

Slake's face revealed nothing.

"You wouldn't happen to know where Tequila Abernathy is, would you?" Benedict added.

Again, not so much as a blink from Slake.

"Well, since Marty isn't around, he won't be able to complain if we break a few things," Jack grinned. "There's no one here but you and us Hector. Who would believe you when you said two cops came in and poured every bottle of liquor on the floor? It's the word of two upstanding officers of the law versus a convicted baby-raper."

To emphasize her point, Jack knocked Slake's glass of club soda off of the bar and across the room. It fell with a tinkling of broken glass. Slake gave Jack a bored look, showing no fear.

"I'll go double check," Slake said, disappearing through a door next to the back bar.

Benedict looked at his partner.

"Scary, Jack. I got Dirty Harry vibes."

"I never liked these organized crime types," Daniels said. "Not only are they scummy, worthless warts on the face of society who think they're above the law, but they make so much more money than I do."

Benedict looked around the empty club, idly wondering what a place like this pulled in a night. And how much Marty padded that sum with laundered book money. *Marty probably paid more in taxes a year than I make,* he thought. His stomach gurgled in sympathy.

"I think I had too much pizza." Herb stifled a belch with his fist.

"No kidding."

Herb dug the bottle of ulcer medication from his pocket and popped two pills. Jack watched, fascinated.

"You can swallow pills without water?"

"Sure. Can't you?"

"No. They get stuck in my throat. Then I'll go and drink something, but they still feel stuck there."

Herb nodded. "That's happened to me before. But not with pills. Turkey."

"Turkey?"

"Day after Thanksgiving, grabbed a piece from the fridge, it was like swallowing a dry sponge. Felt it in my throat for a week."

"That happened to me with cold pizza once. Sometimes I think I still feel it."

"You ever throw up through your nose?"

"Sure."

"That burning stomach acid sensation, all the way up through your nasal passages."

Jack frowned. "I hate that."

"Got the stomach flu once, after eating spaghetti. Threw up, and had a noodle hanging out of my nose. Just hanging there, swaying back and forth, burning like hell."

"What did you do?"

"Nothing. Dog came by, took care of it for me."

One more reason not to get a dog. Jack immediately felt guilty for the thought.

"Alan wants to get a dog. I'm not a pet person. But maybe if I got him one he wouldn't be mad at me all the time."

"Jewelry works too."

"Jewelry?"

"If you're going to buy someone's love, think big. And you don't need to take gold and diamonds for a walk at 2 a.m."

"Point taken. Think I should get him some earrings?"

"Only if they come with a matching necklace."

They waited several more minutes in silence before Slake came back through the door marked PRIVATE.

"Nope. Checked everywhere. Marty isn't around."

Jack's spine stiffened. "Maybe we should check for ourselves."

"I wasn't aware you had a warrant."

"We don't need a warrant. We entered on suspicion of a felony after hearing screams coming from behind the door."

"Impossible," Slake said. "The door is sound proofed."

"Maybe it wasn't screams. Maybe we smelled marijuana. In fact, your pupils look kind of dilated, Hector. I have a strong suspicion you've been smoking the wacky tobacky. What do you think, Detective Benedict?"

"He does have that certain spaced-out look often associated with the Devil's oregano. And is that smoke coming from behind the door?"

Jack and Herb started towards the door but it opened before they reached it. Walking through was a man that Jack IDed as former Chicago cop James Leman.

"Hi, Leman. Liked the criminal element so much you decided to join full time, huh?"

"Take off, cop, unless you've got a warrant."

Jack considered the situation. Making a mockery out of Slake if anything came of this would be pie. With another witness, one who used to be a cop, Jack wasn't sure she could get away with it. Even though it was a cop kicked off the force for excessive brutality. Leman had worked Vice, and knocked around hookers to get freebies. Jack didn't like pimps, especially ones with badges.

"We want to talk to your boss. Routine questioning in a Homicide investigation."

"Homicide?" Leman raised an eyebrow. "Who died?"

Instead of answering, Jack said, "What happened to your shoulder, Leman?"

"A little accident."

"That accident didn't happen to be named Tequila, did it?"

Leman's lips pressed together.

"No wonder you couldn't cut it as a cop, Leman. Can't even handle a little shrimp half your size."

"Fuck you, *Detective*."

Jack's lack of sleep, coupled with the problems at home, left her feeling mean.

"Does it hurt, Leman? Your shoulder?"

"What's it to you?"

Jack didn't narrow her eyes, or pivot her hips, or twitch or lean or do anything else that telegraphed her move. Leman was caught totally by surprise when Jack drove her palm hard into the ex-cop's bandaged shoulder. He fell back into the doorway and Jack walked right over him and marched up the stairs with Benedict in tow and Slake scurrying behind.

The stairs led to a hallway, and Daniels heard conversation coming from the office at the end. She made her way to it quickly and announced her arrival by walking right in.

There were two men in the room, Marty Martelli and a man that Jack didn't recognize from Marty's files.

"Who the hell are you?" Marty demanded.

"They pushed their way in Marty," Slake said, looking at Daniels with undisguised venom.

"See, Slake? Marty's right here," Jack said. "Not only are you a baby-raper, but a lying little gofer as well. Would you stand on your head if Marty told you to?"

Slake murdered Jack with his eyes.

"I asked you a question, cop."

Daniels turned her full attention to Marty the Maniac.

"And I'll answer your question. I'm Homicide, Detective Daniels out of the 26th. And now I have a question for you. Did you order the murders of Vincent and Marie Binkowski?"

Marty made a face. "What the hell are you talking about?"

"You want to call a lawyer first?"

"Who the hell are Vincent and Mary Binkowski?"

"*Marie.* One of your men, Sam Terco, shot them both last night. We've got him in custody now. You hire men with loose lips, Marty."

"Detective Daniels," Marty had a placating smile on his face, and Jack was positive that she wasn't going to get anything out of him. "I'd be more than happy to answer any questions you may have, but right now I'm in the middle of a business meeting."

"And who might you be?" Daniels turned towards Royce.

Royce simply grinned, giving the Detective a peek at his fangs.

"You're never too old for braces," Jack told him.

"Are you the same Detective Daniels that broke that serial killer case a while back?" Royce asked. "You're a legend in Chicago. You know, I'm a bit of a legend too. The name is Royce."

"Never heard of you."

"But I'm sure you and your comrades have come across my work on many different occasions, being in the division of police that you are."

Jack moved closer to him. "Are you confessing to murder, Mr. Royce?"

"What would give you that idea, Detective? I've said nothing of the sort. And I'd repeat that denial fifty-six times, if necessary."

Jack stared hard at the fanged man. Was this guy really hinting that he'd killed fifty-six people? He had to be bullshitting. Yet Jack saw that look in his dark eyes. The sociopath look. This man was a murderer, no doubt at all. Perhaps someone Marty had brought in to deal with Tequila.

Jack backed up. "My mistake then, Mr. Royce. I've dealt with enough killers to know you don't have that hard-edged look about you. You'd probably faint taking a mouse out of a trap."

Royce's vampire grin fell off his face.

"It was nice meeting you, Detective. Perhaps we'll meet again, and I'll be able to add a few more denials to my list."

"I doubt it, Mr. Royce. I deal with killers, not liars. Now Marty the Maniac here, he's the real item."

"You accusing me of murder now, Daniels?" Marty warned. "You think this gung-ho bullshit is going to work with me? You'll be off the case by the end of the day, bitch. Now get the hell out, I'm sick of your bullshit."

Jack slammed her palms down on the desk and leaned forward, getting in the Maniac's face.

"I know about Tequila, Marty. I know you're after him. And if he turns up dead, a blind man would be able to follow the trail straight to you. It happens with you old-timers, Marty. You get sloppy. You lose control. Even outside help like this pathological liar Royce won't be able to fix it. You're heading for a fall, and I'll be there when it happens. If you think I'm a bitch now, wait till I get your fat ass in my interrogation room."

"Get out!" Marty screamed.

Daniels smiled cordially at Marty, at Royce, and at Slake, and then she and Herb left the office. They met Leman in the hallway, holding his shoulder.

"You little—"

He didn't get to finish because Jack threw another palm at Leman's bad shoulder, putting her body into it and spinning the ex-cop to the floor.

"Am I a vicious person, Herb?" Jack asked, stepping over Leman.

"Not at all. You're a pussycat."

"Then why is it I got the biggest kick out of smacking that dirtbag around?"

"It's probably just too much caffeine."

They took the stairs down to the door and exited through the bar.

Daniels waited a moment before putting the car into gear after starting it. Her hands were still pulsing from the adrenaline rush, and she was thinking through her recent actions and wondering if they'd come back to haunt her. Jack Daniels wasn't a strictly by-the-book cop, but she was honest, and she didn't like trampling over people's rights or engaging in police brutality.

"Seriously, Herb. Did I push it too far in there?"

"I think you met a resistance with an equal amount of force."

The answer satisfied Jack, and she pulled into traffic.

"What'd you think of Mr. Royce?" she asked her partner.

"Scary son of a bitch. I think I've heard of someone named Royce, but I'm not sure where."

"We'll run his name, see what comes up. What stone do you want to turn over next?"

That was how police work went sometimes. Just keep turning over stones and watch if anything scurries out from under them.

"Let's find Frank Michaels, get him to ID Slake. I liked that creep even less than Mr. Royce."

Benedict radioed the surveillance team watching Michaels's apartment, only to find he hadn't shown yet.

"Do you think we scared Marty off Tequila's trail?" Jack asked.

"Hell no. You see Marty's eyes bulge when you mentioned Tequila's name? He wants that guy, bad."

He's not the only one. Jack wanted him too. Tequila was the cause of all this violence, and once they got him, Jack knew the violence would stop. But as long as Tequila was free, there would be more bodies. Jack was sure of it.

So where the hell was he?

CHAPTER 27

Tequila parked the stolen Trans Am two blocks away from Slake's house in a strip mall lot. He had no plan of action, because there were too many variables. The first move would be to see if Slake were home or not, and then go from there.

Most of Palatine, as was typical of all Chicago suburbs, was residential. Ranks and files of houses and housing developments, interspersed every so often by a convenience store. Slake's neighborhood was woodsier than most, with full grown trees and bushes separating the half-acre lawns from house to house. Tequila walked along the well-kept sidewalk, his feet crunching on the salt that the township had spread out to melt ice. When he came up on Slake's address he cut across the neighbor's lawn and entered the property via the backyard.

It was a mid-sized ranch, white and gray wood paneling and black tar shingles. Tequila couldn't picture a psychotic like Slake living in it. The house was better suited to a young yuppie family or a wealthy elderly couple. But everyone had to live somewhere. Every spider had a web.

He sprinted over to the side of the home and crouched next to a window. It was curtained, preventing Tequila from seeing inside. The next window he tried was similarly draped.

He moved cautiously around the perimeter of the house until he reached the back of the adjacent garage. Like most garages, it had a rear door leading into the backyard, and at the top of the door was a window. Tequila peeked in. The garage was empty. Tequila recalled the front of the house, and Slake's silver Monte Carlo hadn't been parked in the street or the driveway. He probably was with Marty, helping with the search.

Still, no reason to get killed because of a bad assumption. Tequila hit the button and demagnetized his holsters, and he walked around to the front of the house and rang the doorbell.

No answer.

He rang again to make sure, holding his ear to the door, listening for movement.

Nothing.

Tequila went around to the backyard again, thinking things through. Either no one was home, or no one was answering. If Slake had owned a dog, it would have barked or at least come to investigate the doorbell. He scanned the backyard for dog crap and found none. His guess was that the house was probably empty.

He chose a backyard window, breaking the glass with his elbow and then clearing the excess off the pane with the butt of a .45. Heaving himself up easily, Tequila pulled through the opening and landed hands first inside Slake's bedroom.

Getting to his feet, he took a look around. It was a normal bedroom; a dresser, a closet, a four poster bed. Except this four poster bed had chains and shackles attached to the posts. Tequila searched through the drawers and wasn't too surprised to find several whips, black leather masks, ball gags, and a riding crop. There was also a rusty car antenna, and a black box with a handle that Tequila figured out was a hand crank electric generator, complete with clamps to enhance anyone's perverted sex life.

He opened the bedroom door and looked down the hall into the kitchen. Two things caused immediate panic in Tequila. The first was the sight of five oversized dog bowls all lined up on the kitchen floor. The second was movement behind him.

Tequila whirled around, the .45s in his hands, and fired as fast as he could.

The first of the pit bull mastiffs, as broad in the chest as Tequila and weighing damn near as much, was already in mid leap when the bullets thudded into its body. Tequila shot it three times from each gun, but momentum propelled it onward and the animal slammed into him with the force of a football tackle.

Tequila fell back, trying to push the dog off of him. It wasn't quite dead yet, and it snapped its massive jaws feebly at Tequila's neck. While he struggled with the beast, he felt white-hot pain surge through his left ankle as another dog bit into his foot.

Screaming, Tequila emptied his right .45 into the biting pit bull's head. The dog fell back, taking Tequila's shoe with it. Sensing movement behind him, Tequila swung around his left .45 and fired four times at the charging black form. He hit the dog in both front legs and twice in the mouth. The animal fell forward and ate the carpeting, choking on blood.

With the last bullet in the gun, Tequila delivered the coup de grace into the forehead of the first dog still quivering on top of him. With a sharp explosion of gore the beast went limp and Tequila pushed the dead weight off his lower body, gaining his feet.

He hadn't brought extra clips with him. He had figured if he couldn't kill Slake with fourteen bullets, then a few more wouldn't help much. So he holstered his .45s and took Terco's back-up .38 from his waistband.

Two dogs dead, one out of commission. But there were five bowls in the kitchen. Where were the other two?

Tequila whistled, hoping to draw them out. He wasn't surprised that it didn't work. These dogs were highly trained. They didn't bark. They didn't make any noise at all. And they'd flanked him on both sides like a wolf pack. The other two were probably watching him right now, waiting for the right moment to pounce. The thought made Tequila's bladder feel tight.

Tequila looked down at his wounded foot. It was covered in blood, but that might have been the animal's. Walking slowly, he eased past the dying pit bull whose legs he'd practically shot off. It was gagging, pushing itself slowly forward with its rear paws. Tequila ended its pain with a quick switchblade slash across its throat, then advanced in a crouch to the kitchen.

He immediately recognized it as a bad move. The kitchen had four different entry points; the hall, the foyer, the living room, and the dining room. Tequila couldn't cover them all at once. Acting quickly, he went into the dining room and the fourth dog sprung from its hiding place.

One hundred and twenty pounds of highly-trained, finely-tuned killing machine. It pinned Tequila down and went straight for the throat, its claws digging furrows in Tequila's chest and its slobbery breath smelling like meat gone bad.

Tequila tucked his chin in and twisted his body, letting the dog sink its long teeth into his shoulder. He couldn't bring the gun up to the beast's head, but he got it to chest level and fired five times.

The animal continued to gnaw on his shoulder, seemingly unaffected by the five slugs in its body. That was the difference in stopping power between a .38 and a .45. Tequila shifted his body and rolled hard, breaking the dog's pin. He came out of the roll with the switchblade in one hand and the gun in the other. The dog was on him before Tequila could get to his knees, but this time when the huge head lunged to tear out Tequila's throat, he thrust the knife under the V of the creature's jaw and through the top of its snout.

The dog tried to open its mouth but found it skewered by a seven inch blade. It brought a paw up to its face and scraped at the knife, repeatedly filleting its own foot on the exposed point. Tequila took advantage of the dog's confusion and pushed the revolver between the animal's eyes, firing point blank.

The dog's head jerked back and it flipped onto its side, legs jerking spasmodically. Tequila placed his foot on the canine's muzzle and yanked his knife back out. His shoulder was on fire, and he chanced a quick look and saw at least three puncture wounds that would require stitches.

But that wasn't his biggest worry at the moment. There was one more dog in the house, and Tequila didn't have any more bullets.

He stuck the empty .38 back into his waistband and spun around, eyes and ears on alert. He held his breath, listening for any sound that would indicate where Number Five was hiding.

Seconds ticked by. A minute. Two. The blood seeped from Tequila's shoulder, down his side, wetting his sock. He didn't hear a damn thing.

Maybe the fifth dog was at the vet. Or maybe it recently died. Or maybe it was locked in the basement, or was hiding from the gunfire.

Or maybe it was...

Tequila cocked an ear to the kitchen, detecting the faintest sound of slurping. Treading as silently as possible, he made his way to the dining room door.

He saw it in the hallway, next to the body of the first dog he'd killed, its snout buried in the ripped open underbelly.

Eating. It was eating its fallen pack member. Tequila wondered why a trained attack dog would bother stuffing its face when there was an intruder in the house. When the dog looked up at him, he realized why.

It was covered with scars. They streaked its fur, long jagged welts and bare spots, some still unhealed. Tequila knew that one of the best ways to train attack dogs was to teach them to fight their own kind, preferably dogs bigger than themselves. To give the smaller dogs a chance, the bigger one was usually tied up or muzzled.

This was the training dog. Though it was the largest, its will had been systematically broken by the attacks of the others. Now that the others were gone, it was top dog again, and it had taken advantage of the fact by gnawing on the body of one of its tormentors.

It stared at Tequila, fangs dripping gore. The years of pain were over. It could finally fight back. The beast leapt casually over the carcass and began moving slowly down the hall. Stalking. Head low, ears back, tail straight.

Tequila had never known unfettered, primeval terror until this moment. The dog had to weigh twenty pounds more than he did, and the switchblade he clutched seemed like a toy. The dark, massive figure advanced, its eyes never leaving Tequila, bloodthirsty and intent.

Tequila considered backing up and locking himself in the dining room. The only problem was it had two more doors, both of which were open. The beast would undoubtedly get in one while he was closing the others.

"Sit!" he commanded the dog.

The dog didn't sit. It continued coming at him, low on its haunches, like a lion in the grass.

Since there wasn't any place to run, and fighting was suicidal, Tequila decided on a different approach. He tucked away his switchblade and remagnetized his holsters.

Then he ran at the dog.

The dog bowed down, snarling, ready to spring. Tequila tried to pretend it wasn't there, concentrating on a floor exercise routine from years ago. After five steps he dove into a hand spring, bounced from his hands to his feet, flipped into one more hand spring, and then pushed hard off his toes and executed a double summersault in the air, going over the head of the jumping animal and landing several feet behind it.

The dog spun fast and sprinted after Tequila, but Tequila was already tearing ass over to the bedroom, not having bothered to stick the landing for the required three seconds. He beat the dog to the door and slammed it as the animal leapt.

Tequila had been braced for the hit, but the weight and force of the animal bounced the heavy door off of Tequila's chest and sent him sprawling backwards over Slake's bed. The dog recovered from its encounter with the door and shook its patchwork body, lunging into the bedroom after its prey.

In the instant it took to the air, Tequila saw his own horrible, screaming, bleeding death, and he cried out in fear and anger.

The pit bull landed front paws first on Tequila's chest, forcing the air from his lungs, interrupting his war cry. Tequila shot his hand out at the dog's throat and tried to keep the snapping jaws away from his face. It was like wrestling with a bear. The dog shook angrily, its mouth jerking open and closed like a steel trap, spittle and gore showering hot and wet over Tequila's face. The animal went for Tequila's arm, and he adjusted his grip so one hand pushed away the jaw and the other clamped tight on the huge neck. The dog was stronger, and Tequila's arms were slowly being forced back. Seeming to sense victory, the dog increased its efforts, razor sharp teeth inching ever closer to Tequila's unprotected throat.

The leather collar around the dog's neck jingled its tags, and Tequila saw the dog's nameplate and failed to laugh at the irony that his adversary's name was Happy.

Tequila curled his legs up to him and tried to kick Happy backward. The dog countered by shifting its weight, attacking Tequila from the side rather than from directly on top. When the man's muscles began to spasm with effort, he changed tactics.

Tequila jammed his left hand into the dog's mouth, deep into its throat, trying to cram his fist into the hinge of its jaws so they couldn't bite down. Then he used his other hand to dig his thumb into Happy's right eye.

The combination of the two caused Happy to choke and back off, shaking the offending hand free. But it didn't pause to lick its wounds, and as Tequila got to his knees, Happy lunged again.

This time Tequila let Happy have his right arm. As the dog clamped down, he drove his index finger hard into Happy's left eye, effectively blinding him. Then Tequila fell back onto his butt and got his feet in front of him, rolling with the dog and then kicking up with his legs. Happy flipped over him and onto its back.

The dog released Tequila's arm and growled like some prehistoric monster, its jaws snapping audibly on empty air. Tequila rolled to his stomach and freed the switchblade from his pocket. He'd blinded the dog, but supposedly a blind dog was even more dangerous than one that could see. Tequila didn't know if he believed this or not, because he couldn't see how Happy could possibly be any more dangerous.

The dog, working by smell, pounced on Tequila. He jammed the switchblade up between Happy's ribs and tried to jerk it sideways, but the ribs were too big and the blade became stuck. Releasing the knife, Tequila held tightly onto Happy's right paw and wedged it hard under his armpit. Then he rolled.

Happy's foot bent, and then snapped. It howled, which was an even more horrible sound than its growling, and its teeth found Tequila's wounded shoulder and dug in deep.

This time Tequila howled. Still holding Happy's broken paw, he twisted it viciously, using the leverage to force the dog backwards. Judo worked with dogs like it worked with people, and Happy released its bite and turned over onto its back.

Tequila brought a knee down hard onto Happy's ribs, and then let go of the dog and jumped onto Slake's bed.

Happy righted itself and sniffed the air for Tequila. It hobbled toward the bed on three legs, its whole body shaking with rage, the switchblade sticking grotesquely from its ribcage.

Tequila picked up the shackle nearest him and shook it at the dog, letting it hear the chains rattle. The dog jumped onto the bed and Tequila snapped the handcuff onto Happy's wounded front paw, above the knee. Then he rolled away, off of the bed, and across half of the bedroom floor.

The dog howled, finding itself chained to the bed by its injured limb. It pulled and yelped and then began to dig and bite at the pillows. After mauling the pillows it tore into the sheets and the mattress, whining like the damned.

But the shackle held.

Tequila crawled out of the bedroom and headed for the bath. As he'd expected, Slake had a first aid kit in the medicine cabinet. Most men of their profession had one. Tequila dug into it and filled the sink with water.

First he washed away most of the blood on his wounds, and then searched for a bottle of hydrogen peroxide to disinfect them. Unfortunately, he only found rubbing alcohol. It stung so bad his eyes watered.

His foot turned out to have only minor injuries, but his arm and shoulder had ragged tears in them that required stitches. Luckily, Slake had a surgical needle and thread.

Tequila found a bottle of Demerol and a syringe—would have been nice to have found it before the rubbing alcohol ordeal—and injected himself wherever he hurt, which was almost everywhere. Then he did some quick stitch work and bandaged his wounds tight as he could. Slake had a pharmacy worth of drugs, and Tequila helped himself to some Vicodin, amphetamines, and amoxicillin. He took three of each, pocketing the bottles, along with the syringe and the Demerol. Tequila hoped that the dogs had all of their shots. From the way they were trained, he figured they must have. Slake would have spared no expense on these killers. You don't spend two grand training a dog so it can die of heartworm or rabies.

Tequila left the bathroom and found his shoe in the hallway. He slipped it back on, wondering what to do next. He didn't have any weapons left, and he certainly wasn't in any shape now to take on Slake barehanded. He needed to rest.

Happy howled from the bedroom.

Tequila made his way through the house, intending to leave through the rear garage door. Entering the garage, he was hit with a wave of stink. Butcher shop stink. Dead person stink. He flipped on the light.

On a workbench in the corner of the garage was a meat grinder, industrial-sized. Put the meat in the top, turn the crank, and hamburger came out of the holes in the side. Next to it was a plastic garbage bag, something lumpy inside. Tequila went over for a closer look.

In the bag were a leg, two arms, and a severed head. The temperature in the garage was below zero, but the parts weren't frozen solid. Tequila dumped them onto the workbench.

Whoever this individual was, Slake had dismembered him and was grinding him up into peopleburger. The residue on the meat grinder attested to this. Tequila guessed that Slake probably then fed the butchered corpse to his dogs in their oversized bowls. It was one of the more unique ways Tequila had ever heard of to dispose of a corpse.

He stared hard at the frosted-over face and didn't recognize it. But on the right hand of the dismembered arm was a tattoo. A tattoo of a Monarch butterfly, almost identical to the one he had.

So this was how Tequila had been so neatly framed. Slake and this guy had been the ones who robbed Marty. But Slake must not have wanted to split the take, and this was how he dealt with his partner in crime.

Tequila realized his discovery hadn't changed anything. He was still going to kill Marty, and the rest of them. If anything, Tequila was even more enraged at Slake for starting this whole damn mess. Not only had the bastard raped his sister, but he was also responsible for the opportunity to arise.

He looked around the garage, thinking.

"Where would I hide a million dollars?" Tequila said aloud. His words echoed through the freezing garage.

He went back into the house and began to tear it apart. Closets. Furniture. Cabinets. Drawers. Nothing.

Then he checked the basement, and finally the garage, coming up empty on all accounts. He had almost assumed that Slake had hid the money elsewhere when he realized the house had no porthole to the attic.

Slake's ceilings were flat, but his roof was beveled. That implied space between the ceiling and the roof. Usually houses had an access porthole, with a folding ladder that could be pulled down to climb into this storage area. Tequila hadn't seen such a porthole.

But in the kitchen he found a patch of ceiling that was whiter than the rest. He brought a chair over and stood on it. There was a new paint smell, and it was slightly tacky to the touch. Tequila squinted and made out a faint indentation in the shape of a three foot by three foot square. He pushed up in the middle of the square and it lifted up on hinges, the new paint in the cracks flaking away.

Slake had concealed his attic entrance, and then recently painted over the seam to hide that as well. Tequila pushed the trapdoor up until it fell inside the attic, and then pulled himself up after it.

Four suitcases were under a sheet, balanced on the rafters. Tequila didn't even need to open them to know they were filled with money. He pushed them through the porthole and down into the kitchen.

Back on the ground floor, Tequila hauled the suitcases to the front door and unlocked it. He'd drive his car up and then throw them in the trunk. The money meant little to Tequila, but he welcomed the anguish it would cause Slake.

He was almost out the door when a thought occurred to him. Slake had obviously been the thief, but Tequila could have sworn it was Marty who sent him after Billy Chico. Could Slake somehow imitate Marty's voice?

Driven by curiosity, Tequila went back into the living room. Nestled next to the entertainment stand was a computer. Tequila turned it on and watched as the latest version of Windows was booted up.

He scanned all of the items on the main menu desktop, and wasn't too surprised to find a file marked *Voice Generator*. He clicked the file and it booted up.

Voice Generator had several different options, among them were *Record, Synthesize, Pitch, Tone, Volume, Enunciation, Elocution, Emphasis, Dialects,* and several dozen saved files. Tequila clicked a file marked *Chico* and Marty's voice came through the computer's stereo speakers.

"Tequila, Marty. I've got a line on a two grand loser named Billy Chico. He's at 3342 Randolph, apartment 405. Thin guy, thirties, long black hair. Take him tonight."

That was the exact phone message Tequila had gotten yesterday on his day off. Somehow Slake had synthesized Marty's voice, either by recording it first or by trial and error with this software.

He clicked another file called *Me*. This time Slake's voice came through the speakers.

"Marty? It's Slake. My mistake, I hit the wrong number on my speed dial."

Tequila played it again, wondering what it meant. He was stumped, until he noticed the Timer option on the menu. He selected it and read through the instructions, and then he understood.

While he'd been robbing the vault, Slake had his computer call up Marty and play the *Me* recording. Slake had given himself an alibi while committing the crime. Marty couldn't expect Slake to be in the vault and calling him with a wrong number at the same time.

Tequila selected the record feature and put his face to the microphone.

"It's me, Slake. Don't bother with replacing the dogs I just killed. You won't live long enough to train them."

He named the file *Hey Asshole* and then played the message back to see if it worked. It did.

Tequila left the computer on and headed for the door when he noticed something was wrong. It took him a moment to place what it was.

Happy. The dog hadn't howled for a while. Maybe the beast was dead, but Tequila's imagination suggested something else.

There was movement to his right, and Tequila twirled around and saw the dog limping towards him, its muzzle soaked with blood, its leg severed at the knee.

Happy had chewed off its own foot to escape the chain.

Tequila ran, but the dog was surprisingly nimble on three legs and began to gain on him, sniffing the air before it. Chancing a look behind him, Tequila saw Happy was almost at his heels and he made a quick left and ran two steps up a wall and then back-flipped over it, landing behind the dog.

Happy heard the sound and spun to snap at it, but Tequila was already midway through a reverse kick and he connected solidly with the dog's head, knocking out three of its fangs. Then Tequila followed up with a punt to the switchblade, still jammed in Happy's ribs, ramming the hilt in three more inches. The dog yelped, and Tequila made a fist and threw a haymaker punch to the side of Happy's head, knocking the animal over.

Happy rolled to its feet, eager to bite the thing that was hurting it so. For the first time in years it was free to fight back, and it wasn't giving up yet. Springing off its powerful hind legs, Happy lunged through the air and hit Tequila dead center, knocking him backward. The dog began a biting frenzy, desperate for some flesh to sink its teeth into. Tequila fended off the mouth with his fists, but after four punches they became ripped on the dog's teeth, and the blood made Happy even crazier.

Tequila held the muzzle away with one hand and the other roamed Happy's torso for the switchblade. He touched it once, but it was too slippery with blood to pull out.

The dog's teeth found Tequila's throat.

Tequila pushed as hard as he could, and then tried to roll, but the dog stayed on top of him. He could feel the needle sharp fangs closing on his neck, the rancid dog breath clogging his nostrils.

His hand touched the knife again and Tequila yanked it out, bringing it up driving it hard through Happy's blind right eye.

The blade slid through the socket and into the brain, and Happy jumped off Tequila and began to gallop in circles, making a high keening sound like a baby crying. Tequila checked his throat and found only minor damage. He got to his feet slowly, staring at the crying dog, trying to think of a way to end its suffering. He didn't want to get close to it again, because the dog was still dangerous as hell.

Luckily, he didn't have to. With one final cry, Happy fell over, kicking its three legs out like pistons. Gradually, the kicking slowed down, and then stopped.

Tequila left it there, exiting out the front door of the house. The cold air invigorated him, and the walk back to his car went quickly. Once inside, he popped two new clips into his .45s and then headed back to Slake's house. He parked in the driveway, popped the trunk, and went to the front door.

Happy, the hound of hell, lunged at him as he entered, the knife still embedded deep in its head.

Tequila shot him seven times, and the dog went down for good. He loaded the suitcases into his trunk, and then left Slake's house, somewhat surprised that his gunshots hadn't drawn police. Either the houses were too far apart, or everyone was at work, earning the money needed to live in such a nice suburb.

Tequila drove for a while, looking for a place to rest and a place to stash the suitcases. He realized two things during his wandering. The first was that he had to get some new clothes, because these were so ripped up and bloody he wouldn't last thirty seconds in public before being arrested.

The second was that he never, ever, under any circumstances, wanted to own a dog.

CHAPTER 28

Slake headed home for the evening, leaving Marty in the hands of his newest golden boy, that asshole Royce. The way they looked at each other Slake wondered if they were in love. He wished he could end this stupid charade and just take off with the money, but his plan required him to stay with Marty for two more months. Then he could leave, with the Maniac having no idea it was Slake who took the Super Bowl cash.

The whole plan had gone perfectly. He'd set Tequila up, cleared himself, killed his partner, and hid the money without any problem at all. The only loose end was Tequila, but that little son of a bitch would get his soon enough. Once Tequila was dead, Slake had no more worries. Even the witnesses had been eliminated. That moron Matisse had taken care of Tequila's retard sister, and Slake had killed Tequila's nosey doorman early this morning, along with the dumb prick's wife.

When Slake had gone back to Tequila's apartment to grab his sister, as dictated by Marty, he ran into the cop party going on. Something had gone wrong. So Slake waited, and when he saw Frank the doorman leave with a police escort. Slake followed them home.

Then, when the cops left, he simply knocked on their door. When the woman answered, he cut her throat. Her husband gave him a bit of a chase around the kitchen table, but in the end he caught him too. All the while the coon was pleading with "Mr. Collins" not to hurt him. Slake smiled at the memory.

He drove his silver Monte Carlo at three miles an hour above the speed limit down the expressway, exiting on Route 53 to Palatine Road. Slake liked Palatine. He liked being the snake in a town full of mice. But he had no plans to stay when his two months were up.

Slake was going to Mexico, to a little town called Frendes near the southern border. It was a very poor town; so poor, Slake knew, that families would sell their adolescent children if the price were right. Slake had enough money to buy hundreds of kids, to use and dispose of at his whim. He'd live the rest of his life a happy man.

He pulled into his driveway, opening his garage door with the electronic box on his visor. As the light came on, Slake was hit by a wave of panic. The remaining body parts of his ex-partner were spread out over the workbench, and Slake was positive he'd left them wrapped in a garbage bag.

Slake got out of the car and closed the garage. He took out his 9mm and forced the panic back. If someone had broken in, they'd be dead. His dogs would have taken care of them. There wasn't a problem.

He went into his house and called.

"Bashful! Doc! Dopey! Grumpy! Happy!"

No dogs came.

Slake called again, but they didn't run up to greet him as they always did when called.

Full blown fear enveloped Slake, but even stronger than that was the urge to know what was going on. He crept cautiously into the house, his ears peeled, his pistol on full cock.

When he saw the first dog's body, he went ice cold.

When he saw his attic porthole open, he began to scream.

CHAPTER 29

Jack Daniels lay awake in bed, staring at the ceiling, mad as hell.

They'd taken her off the case.

At first, she couldn't believe it when Captain Bains told her. Jack had been pulled from cases before, but only to be put on a more important one. Never, in her entire career as a police officer, had she been yanked because of politics.

Bains had orders from high up. Really high. Jack could see how much her boss hated to pass them along, but the man had a family to feed just like everyone else.

Good old Marty the Maniac had made good on his threat after all. Not only was Jack off the Billy Chico case, she was off the related Binkowski case and the Tequila case.

At first, Jack had raised a proportionate amount of hell. She demanded to know where the order came from. Bains stayed stoic and wouldn't say. Recognizing futility, Jack relented and chose to take her yearly vacation starting tomorrow.

The ramifications sunk in later that evening. After the obligatory fight with her husband about her long hours, Jack became paranoid. Not about her marriage falling apart, but about the Outfit's obvious hold over the Chicago Police Department. There was some deeply embedded corruption in the CPD, and no one was trying to stop it.

Well, that ended tonight.

Daniels, like her mother, became a cop because she wanted to make the world a better place. To serve the public. To protect the innocent, and arrest the guilty. She didn't become a cop to work for mobsters, or to work alongside others who did. This situation needed to be fixed. And the key to fixing it was finding Tequila.

She'd been thinking about it all night, trying to guess what Tequila would do next. Tequila's stay in the shelter last night proved he wasn't going to run. He was going to stick around. To avenge his sister's death. And to do that he'd have to go after the king pin himself. Tequila was going to try for the Maniac.

Let the cops stake out the homeless shelters, waiting for Tequila's return. Jack was going to stake out Marty Martelli's place. Maybe it would take some time, but Daniels knew Tequila would make an attempt, and the best place to try for him was at home. At *Spill*, Marty was surrounded by bodyguards, guns, and people. But killing a bear was easy if you got him while hibernating in his cave.

Jack assumed Marty was aware of this as well, and would take appropriate measures. So Jack's plan was to nail Tequila before he put a foot on Marty's property.

And once she found him, she'd go to the Feds. They loved being invited to any party that had the faintest whiff of police corruption. Tequila would talk—after all, he wouldn't have any allegiance to employers who killed his sister and were trying to kill him. Arresting Marty the Maniac would be sweet, but Jack's real agenda hit much closer to home. She wanted the bad cops. She wanted them so bad she could taste it.

Jack tossed and turned and tossed some more, and sleep and Jack kept orbiting around one another like two sparrows in a death duel. Finally, the Homicide Detective gave up and went to get dressed.

If she was going to stake out Marty the Maniac, she might as well start tonight.

After all, it was her vacation, and she didn't want to sleep it all away.

She was pulling on a pair of slacks when the phone rang.

"Daniels."

"Hi, Jack. It's Herb. Hope I didn't wake you."

"You can't sleep either?"

"Mandatory vacation sounds like it should be heaven, but I feel like my balls were just lopped off."

"I don't have balls and I feel the same way."

"Call me paranoid, but I don't know who to trust anymore. Except for you."

Jack was honestly touched. "Thanks, Herb."

"Don't take it personally. It's because you're a woman and pretty much everyone excludes you from everything. It's called an *old boys network*, not a *unisex network*."

"So no one would trust me with mob payoffs."

"Exactly."

So much for being touched. "Why should I trust you, then?"

"Because I'm naturally honest. And because I keep you in the loop with all the dirt."

Jack grinned. "Tell me you've got something."

"You didn't hear this from me. And I can't pursue this with you, because the wife got all excited once she heard I had time off and already booked us on a flight to California tomorrow to visit her parents."

"Spill it."

"You know district gossip. Well, actually you don't, because everyone is tight-lipped around you."

"No one likes me. Got it. Move on."

"Well, after we got yanked, I made a few *inquiries*." Herb lowered his voice. "It's possible the Outfit has the assistant police superintendent in their pocket."

Jack grunted. "That's ridiculous. They can't own someone that high up."

"This Tequila guy is being charged with not only the Chico murder, but the Binkowski murders, and the murder of his own sister."

Jack shook her head. "That can't be right. The evidence—"

"The evidence is *gone*, Jack. And it gets worse. Frank Michaels, the doorman at Tequila's place, was just found dead in his apartment. His wife too. A neighbor was complaining about the smell and the landlord went in. It happened sometime early this morning."

"How?" Jack was stunned. They'd been trying to get in touch with Frank all day, to ID Hector Slake's picture. But Jack hadn't guessed the man was dead.

"Knife. Probably the thin guy who killed China Johnston and Mitch Comsteen."

"Hector Slake."

"Could be. We'll never know now, without a witness to ID him. We should have put someone on him right away."

"Especially after the Binkowski murders. Goddammit, Herb, why weren't we thinking?"

"We did think. We had men on Frank Michaels, but just too late. Who would have figured they'd go after the doorman, Jack? This is turning into a 1930's gangster movie."

"They charge Tequila with this one too?"

"No. They're calling it a murder/suicide. But I talked to the Homicide dick in charge. Woman was stabbed eighteen times. Man was stabbed through the *eye*. How many people off themselves with a knife through the eye?"

Jack felt her stomach drop. "Maybe you're right to get out of town, Herb."

Herb laughed. "I'm leaving because of Bernice, not because I fear for our lives. I think we're safe, Jack. Cops may turn a blind eye for some cash, or cover up some Outfit business, but I can't picture boys in blue killing one another."

"How about girls in blue?"

Herb was silent.

"Thanks for the word, Herb. If you hear anything else, let me know."

"I'll keep my ears open. And… be careful, Jack."

Daniels hung up, the weight of two more souls heavy on her conscience. Frank must have been killed shortly after coming up with the Identikit drawing of the thin man calling himself Mr. Collins. How could Jack have known they'd get to him that quickly?

But she should have known. She should have put a watch on him.

Not that it would have mattered. If the corruption went that high up, there's nothing she could have done.

But there was something she could do now.

Jack found a shirt and worked her way into it. She put on her heavy coat, grabbed her gun, some extra speed-loaders, and her stake out kit, which was a bottle of water, three candy bars, and a coffee can to piss in. Then she left the apartment..

The cold, freezing night welcomed her as she got on her way.

CHAPTER 30

The night labored on, and as Tequila slept his rage burned hot in his dreams.

There were no homeless shelters in the suburbs. The police picked up anyone wandering the streets and escorted them out of town. If they returned, they were arrested for vagrancy, and not handled very nicely while serving their term. So the suburbs didn't have the homeless problem that the city did, and Tequila had no anonymous place to stay for the night.

The problem with motels was that they kept records. Even if he gave a false name, Tequila figured both the police and the Outfit were checking every hotel and motel in Illinois, looking for him. A desk clerk would talk, and Tequila would get nailed. His size, and the condition of his clothing, would make him memorable. And even a sizeable bribe to erase the desk clerk's memory would pale next to the Mafioso threat of cutting off his gonads.

So he eschewed hotels in favor of a different idea.

Earlier, in a strip mall in nearby Hoffman Estates, Tequila found a thrift shop. It sold second hand furniture, old books, and most importantly used clothing. Tequila had cleaned himself up as best he could in a gas station bathroom, but he still looked like a ragged, tattered, beaten man. That image would be conspicuous at JC Penny's, but wasn't out of place at all at a charity run resale shop.

He'd found a pair of jeans that fit loosely, and bought a belt to go with them. He had also bought a sweat shirt, a watch cap, and a black down-filled camping jacket. The elderly woman who rang up his purchase was a volunteer, as were the two other old ladies in the shop, and none of them gave him a second glance. His purchase amount came to fifteen dollars and some change. He'd gone back to the fitting room—an alcove in the corner of the store partitioned off by a sheet on a pole—and changed into his new but used clothes.

Looking like a normal person again, Tequila next went to a Burger King and kept ordering cheeseburgers until he was full. The pain from his various injuries had gotten worse, so he took four more of Slake's aspirin. After the restaurant he visited a clothing store and bought underwear and socks and a new pair of Nikes. Again he brought his purchases into the dressing room to change.

Next he'd gone to a U-Store-It and rented a locker for a year under a false name. He'd told the clerk he'd forgotten his driver's license, and had given him a fifty to smooth things through. The suitcases of Slake's money went into the locker, and the lock on it was a combination Tequila memorized and then threw away.

Fatigue was beginning to gnaw at him as it got dark. He'd longed for a soft bed and some sleep, so that's what he sought out. His next stop was a furniture store, and he found one in Schaumburg. It was a sprawling establishment, selling everything from dining room sets to outdoor pools. Tequila had been accosted by three different sales people, all overly helpful. He'd waved them off, saying he was just browsing. Eventually, the sales staff no longer noticed him, and the customers began to thin out.

A half an hour before closing time, Tequila was walking through the bedding section, all alone. Making doubly sure he wasn't being watched, he dropped to his chest and scurried under a queen sized bed. He made sure the dust cover was unruffled from where he entered, and then he'd simply waited for the lights to go out.

When they went out, he waited another half an hour just to be safe. Then he crept out from underneath the bed and fell asleep on top.

It wasn't the Ritz, but it got the job done.

The nightmares of Sally were overshadowed by the beatific dreams of his vengeance. While his body rested and began to heal, his mind wracked itself, subconsciously ripping Marty and his whole gang apart.

He slept until the next morning, when the opening manager woke him by turning on all of the lights. Tequila then got off the bed, made his way to the front door, and left without ever being seen.

He went back to the same Burger King as yesterday and got coffee and breakfast, using the bathroom when he'd finished. He wanted to take a shower, but the last one had turned out disastrous, so it would have to wait until he thought of a better alternative. He settled for a five Demerol injections, two Vicodin, three amphetamines to counteract the drowsiness, and a few antibiotics.

Rested, fed, and feeling mean, Tequila made sure all of his weapons were locked and loaded, started up the car, and headed for Marty the Maniac's to give the bastard a wake-up call.

Marty lived in a McMansion on the outskirts of Evanston. Three stories, eighteen rooms not including baths, and the obligatory kidney shaped pool. What self-respecting mobster didn't have a pool these days?

The drive took forty minutes. During that time, Tequila tried to come up with some semblance of a plan. Marty was undoubtedly waiting for him, with enough hired guns on the premises to obliterate an entire housing development. Much as Tequila wanted to storm in and strangle the bastard, he'd likely get killed before he even set foot in the house.

The way to go was reconnaissance. He would have to study the grounds, count the guards, wait for the right moment, before he had an opportunity to kill Marty. His boiling blood screamed for instant gratification, but he pushed rash thoughts aside. Best let them simmer a while longer, and then release them when he had the chance. Now wasn't the chance. First he had to get the lay of the land straight.

Parking almost a half mile away lest Marty have guards roaming the block, Tequila put his shoulder rig on under his camping coat. The coat was big and hid his guns effectively. Terco's .38 went into the back of his belt, along with six extra clips and eighteen speed strips. He got out of the car and stepped into the miserably cold day, frost seeming to form on his exposed skin almost instantly.

Evanston was a much older suburb than Palatine, and consequently it looked like Palatine would look in fifty years. The houses weren't as flashy, but ivy and towering oak trees gave them a classier cast. Tequila strolled past one beautiful home after another, hands shoved hard in his pockets, his objective clear in his freezing brain.

When he reached the edge of Marty's property—the northeast corner of a wrought iron fence that covered his boss's two acres—he heard a car start up. Turning over his shoulder, he saw a plain blue sedan pull out of its space on the street fifty meters away, heading towards him. It was a Nova. An old Chevy Nova. None of Marty's drones would drive such a crappy car. That meant cop, unless this was just some kind of strange coincidence. Or maybe the car was stolen...

Tequila made out a single figure in the car as it came closer. Cops usually worked in pairs. So did wise guys. A sudden panic seized Tequila as he pictured a man hunched in the back seat with a machine gun. Tequila had nowhere to run, standing next to a fence. He could only move on the sidewalk, which was adjacent to the road, where he was easy pickings for a drive-by shooting.

Digging into his rig, he came out with both .45s. Maybe he'd have a chance at them before they were able to gun him down. He pointed one barrel at the driver and one barrel at the back seat passenger window, but the driver— a woman—didn't even look at him and drove right on by without incident.

Tequila watched the car turn the corner in the distance. Better safe than sorry. He put his guns back in his rig and walked along Marty's perimeter.

The fence covered all four sides of the property. The motorized gate was unmanned, using rollers rather than hinges. It opened with a garage door opener, Tequila had recalled during a visit to Marty's a few months back. Marty had his collectors over for swimming and poker several times a year, and attendance was mandatory. Tequila didn't mind because he usually won at poker. He bluffed extremely well and was equally adept at spotting bluffing in others.

But those days were long gone now.

Tequila hadn't noticed any unusual activity on Marty's grounds during his walk, but that didn't mean he was alone in there. Tequila needed a closer look and a possible peek through the windows to see what he was up against.

He didn't see the security camera, hidden in the gate post. But when he passed through the camera's line of sight he was seen by Leman, who was sitting by the security monitor in Marty's house hoping for such a longshot.

Oblivious to this, Tequila sighted on a portion of the fence next to a copse of trees on Marty's property. The fence was eight feet high with spires on the top, but scaling it would prove little difficulty for a gymnast. Tequila planned on climbing to the top and then dropping down on the other side, his ascent hidden from the house's view by the oaks.

He was putting his hands on the wrought iron bars when he saw the woman approaching at the right.

She was medium build, in a black overcoat, walking towards Tequila at a brisk pace. The woman from the Nova. It wasn't unheard of for the Outfit to employ women for wet work. A bullet was just as deadly whether the shooter had one X chromosome or two.

Tequila stepped away from the fence and began to walk at the woman, meeting her eyes, waiting for her to telegraph something. Would she try to draw on him? Tequila wasn't worried about that, because whoever this was, he knew himself to be faster. But not yet. There was always the chance it was just some moron out for a walk, and if Tequila pulled his .45s, the woman would no doubt run to the cops with a description.

As she drew closer, Tequila noticed two things about her. The first was that she was attractive—mid thirties, pleasant face, nice legs. The second was that the woman was smiling whistling to herself.

They got within ten feet of each other and the woman stopped. Tequila stopped as well.

"Shitty day for a walk," the woman said. Then she smiled.

Tequila didn't answer. He searched for something in her face that indicated approaching violence, but didn't find it. That proved nothing. A lot of the real violent types smiled while they worked.

"I'm sure you're armed," the woman continued. "But I'm betting on the fact you won't kill a cop. Homicide Detective Jack Daniels out of the two-six. Mr. Abernathy, you're under arrest for the murder of Billy Chico. Could you please drop your weapons and put your hands on your head."

Tequila didn't buy it. This wasn't how cops arrested people. He'd seen the group in his apartment hallway. Where was the whole battalion, rushing at him with Kevlar vests and tear gas?

He pulled his .45s in the blink of an eye.

The woman didn't flinch.

"You're pretty fast," said the woman claiming to be Detective Daniels. "Me? I'm not so fast. See?"

Moving slowly, Daniels pulled her coat back, revealing a badge hanging around her neck on a cord. She also revealed her shoulder holster.

"You're not going to arrest me."

"Honestly? I don't want to arrest you, Tequila. I want to bring you in. Federal custody. You don't matter to me. I want Marty, and the cops on Marty's payroll. You can help me get them, then you get a new name, new location, new life."

"It doesn't work that way. They'd find me."

"We can put them away."

"Not all of them. The Outfit is a hydra. Cut off one head, two others spring up."

"We can protect you."

"I don't want protection," Tequila said. "I want them dead."

Tequila took a step backward. The easiest way out of a standoff was to leave. If the cop reached for her gun, he would just shoot first.

"Look, Tequila. I know you've got guts. I was there when you took the dive out of your apartment building. That was a risky move for even the most experienced skydiver. How experienced are you anyway?"

"That was my first time. I didn't like it too much, and I doubt I'll try again."

Daniels stared at him for a moment. Tequila took another step back.

"Guts aren't enough here, Tequila. You've got an army after you. The wrong cops catch you, you're dead. The mob catches you, you're dead. I'm the only friend you've got."

"I don't need friends."

Tequila took one more step back. In a moment he was going to sprint across the street. This woman wasn't fast enough to catch him.

"Killing those responsible for Sally's death won't bring her back."

Tequila blinked. He felt a lump in his throat, so big it made his other various aches and pains seem trivial.

"She..." His voice wavered, but he got it under control. "She was innocent."

"I know. But even if you kill them all, it won't take the hurt away. You have to let us handle it."

"Marty owns cops. He probably owns your boss."

"Let me bring you in, and we'll take them all down."

"I can't."

"You're going up against fifty or more. You'll get killed."

"Then I get killed."

"Come in, Tequila. Help me put Marty, and Slake, and the rest of them away for what they've done to your sister. You want revenge? Send them to jail and every week send a postcard. That's the best revenge."

Before Tequila had a chance to answer, two things happened. The first was that Marty's automatic gate began to open. The second was that a black Lincoln sedan came barreling around the corner, squealing tires, heading towards Tequila and Daniels. Tequila turned at the car and emptied both clips at the driver's side passenger window, where a gun barrel was peeking out.

The car swerved right and went up onto a neighbor's lawn. Tequila was jamming in two new clips when another car, coming through Marty's gate, swung out onto the street.

Daniels drew lightning quick and fired four shots, all into the engine block of the approaching Mercedes. Steam from the punctured radiator blew the hood off the Benz, and Jack yelled at Tequila.

"Two more cars coming! I'm parked half a block away!"

Tequila nodded and ran with Jack, hearing the sound of automatic weapon fire stitch a path behind him. Daniels surprised Tequila by keeping pace with him as they sprinted. Maybe the woman had some pep in her after all.

They rounded the corner and both dove at the ground. Parked next to Jack's car was another black sedan, two men standing on either side armed with wicked looking Kalishnikov AK-47s. The cop and the gymnast fired at the same time, but they both shot at the same man. He dropped, but the other scurried behind the sedan and held down the trigger on the automatic, kicking up dirt and rocks several feet before the duo. The man emptied his thirty round magazine and stopped to reload.

"I'm parked two more blocks down," Tequila yelled at Jack.

She nodded. Tequila took off across the street with Jack in pursuit.

Automatic weapon fire sounded off behind them, and ahead came another black sedan. The two cut across someone's lawn and then onto another street, running like mad.

They made it to the Trans Am without being shot at again, but more screaming tires in the distance confirmed Marty's men hadn't given up their chase.

"I thought you drove a Caprice," Jack said, getting in the passenger side.

"Stolen," Tequila answered. "If it bugs you, you can walk."

The black sedan rounded the corner and came straight at them, mirrored glass reflecting the aged trees it was rapidly passing.

"I'll arrest you for it later," Daniels said.

Tequila punched it in reverse, tires shrieking and laying down two long streaks of rubber. Jack popped in a speed loader and cranked open her window, leaning out and shooting at the oncoming sedan. The sedan swerved off the road, and Tequila yanked Jack into her seat and turned the wheel harshly. The Trans Am spun around and Tequila jammed it into drive when it reached 180 degrees. Then he hit the gas again and they were going forward.

"Nice," Daniels said. "But can you parallel park?"

Tequila allowed himself a small grin, but it faded when he saw two more of Marty's cars approaching from the left. He punched the accelerator and beat them to the intersection, but they swung into pursuit.

The rear window of the Trans Am shattered with a gunshot, spraying Tequila and Jack with cold glass. Daniels turned around and fired two rounds at the first sedan, hitting the windshield dead center. The car careened left and smacked hard into an eighty-year-old oak tree. The tree won, spitting the occupants through the front window and onto some rich guy's lawn.

"We should buckle up," Jack said.

Tequila looked in the rearview and then put his seatbelt on. Jack did the same. The other sedan dropped back as Tequila hammered down on the gas. But the street he was on made a sharp turn, and he was forced to slow for it.

Another turn followed that, and then Tequila found himself out of the residential area and on busy Kedzie Avenue, heading into Chicago.

He slammed on the brakes as traffic ahead of him stopped at a red light. The sidewalk was too narrow to drive up on, and the oncoming lane was full.

Jack and Tequila turned to look through the missing rear window.

Three more sedans were coming fast.

"You're a cop," Tequila said. "Arrest them."

"You want to take my badge and give it a try?"

The light remained red.

Tequila squealed tires and pulled the Trans Am into oncoming traffic.

Cars honked, swerved, and smacked into each other, blocking off the entire lane. There was no place left to go. After slamming on the breaks, they abandoned the vehicle and ran for it.

From Kedzie they cut down a side street and through an alley. The alley let out into another alley, underneath the el tracks. As they raced towards the open street ahead of them, three men with machine guns appeared to block their path.

Gunshots riddled the brick wall to the right, and Tequila and Jack dove behind a Dumpster. As they ducked down, holding their heads, round after round of automatic weapon fire clanged against their temporary cover, so rapid that the Dumpster sounded like it was being hailed on.

Then, as abruptly as it began, the gunfire stopped.

"I made out at least six," Jack said, counting how many weapons were being fired at them.

"Seven."

A look passed between them. They had no chance against odds like that.

Tequila took in his surroundings: The Dumpster, the alley wall behind him, the el tracks overhead.

"Window." Tequila pointed to a wall ten yards in front of them, across the alley. The window had rusty security bars preventing entry, four bars in all.

"It's barred."

"What are you loading? Sounds heavy."

"Hollow points."

Tequila raised an eyebrow. Jack shrugged.

"For when I go hunting. You never know when you'll run into a deer wearing a bullet proof vest."

"Can you hit the bars?"

Jack squinted at the target. "You mean shoot them off?"

"Yes."

Jack extended her gun arm towards the barred window, lining up the sights. She squeezed off a round, and it ate into the brick wall an inch above the bar. She fired again, this time below it, and the iron bar toppled out of its mortar and clattered to the sidewalk. She emptied the spent brass from her cylinder, popped in a speed loader, and repeated the process with two more bars.

"Marty wants me alive!" Tequila shouted, not pausing to be impressed by Jack's shooting. "You assholes kill me, Marty will have your balls!"

Then he turned to Daniels and said, "That window is about four feet off the ground. You'll have to dive through it. Can you make it?"

"I don't have any Olympic medals, but I'll manage."

Tequila took one of his .45s and shot the window, shattering the glass.

"You go first. I'll cover you. Then you cover me when it's my turn."

Jack nodded, reloading her .38.

"You have a back-up piece?" Tequila asked.

"No."

Tequila reached around his belt and handed her Terco's .38. Jack eyed it oddly.

"This yours?" she asked.

"It is now. You ready?"

Daniels stuffed the gun into her holster and nodded.

"I give up!" Tequila yelled.

He stood up behind the Dumpster and began firing both .45s while Jack took off towards the window.

Feeling bullets whiz past her legs, Daniels made the window in ten steps and dove face-first through the opening and into blackness.

She hit the inside hard, banging into something, and scraping her face on the rough wooden floor. Her .38 skittered across the ground into the darkness, and motes of light appeared before Jack's eyes.

The booming sounds of gunfire brought her back. Rather than search for her revolver, she took the spare Tequila had given her and wobbled back to the window. Peeking through the lower corner, Jack stuck the gun out and fired wildly in the direction of the alley's opening. She watched as Tequila sprinted towards her, both of his guns firing like mad.

Slugs tore up the ground at Tequila's feet. The Mafioso had obviously heeded his warning and were shooting at his legs, trying to wound rather than kill. Tequila was almost home free when a bullet caught him high in the hip, spinning him around and to the ground.

Tequila looked up at the window, just five feet away.

"Drop your guns, Tequila!" said a voice he didn't recognize, "Or I'll shoot your knees off!"

To prove his point, the unknown man shot the tip off of Tequila's left gym shoe. Tequila sighted where the shot had come from, around the alley corner forty yards away.

Tequila figured that was the guy who'd winged him. He looked at his thigh and saw the bloody tear in his jeans, meat showing through. A helluva tough shot on a target moving as fast as he was. Tequila knew that the man could easily put a few more in his legs without killing him. And Tequila didn't have the proper angle to shoot the guy back. He was trying to figure out whether to try for the door or go down firing when five shots rang out from the window.

Tequila noted that the first shot bit a chunk out of the brick corner where the unknown man was hiding. Jack was firing at the sharpshooter, giving Tequila a chance to make it.

Tequila took the chance.

Gaining his feet, he took three quick steps and threw himself through the broken window, smacking right into Daniels, the both of them crashing to the floor.

It took a moment for Tequila to get his bearings in the darkness. Both guns were still in his hands. He quickly jammed in two more clips and took off his belt, winding it around his bleeding thigh in a tourniquet.

"Nice shooting," he told Jack.

"Your gun. The sights are off, by the way."

"I know."

They squinted at their surroundings. The dust and the darkness made Tequila realize that wherever they were, it was abandoned.

"We've got to find a door," Jack said. "They aren't going to waste any time coming after us."

"You smoke?"

"No. You want a cigarette now?"

"I want a lighter."

A flame appeared before Jack's face, illuminating it.

"Matches do? I picked up a pack at *Spill* yesterday. The only useful thing I got from that place."

Using the light as a guide, Jack located her dropped .38, and then the two walked off into the darkness.

Outside, bits of brick embedded in his forehead from Jack's shooting, a man named Royce quietly raged.

CHAPTER 31

Marty the Maniac Martelli had to restrain himself from clapping his hands together in glee. Tequila, and that idiot cop Daniels, were trapped. Trapped in an abandoned warehouse. All the exits were covered. There wasn't any way out.

And the best part of it all was that they were in the 12th District.

Marty's District.

He owned the captain here. Owned him like an appliance. A simple phone call had made it clear that absolutely no cops would be deployed to the warehouse, no matter how many shots were fired.

It was so damn perfect that Marty couldn't control the grin on his flabby face. He hit the hang-up key on his cellular phone and stood up from his living room sofa, so excited he could no longer sit.

"What happens to the cop?" Leman asked his smiling boss. Leman wasn't averse to wasting someone now and then. He'd done his share through the years. But murdering a Homicide Detective went above and beyond simple clean-up duties. That could bring down some serious heat, even if Marty did own the assistant super.

"She disappears," Marty replied. "After I got her booted from the case, she took her vacation, for chrissake. This bitch isn't even on city time. We do her, dispose of the body, and no one ever hears of the assbag again."

"She's still a cop, Marty."

Marty lost his grin, looking hard at Leman.

"You think I haven't wasted cops before, dumbshit? I was killing cops when you were in grade school picking your zits."

"As long as it's not me who does it." Leman folded his arms in conviction.

Marty slapped him hard across the face, sending him reeling.

"Since when did you grow a spine? You do what I tell you, when I tell you. If I say go shoot your own mother, you'd better ask if I want a head shot or a gut shot. Understand?"

Leman stared at his boss, the shame from the slap hurting more than the actual physical act. Why didn't he get any respect? Wasn't he the one who spotted Tequila on the grounds in the first place? Wasn't he the one who gathered the troops while Marty was off doing god knew what with that dickhead Royce? Wasn't he the one who figured out Tequila's companion was Detective Daniels, simply because he recognized Daniels's car from yesterday at *Spill*?

To hell with this. To hell with all this crap.

"I quit," Leman said.

Marty's face became a darker shade of pissed.

"You what?"

"I quit. I'm sick of you treating me like garbage. You wouldn't even have Tequila cornered if I didn't see him on the monitor. This is bullshit, Marty. I'm not putting up with it anymore."

Leman stood up off the chair, staring face to face with his former employer.

"Mail me my check."

Then Leman made a mistake. A mistake of pride. Intending to show contempt for Marty, he turned his back on him to walk out of the room.

Marty pulled the .38 from his waistband, shaking with rage. He'd never been so insulted by an underling. Ever. He cocked the gun, and to Leman it was as loud as a trumpet blast. The ex-cop stopped in his tracks and turned slowly.

"No one quits me," said Marty the Maniac.

Leman stared at his death down the barrel of the .38 and cursed his stupid pride.

"You don't have to shoot me, Marty," he said, trying to keep his voice steady. "All you have to do is acknowledge my accomplishments now and then. Why should I stay with someone who insults and degrades me all the time? Would you?"

The silence that ensued lasted forever to Leman. Finally, Marty dropped the angry face and his features eased.

"You're right, Leman," Marty said. "I should treat my employees a little better. I'll do that from now on."

Leman, sensing a reprieve, felt relief cascade over him in a shower.

"That's all I mean by it, Marty. You know I love working for you. But I bust my ass. Just a pat on the back and an *atta boy* every now and then would mean a lot."

"Fair enough. Atta boy, Leman."

"Thanks."

Marty fired twice, putting two bullets into the ex-cop's chest. Leman's expression wasn't of pain or horror. It was one of complete and total surprise. He held the expression as he dropped to his knees, clutching his heart. If Marty had bothered to check, he would have found the same expression on the man after he'd fallen face first to the floor and died.

But Marty didn't bother to check, and when two of Fonti's men came bursting into the room after hearing gunshots, Marty directed them to dispose of the body.

After he got Tequila he'd do it all differently. No more incompetent idiots for collectors. Out of his last five, one had robbed him, one had gotten killed, one had been arrested, one had tried to quit, and the last one was off trying to kill the one who got arrested.

He doubted Slake was up to the task, but he didn't care too much. If Slake didn't kill Terco, then Marty would get Terco in jail. He had a thousand friends in prison, all of whom would be honored to pull a job for him. Terco was as good as dog meat, whether Slake nailed him or not.

Marty picked up his cellular and dialed, cursing at Fonti's men because they were leaving a trail of gore across his oriental rug.

"Yeah?"

"I don't want no blitz with everyone rushing in," Marty said. "That's messy, too many possible mistakes."

"Then how do we get them out?"

A grin curled around Marty's lips. "Just send Royce in."

"Alone?"

"Alone. Tell him to get rid of the stain, without ruining the shirt. Bring the shirt back to me."

"What should be done with the stain after removal?"

"Put it someplace where it will never stain anything again," Marty said. He was very careful on cellular phones, because the airwaves could be recorded and used as evidence without a warrant. The last thing Marty needed right now was some bonehead with a ham radio listening in to his order to kill a Chicago Homicide Detective.

"Will do, Marty. I'll go tell him."

Marty hung up. He felt an odd mixture of power and relief. The first major crisis in his professional career was nearing an end. He'd weathered it well, and learned a few things that needed to be learned. After Tequila gave him his money back, Marty would rebuild. He'd only hire pros from now on, not ex-cops or former gymnasts. He'd be more careful who he trusted, and add more security to *Spill*. Valuable lessons, all of them, and well-earned.

Marty smiled again, this time thinking about Tequila and that cop, all alone in the big, dark warehouse. With Royce coming for them.

Marty wished he could be there to see it.

But the second-hand details would be just as good. He looked forward to hearing the story from Tequila's own lips.

And Tequila would tell.

When the Maniac was done with him, Tequila would tell all.

CHAPTER 32

Jack Daniels cursed as the match burned down to her fingers, singeing them with a crackling hiss. She lit another, looking for something in the room to use as a torch. After all, they couldn't find their way out of there without light, and none of the wall switches in this place worked. They probably hadn't worked for ten years, judging from the musty smell and the layer of thick dust over everything.

There was a sound of snapping behind her, and Jack whirled. Tequila was holding a leg he'd broken off a chair. He was winding a tattered piece of curtain around it.

"Try this." He handed her the make-shift torch.

Jack lit the curtain, and they both recoiled from the noxious fumes it produced. But it was light, and held at an arm's length it did a fair job of illuminating the room they were in.

It was an office, kitty corner to the other office they'd entered via the broken window. With the aid of the torch Jack easily found the door, and walked out into a large open area, ranks and files of towering shelves stretching off in all directions.

"It could be worse," Jack told Tequila. "There are plenty of places to hide out until the cops show up. With all of that gunfire, they'll be here any minute."

"Not in this District, they won't. Marty owns it. There won't be any cops."

"He can't own a whole district."

"Do you hear any sirens?"

Jack strained her ears, but all she heard were the empty echoes of the huge warehouse.

"He can't own a whole district," Jack said again, but her voice lacked conviction.

"Marty's men will be coming in soon," Tequila continued. "We've got to dig ourselves in. Especially with that sharpshooter they've got."

"Do you know him?"

"No. You?"

"I think it's that creep I met yesterday with the vampire fangs. Royce is his name. Ring any bells?"

"I've heard of him. If he's as good as what they say, he'll be a problem."

"No shit. Maybe you can try pretending to be holding people hostage."

Tequila squinted at her. "I needed time to get the parachute on."

"I'm sure. Anyone ever tell you you're a little crazy?"

"No. Anyone ever tell you you're a pretty good cop?"

"Only me. And I only have to remind myself a few times every hour. One day I hope to start believing it."

Jack handed the torch to Tequila and loaded both .38s with her hot rounds. Looking closely at the gun Tequila had given her, she asked once more where he got it.

"Awful nosey about that gun."

Jack said nothing. She knew the Binkowskis had been killed with a .38, and had a strong feeling that this was the one that did it. Daniels had pretty much proved that Terco was the murderer, but if this was the weapon, why did Tequila have it?

Tequila noted Jack's hesitancy.

"I got it off a former associate named Sam Terco. I believe it's registered in his name."

"When did you get it?"

"Early yesterday morning, after kicking his ass."

Jack felt a tinge of relief. She wanted to believe Tequila, because she was starting to like the guy. Strange, considering he was a leg-breaker for the mob, and a murderer as well. But Jack sensed something more there. Originally, she thought he was a sociopath. Now, she wasn't so sure.

Maybe it was those pictures that Sally Abernathy had drawn for her brother. Hundreds of them, preserved in his floor safe. So valuable to him they were locked up.

Tequila went off to a row of shelves and leaned hard into them. Jack saw what he was doing and lent her weight to the effort. The two toppled over a high section, sending it crashing hard to the cement floor.

Climbing into their new bunker, Jack and Tequila found themselves sandwiched by two long planks of sheet metal, three feet high. Their sides were still vulnerable, but they detached two other shelves and made themselves a bulletproof metal cubical, with enough room for both of them to move around in. They had no top, deciding to leave it open to allow for shooting back.

After creating their Alamo, Tequila and Jack counted their ammo.

"Fifteen rounds," Jack said.

Tequila handed her five speed loaders of six rounds each for the .38. He counted thirteen rounds for his .45s. Not enough to invade a country, except for maybe Belgium. But possibly enough to hold off the first round of the siege.

Jack stamped out the torch, and they waited in darkness, letting their eyes adjust, listening for sounds.

"Do me a favor," Jack whispered. "Since we might get killed here, lay it all out for me. How'd you piss Marty off so bad?"

"He thinks I stole some money."

"Did you?"

"I was set up by an asshole named Slake."

"I met him. You're right."

"That he set me up?"

"That he's an asshole."

"It was a good frame, I'll give the bastard that. But I got away and screwed up his plans."

"Through the heating ducts."

Jack noticed Tequila had turned his head to face her in the darkness.

"How did you get on to me?" he asked. "I normally don't make mistakes."

"You first. You killed Billy Chico, right?"

"He drew on me, it was shoot or get shot."

"How about the Binkowskis?"

"Who are the Binkowskis?"

"The owner of the liquor store Chico was trying to rob. And his wife."

"Is that how you made me? That old man talked? I'd figured him for the greedy type, thought he'd try to rip off his insurance company instead of fingering me."

"I can be very persuasive," Jack said.

"I bet. So what about the Binkowskis?"

"They're dead."

Tequila put two and two together.

"Killed by a .38," he said.

"Maybe this one, that you said is Terco's. We're holding Terco for their murder. If this gun is registered in his name, we've got him cold."

"So Binkowski gave you a description, and you ran me through the computer and came up with my dropped assault charge from a few years back."

"Right. IDed you from the tattoo on your hand." Jack saw Tequila's silhouette nod in the darkness.

"You're a good cop. Don't you guys usually travel with partners, and have back-up?"

"I was taken off your case yesterday. Technically, I'm on vacation. No one knows where I am."

Tequila frowned. "I take back the *good cop* comment."

"Give me the rest of it," Jack said. "The whole story, starting after the liquor store."

Tequila ran it down. He wasn't quite sure why he was telling Daniels all of this, but he did anyway. Maybe it was because he was damn near certain Jack would be dead within the next hour. But part of it, he knew, was because he sort of liked the cop. Or maybe respected was the better word. He was feeling toward Daniels what he used to feel towards his Olympic coach.

So Tequila told her about the frame, and about finding Matisse in his apartment with Sally and China dead, and about spending the night at the shelter, and fighting with Terco at the health club, and going to Slake's and finding out he'd been the one who framed him. He told Jack everything, only leaving out the part about hiding the money. If Jack knew Tequila had the money, Marty might be able to drag the information out of Jack. If and when Marty finally caught Tequila, Tequila would die before he let that fat bastard have his money back.

"Rough couple of days," Daniels said when Tequila finished his tale. "When we get out of this, and you testify, you'll probably be free and clear."

Tequila didn't bother telling her that they weren't likely to get out of this.

They were silent for a minute, listening for sounds.

"Were you the one who got that killer a few years ago?" Tequila asked quietly. "I remember the cop's name was Jack Daniels. That's a tough name to forget, especially for someone named Tequila."

"That was me. Jack Daniels. Originally Jacqueline Streng. Daniels is my married name. You can guess what people buy me every holiday. I've got enough whiskey in the house to get Wisconsin drunk. How about you? Tequila is on your driver's license, FOID, birth certificate."

"I was born almost six weeks premature," Tequila said. He'd never told anyone this story, possibly because no one had ever asked. "I was only eighteen ounces at birth, and jaundiced from liver failure. Neither of my parents expected me to live, so as a joke my father put the name Tequila on my birth certificate. Because I was yellow and about as big as a shot of tequila."

Tequila stopped there, not bothering to go on about how his mother ran off the next day, not able to bear watching her new son die. A Down Syndrome baby and a preemie, plus living with an abusive husband, was too much for her. Tequila had never even seen her picture, and only knew her name was Maxie because his father had cursed her for years after she'd left.

"When did you get the tattoo?" Jack asked, changing the subject.

"When I started working for Marty."

"After leaving the YMCA," Jack filled in. "Why a butterfly?"

Tequila thought about the question for a moment.

"Because that's what caterpillars turn into," he finally answered.

There was a noise in the distance—a door being kicked in. The two turned towards it, senses heightened and guns pointed.

"Here we go," Jack said under her breath.

But there wasn't any sudden influx of gun-happy Mafioso rushing in. There was nothing. They strained their ears for sounds of footsteps, but only heard their own breathing.

"Royce," Tequila whispered. "He's coming in alone."

That didn't make sense to Jack. If Martelli had all those men available to him, why'd he only send one in?

To Tequila, it made perfect sense. The more goombas running around shooting off their pistols, the more likely Tequila would be killed and unable to disclose the whereabouts of Marty's cash. Sending in a single, trained professional was Marty's best way of getting Tequila out of there alive.

Or so Marty thought.

Tequila had other ideas.

"Royce!" he yelled at the top of his lungs. Jack tackled him, the pair banging hard into the metal shelf.

"Are you crazy?" Daniels hissed.

Tequila broke Jack's hold with an elbow into the ribs and leapt out of their enclosure.

"I hear you're the best, Royce! Is this what the best does, sneak up on two unarmed people in the dark?"

A chuckle came from Tequila's right, and he crouched down and pointed both .45s in that direction.

"You're supposed to be a real hotshot," Tequila said. "I bet you five bucks I can kick your ass."

Sound to his left. Tequila aimed at it and fired six shots at about chest level.

"You call that unarmed?" Royce asked from the opposite direction.

Tequila spun and fired another six from where the voice came from. Royce had obviously thrown something to make the first noise.

"You're at a disadvantage here, Royce. You can't kill me. How can you guarantee wounding me in the dark?"

Jack stared at Tequila's dark form from the bunker, wondering if his plan had any merit. He was trying to draw Royce out, but Royce was too damn smart. Jack tried to think like Royce, wondering how she would subdue Tequila, and when she figured it out the hair on the back of her neck stood up.

I'd take the cop out first.

Daniels whirled at the sound to her left, bringing up her .38. It was kicked roughly from her hand and went skidding across the warehouse floor.

Jack sprang over the top of the metal shelf at the kicking form, tackling him mid-body, pinning him to the ground. She brought her fist down hard into Royce's face, feeling teeth bend and snap.

The gun went off next to her ear, the sound so loud and painful it hurt almost as much as getting shot. She rolled away, her hand pressed against the side of her head, trying to stop the agony.

Then she felt a spike drive into her back, and realized she had been shot, and that her earlier assessment had been wrong.

Being shot did hurt worse.

She dropped the gun and darkness took her.

CHAPTER 33

"I killed your cop buddy, Tequila." Royce was crouching behind the metal shelf. "Tell me where the money is, I'll let you go."

"Jack!"

No answer.

Rage bubbled up in Tequila. Jack had been a decent person. She shouldn't have died like that. If only he'd kept his cool, stayed in the enclosure...

"The money, Tequila."

"Ask Slake. He's the one that stole it. Check his house out. In his garage, there's a body with a tattoo like mine. He set me up."

"Then you have nothing to fear from Marty. Throw down your guns, we'll talk this out."

Throwing down his guns was suicide. The Maniac wouldn't care if Tequila took his money or not. He'd torture him to death anyway.

But Tequila was out of ammo, so the guns were worthless. If he pretended to give up, maybe he'd have a chance at taking Royce one on one. He'd heard legends about this man, how unstoppable he was. A one man army. Tequila didn't doubt Royce was good, but did he have an enormous ego to match his talents?

Only one way to find out.

"I'm tossing over my guns."

They clattered to the factory floor somewhere near Royce's direction.

Then Royce yelled, "Light!"

All at once, the lights went on in the warehouse. Old, incandescent lights, many of the bulbs broken, but still enough to illuminate the entire storage area.

Tequila squinted against the glare, feeling exposed but keeping his posture erect and his hands raised. His stare locked on Jack, lying face-down a dozen yards away, her back a bloody mess. Then his eyes found Royce.

"Didn't I see you in the Wizard of Oz?" Royce asked. "You're one of the Lollipop Kids."

His grin was bloody—the cop had gone down swinging and knocked out a few of his teeth. Good for her.

"And you were on my cereal box this morning. Count Chocula. You don't look nearly as badass as the rumors I've heard. You look like a pussy."

Royce's grin dropped a fraction.

"I can take you easy," Royce said.

He probably could too. The wound in Tequila's thigh hurt like a branding iron was being pressed against it, his ankle had swelled to the size of a grapefruit, and the stitches from the dog bite had opened. The only thing keeping him upright was adrenaline, amphetamines, and bravado.

"You better not try it. Marty wants me bad. It's safer if you just call in the goon squad, surround me. In fact, you should probably shoot my knees out right now. I'm too dangerous for you."

Tequila watched Royce's reaction. A pro, a real pro, would do just what Tequila said.

But Royce did have an ego as large as his talents. He was used to being feared, even exalted. Nobody insulted him. Nobody.

He needed to teach this midget a lesson.

Royce bunched up his fists and stalked over. Tequila moved in quick, feinting with a lunge kick and coming instead with a right uppercut. His fist whirred through open air, Royce dodging the blow and dropping an elbow onto Tequila's shoulder, making his whole arm go numb.

Tequila tucked and rolled away, coming up to his feet and whipping around his left leg in a reverse kick where Royce should have been.

But Royce wasn't there anymore. He was at Tequila's side, throwing a combination punch that split open the smaller man's lip and bruised his right kidney.

Again Tequila rolled away. He found his footing and stared at Royce. The man wasn't even in a fighting stance. He was standing there with his hands on his hips, looking bored.

This time Tequila didn't attack. He let Royce come to him.

Royce did so leisurely, coming within three feet of Tequila before executing a flawless karate kick to Tequila's chest. There had been no telegraphing the move, no way to duck it, no way to block it. The man was fast enough to fight pro.

Tequila was knocked onto his back. Royce casually strolled over and his fist shot out like a snake, grabbing Tequila's right wrist. Before Tequila could pull his hand back Royce had twisted hard and broken his pinky.

Tequila's vision went red with pain.

"Now admit it," Royce said. "You've never seen anyone that fast."

Tequila kipped up to his feet and threw his palm at Royce's chest. He knew Royce would dodge it, but he also knew where Royce would go this time after the dodge. Predictably, Royce rolled away from the punch to the left, and Tequila did a quick reverse kick that smacked the know-it-all look right off Royce's ugly face.

Royce was immediately on guard for the follow-up attack, assuming a classic defensive karate stance.

Well, if the guy knew karate, Tequila would hit him with a little judo.

He tossed a slow hand at Royce, watching for the block. When the block came he grabbed rather than punched.

The grab threw Royce off balance, and Tequila used the momentum to flip the bigger man over his shoulder and throw him across the floor.

Royce hit hard, but was already in motion to gain his feet when Tequila delivered a devastating kick to Royce's ribs.

It wasn't karate at all. It was a football punt. Royce had gotten his hand up to block, but the force from the kick was still enough to strip the air from ghis lungs.

Tequila brought up his foot to stomp on Royce's head, but the fanged man shot out two stiff fingers at the inside of Tequila's thigh, near the injury, prompting white hot agony that doubled Tequila over.

He staggered back and Royce was on his feet again, lashing out with a solid chop to Tequila's head.

Tequila went down.

Royce advanced.

Tequila knew he was outmatched.

Over by the fallen shelves, Homicide Detective Jack Daniels opened her eyes.

"I'm going to break every bone in your legs," Royce told Tequila. "Then I'll use your balls as a leash and make you walk out of here."

Tequila blinked at the double image above him, and brought his knees in tight to his chest, kicking them straight up into the air. The move wasn't karate or judo. It was straight gymnastics. He caught Royce under the chin and sent him sprawling backwards.

Before Royce could recover, Tequila was on his feet and charging. He hit the bigger man with a shoulder tackle and drove him hard into the ground. Pinning him there, Tequila threw punches into Royce's sides, hitting him with all that he had, trying to drive his fists through the man's body.

Unable to throw Tequila off, Royce pulled his knife from his sheath and cut a trail of blood across Tequila's chest. Tequila rolled away, feeling as if he'd been seared with a poker.

Jack reached up a hand, felt the exit wound in her shoulder. The wound was leaking, pretty bad.

Royce lunged at Tequila, the blade dull with Tequila's blood. Tequila parried the lunge with his forearm, getting a razor sharp cut from the elbow to the wrist.

"I'm the best!" Royce screamed. He jabbed at Tequila with the blade, poking at him like a chef with a meat fork, his eyes glazing over with an insane, violent lust.

Tequila backed away from the thrusts, trying to avoid getting cut again. Royce kept moving forward, keeping Tequila off balance, not giving him a chance to plant his feet and throw a solid punch or kick.

Then Tequila's back hit a wall. There was no place else to retreat, and Tequila had no way to stop an experienced knife thrust. He was effectively trapped, and his opponent knew it, breaking into a monstrous smile.

Royce lunged hard at Tequila's chest.

Tequila put up his forearm to block, taking the blade neatly through his arm up to the hilt, between his radius and his ulna. Then, using his bones as leverage, he twisted the knife from Royce's grasp and brought his forearm down across the man's face. The three inches of blade protruding from Tequila's arm raked down Royce's scalp and lodged firmly into the vampire's eye socket.

Tequila grabbed the handle of the knife and pushed hard, through his arm, into Royce's head. Then he brought up a leg and kicked Royce backwards, free of the blade.

Royce sprawled out onto his back, not moving.

Tequila looked at the knife sticking in his arm and almost fainted. He put his head down between his legs to get blood to his brain.

"Pussy," he said to Royce.

Rather than reply, Royce jerked up to a sitting position, gore dripping from his black eye socket, his custom .45 pointed and ready to fire at Tequila's chest.

Then Royce's head burst into a brilliant explosion of red, blood spraying out in all directions like a shaken up beer can. His headless body jerked to the ground, the gun clattering to the floor next to it.

Tequila looked over at Jack Daniels, who was lying on her left side fifteen yards away. The .38 smoked in the Detective's hands.

"Little help here," Jack mumbled.

Tequila limped over.

"Royce!" a strange voice called out. "You get him yet?"

"Can you walk?" Tequila asked Jack.

Daniels nodded, allowing Tequila to help her to her feet.

"Looks like you need a Band-Aid," Jack said, indicating the knife sticking out of Tequila's arm.

"I'm afraid if I pull it out, I won't be able to stop the bleeding."

"Keep it there, then. It makes you look tough."

They stumbled down the aisle, and Tequila recovered his .45s from where he'd thrown them, putting them back into his shoulder rig. Then he tugged the Demerol and syringe out of his pocket. He gave himself two injections, and then offered the last of it to Daniels.

"What is it?"

"Demerol. It'll numb you."

She nodded, and he plunged the needle into her shoulder, next to her gunshot wound.

"Royce!" someone yelled again.

Jack cocked an ear at the voice. Tequila came to her side, also listening.

"So where to, Tequila? We can't parachute out of this one. And all the exits are covered."

"Almost all of them," replied Tequila, pointing up to the thirty foot ceiling. Above them was a skylight.

"Great," muttered Jack. "I get nosebleeds sitting on bar stools that are too high."

"You don't have any blood left for your nose to bleed. Move your ass."

They began to climb up the steel shelving unit, using it like a large ladder. It was hard going. Both of them were badly hurt, and Tequila kept catching the blade of the knife in his arm on boxes, jiggling it around.

Finally, near exhaustion, their endurance almost gone, they made it to the top shelf.

The skylight was still eight feet above them.

It might as well been a thousand feet to Jack. She'd lost enough blood to recognize the early stages of shock coming on. She winced, forcing some of her shirt into the bullet hole to slow the bleeding.

Below them forty armed men entered the warehouse, roaming around like worker ants. It would only be a matter of time until one of them decided to look up.

Tequila stared up at the skylight, trying to figure out how to reach it. There was nothing on the top shelf for them to stand on. Except...

"Get on my shoulders," Tequila said.

Jack rolled her eyes. "You're joking."

"I boost you up there, you pull yourself onto that ledge next to the skylight. Then you can open it and go through."

"How about you?"

"When you get on the roof, lean down and stick your hand through. I'll grab it."

"You can't jump that high."

"I have a better chance than you do. Do you have any other ideas?"

"Yeah. We lie really still and if anyone sees us we just say we're mannequins."

"Get on my shoulders."

"I can't."

Tequila helped Jack to her feet, then squatted down while Jack awkwardly sat on Tequila's back, her legs around his neck.

Grunting with effort, Tequila stood up, Daniels sitting high on his shoulders. Jack reached for the ledge, but it was still a foot away.

"Can't get it."

"Step in my hands."

Tequila locked his fingers together, and Jack placed her right foot in Tequila's palms. The muscles in the gymnast's back were screaming, and his legs began to shake as Jack leaned her weight forward.

"On three," Tequila grunted. "One, two, three!"

Tequila heaved up with all of his remaining strength and Jack jumped out of the man's palms and up to the ledge. She grabbed it and held, and Tequila moved under Jack's swinging feet and let Jack step on his shoulders and hands to hoist herself up.

"They're on the shelf!" someone cried from below.

Sitting on the ledge, Jack fired twice at the lock on the skylight and blew it off. Then she lifted the window up on hinges and climbed onto the roof.

Lying down next to the opening, Jack stuck her hand down for Tequila to grab.

"It's too high!" Daniels yelled. "You won't be able to grab it!"

"Just don't drop me when I do!"

Jack winced. Michael Jordan couldn't have grabbed her hand from this height, and he was over a foot taller than Tequila and had a better vertical jump. He also didn't play basketball with a switchblade stuck through his arm.

"Come on, buddy," Jack urged. "Do it."

Tequila eyed the hand, then measured off ten paces away from it down the long shelf.

He took a deep breath and closed his eyes.

Someone began shooting.

Tequila concentrated on his body. He tried to will the pain away, force back the exhaustion. He was an athlete. He had a job to do.

Win. His job was to win.

He opened his eyes again, staring at Jack's hand.

Win.

He ran forward, hitting the shelf in a cartwheel, turning that into a hand spring, a foot spring, a single flip, and a double, high enough to make the judges catch their breath.

He came out of the double with Jack's arm almost in his face. Reaching frantically with both hands, he caught Daniels by the wrist, his momentum almost pulling Jack down through the skylight with him.

But Jack stayed up, and held on tight. Tequila swung back and forth on the arm, and then got his feet onto the ledge. He levered himself up onto the roof with a smile on his face.

"Nice catch," he told her.

"I think this arm is six inches longer now."

They moved quickly across the rooftop, over to the edge where a Dumpster waited below them.

"Try to land relaxed," Tequila said as they both stared down at the twelve foot jump. "Or else you'll break something."

"We don't want that. Any more Demerol?"

"That was the last of it."

Jack sat on the ledge. "Maybe I'll just stay here, wait quietly for death."

"It's easy. Watch."

He pushed off the edge of the building and floated down to the top of the Dumpster, barely making a sound when his feet hit the metal.

Jack knew she wouldn't float like that. She'd drop like a rock.

He looked up, motioned for her to jump.

"Shit," she said.

Oddly, she thought of her husband. Alan loved her, she knew. But it was a selfish love, about what he could get rather than what he could give. That made Jack defensive and selfish as well. Two people taking, neither of them giving.

It wasn't easy for a woman to rise up through the ranks in the CPD. She knew she spent too much time on the Job. And then, when her husband became resentful, she spent even more hours working rather than go home and fight with him.

But now, staring down at Tequila, she realized if she made half the effort at home that she made at work, maybe her marriage wouldn't be in trouble. Hell, she was jumping off of buildings for her job. Couldn't she come home early every once and a while for the man she loved?"

Jack promised that if she lived, she'd try harder at home.

She left the edge of the building and tried to relax as she fell, realizing in midair what a stupid piece of advice that was.

Jack hit like a sack of rocks, even with Tequila catching her.

"You didn't relax," Tequila said.

"I don't like you anymore."

They scooted off the Dumpster and dragged themselves down the alley. There were no Mafioso to be found. All of them had gone into the warehouse to look for Royce.

The alley let out onto Kedzie, and Tequila ran into the middle of the street to stop a cab. He and Jack got in.

"The nearest hospital," Jack said, flashing her badge at the terrified Hindu driver.

"Yes, ma'am, Misses Police Officer Lady. But please do not get blood on my spotless cab, or my owner with make me pay for it. Do me the honor of putting these pages from the Sunday edition of the Chicago Tribune under you."

The driver handed them the thick Sunday paper from the front seat, and Jack and Tequila spread out the sections and sat on them.

No longer worried about blood stains, the cabbie made good by depositing them at the Emergency Room entrance of Holy Trinity Hospital four minutes later. Tequila handed him a bloody hundred dollar bill, and the duo staggered through the automatic doors and had nurses rush at them from three sides.

Tequila staggered and fell face first to the floor. He was picked up and wheeled off on a gurney.

Jack was taken to surgery.

"I'm a cop," she told a nurse. "That man who came in with me. Make sure he doesn't run away."

Jack was put under and stitched up.

Tequila refused to be put under, got stitched up, and was out the door ten minutes after being given a room.

CHAPTER 34

It took almost a half an hour for Slake to calm down after discovering the missing money. He spent most of that half hour kicking, cutting, and stomping on the bodies of his so-called watch dogs. Finally, beaten and exhausted, he began the task of cleaning up.

Leaving town had occurred to Slake more than once during his rampage, but he didn't have anything to leave town with. The thing to do was to stick around and play it cool. If Tequila had left with the money, Marty had enough eyes throughout the world to find him eventually. If Tequila were still around, Marty would find him as well.

Slake just needed to stay alert and wait for his chance. He had to somehow get Tequila away from Marty without Marty knowing, find out where the money was, and kill Tequila before he could talk.

All wasn't totally lost, just a lot harder.

The next day was case and point for Slake. His objective was to stay close to the Tequila search, but Marty had sent him to go kill that idiot Terco in the hospital. Under police protection yet. It was a near impossible job, and Slake had to bite his tongue not to protest it.

But, if he pulled it off, he would be in Marty's good graces for a while, which would make him privy to all the goings on of the search.

Slake went to Rush-Presbyterian Hospital.

Through discreet observation and a few careful questions to the nursing staff, he found out Terco occupied room 324, bed two, and was guarded by two plainclothes policemen.

Slake tried to recall all the movies he'd seen which involved killing someone in a hospital. Maybe he could dress up as a doctor or an orderly, and give Terco a shot of something lethal. But that would only work while Terco was asleep, because Terco would recognize him. If Slake watched the nurses for a while, he could figure out their routine and slip something fatal into Terco's food or medication, but that would take too long. Slake wanted to be in and out, so he could get back to the search for Tequila.

So, he went with the distraction ploy.

Going into room 302, he found a lone patient lying in bed asleep. Making sure no one was looking, he shot the man four times in the chest and then ran out of the room, gun in pocket.

"A man's been shot!" he screamed. "He's been shot! The guy's getting away!"

As people rushed into the room, Slake stood aside and stepped into the background, passing himself off as a curious bystander.

As he'd expected, both of the cops guarding Terco had come running over, pushing through the forming crowd.

Slake slipped into Terco's room and had the knife to his throat before the big man could so much as utter a single word. He cut deep enough to guarantee death, and then plunged the knife once into Terco's heart just to make sure.

Then he was walking briskly down the hall and to the elevators, stepping into the first one that opened. It was going up, which suited Slake. By now the cops were checking the staircases and the elevators on the first floor anyway. They would expect for him to try to escape, not to go up.

Slake rode the lift to the sixth floor and walked down a series of meandering hallways until he was in the other wing of the hospital. There he took the stairs to the ground floor, where he walked straight to the car he'd parked next to this exit.

He was back at Marty's house fifteen minutes later, just in time to hear about Tequila and that dumb cop being trapped in the warehouse.

"I'm sending Royce in after them," Marty squealed like a school girl, rubbing his palms together.

Slake sat on Marty's couch and waited, occasionally eyeing the blood stain on the oriental carpet. Eventually curiosity got the better of him and he asked Marty about it.

"Leman tried to quit," the Maniac said.

They waited in silence for word from the warehouse. When it finally came, Marty exploded.

"Dead? He can't be dead!" Martelli screamed into his phone.

"His head is gone, Marty."

"Where is it?"

"It's all over the place. One of the men slipped on it and busted his knee."

"So who got Tequila?"

"Tequila got away."

Slake hid his smirk as Marty hurled the cellular phone across the room, shattering it against the wall. The Maniac had to go to his Cadillac in the garage to get his car phone so he could call the men back. Slake tagged along, the seed of an idea germinating in his head.

"What happened to the cop?" Marty asked, barely containing the rage coursing through his veins like speed.

"She got away too."

"I have one more question."

"Yeah, Marty?"

"How do you guys take a shit with your thumbs up your asses?"

"You're the one who wanted to send Royce in alone, Marty."

"Who the hell are you to talk back to me, you cheap dimestore hood? Is this the kind of help Fonti is recruiting these days? When I talk to your boss

I'm going to have him bust your sorry ass down to diaper boy at the Great Oaks Nursing Home!"

"What would you like us to do next?"

"Find him, for chrissakes. Was the bastard at least wounded?"

"We think so."

"Then start checking hospitals. Every damn one in the area. If you guys don't find him, I swear I'll break every one of your goddamn knees!"

Fonti's man hung up. Marty couldn't quite believe it. Forty men had two men trapped, and the two men got away.

Even more unbelievable was what happened to Royce. Marty had been positive nothing could kill Royce short of a nuclear explosion. How the hell had Tequila and that dumb bitch cop managed that one?

It didn't matter now. All that mattered was getting Tequila.

Marty glanced over at Slake, who was staring at him with a smile as wide as a zebra's ass.

"What are you looking at?" Marty demanded.

Slake walked over to Marty and stood right in his face, almost nose to nose.

"A first class, pig-headed, asshole," Slake replied.

Marty's eyes widened with rage. "What did you say?"

"Marty!" Slake screamed as loud as he could, hoping it would carry into the house. "Don't do it!"

Then he pulled Marty's .38 from the Maniac's waistband and shot him in his ugly, gaping mouth.

Marty Martelli's last thought—hammering Slake in the face—flew out the back of his head with the rest of his brains. The spray coated Marty's new Cadillac, which would have pissed the shit out of the Maniac if he hadn't been already dead.

Even as Marty fell, Slake was kneeling over his former boss, pressing the gun into the Maniac's dead hand. Now Slake didn't have to worry about

Marty catching Tequila and finding out the truth. Now Slake didn't have to wait two months after recovering the money to go to Mexico. Now Slake would never have to listen to Marty's fat, ugly mouth ever again.

The guards came rushing in, pistols drawn.

Slake was kneeling next to the body, shock spread across his face.

"I tried to stop him," he said quietly. "I can't believe it."

"Hands in the air!" the first man yelled.

Slake raised up his hands and two men grabbed him, one of them removing Slake's 9mm from his holster. The man sniffed Slake's gun and shook his head. The gunpowder smell wasn't coming from there. He looked down at the pistol in Marty's hand, still smoking.

"What the hell happened?"

"Tequila got away. After Marty got off the phone he ate his gun. I can't fucking believe it."

"Anyone see it?" the man asked.

They all shook their heads. One of them spoke up and said he heard Slake yell for Marty to drop the gun.

"Ah, shit. Someone call Fonti," the man ordered. "Bring him in the house."

They took Slake into the living room and sat him on the couch next to Leman's blood stain. He remained there, guarded by armed men, until Fonti showed up forty minutes later.

Fonti was a short, hairy man in his early sixties. He had great bushy eyebrows and furry ears and a constant twelve o'clock shadow, even after just shaving. He was as ruthless as he was hairy, and he exuded control like only the most powerful men in the world could.

Fonti stared hard into Slake's eyes, boring into his brain and saying with his look that only the truth would do.

"What happened?" the loan shark asked.

By now every soldier in the county had shown up, and Marty's living room was filled with Fonti's men. They were all silent, eyes on Slake.

"Marty broke his first cellular phone because he was so angry Tequila got away, so we went to his car phone in the garage. He talks on the phone for about a minute, gets real angry, and hangs up again. Then he says, *I'm fucked.*"

"He told you you were fucked?"

"No, he said it about himself. Then he pulls his gun and shoves it in his mouth. I yell for him to drop it, but he pulls the trigger."

Fonti continued to stare at Slake, waiting for him to squirm or look away or give any other sign that he was lying.

Slake gave him blank, meeting the man's stare, thinking about killing Terco. That was the secret to lying well, saying bullshit and then thinking about something else entirely.

"You're lying," Fonti said flatly.

"You think I killed him?"

"The thought had crossed my mind."

Slake switched on a liberal dose of outrage.

"Marty was like a father to me!" he screamed, standing up. Five thugs rushed him, pinning him down, but Slake continued his tirade. "I loved him! I loved that man! I tried to stop it! I tried to stop him!"

Slake struggled and screamed, and was eventually forced back onto the sofa, a hand over his mouth. He radiated anger at Fonti, burning holes through him with his eyes for suggesting such a horrible thing.

"Cool it," Fonti said. "I believe you. It all checks out. Marty was losing it. He even killed one of his own men today. I was just checking to see if maybe Marty drew down on you, and you shot in self-defense."

Slake's rage intensified, but Fonti held out a placating hand.

"I know you didn't. We checked your gun. It had a full magazine, hadn't been fired. My men were there right after the gunshot, you couldn't have reloaded. And I highly doubt you got Marty's gun away from him and shot him yourself. The Maniac wouldn't have let that happen. Plus there's no point for you to kill Marty. Why would you do that? There wasn't any reason. He was your boss. He paid your bills."

Fonti motioned for his men to let Slake go. Slake shrugged his shoulders, still doing a slow burn.

"Look," Fonti said, "I admire loyalty like that in employees. Marty messed up big, couldn't deal with it, and he's gone now. We all respected him, and we mourn his passing. You call me in a few days, you can work for me from now on."

Fonti shook Slake's hand, palming his business card to him. Slake dropped most of the anger and let himself appear deflated. He took a long time reading Fonti's card, then put it into his pocket.

"Thanks," Slake said.

Fonti nodded and walked off.

Slake was a good actor, but it took every ounce of effort not to break into a huge, self-effacing grin.

He'd gotten away with it.

All that was left now was Tequila.

And Slake knew exactly how to prepare for him.

CHAPTER 35

Flying on painkillers. Tequila took a cab from the hospital to a gas station a mile away from Marty's house. He used the pay phone to call the Maniac's home number. Tequila had a plan. He'd tell Marty he was sick of running, and set up a meeting to give Marty the money back.

Of course, Tequila wasn't going to give the money back. He was going to buy a rifle and shoot Marty and his goons from three hundred yards away. There was a forest preserve in Elk Grove that he'd driven past which would be perfect for the set-up. He'd plan it for sometime tonight, so he had a chance to scout out the area and buy a rifle with a night scope.

But Marty didn't answer his phone, some unknown man did. When Tequila asked for Marty, the man demanded to know who was calling.

"Guido Fucking Lambini, you schmuck," said Tequila. Lambini was a well-known mafia figure from Detroit.

"I'm sorry, Mr. Lambini. I hate to be the one to tell you, but Marty's dead."

"Dead? Fucking how?"

"I don't know if you were aware of Marty's recent money trouble, but he took a big hit for a large sum, and he cracked."

"How did he fucking die?" Tequila demanded.

"He killed himself, Mr. Lambini. Shot himself in the head."

"I don't fucking believe it." Guido Lambini said *fucking* a lot.

"None of us do. It's a shock to us all. We'll be sure to let you know when the services are being held."

Tequila hung-up. Were they lying to him? Was the Maniac really dead? He didn't buy it. Marty wasn't the type to off himself.

But why would they lie? Did they know he wasn't Lambini?

Tequila dropped another thirty-five cents into the phone and dialed *Spill.*

"It's Slake," Tequila told the answering bartender. "Put Marty on."

"I thought you heard, Slake. Marty's dead. Blew his own brains out. We might not even open tonight."

Tequila replaced the receiver and walked into the gas station to get out of the cold. It was possible Marty had faked his own death, because he knew Tequila was coming for him.

But that was almost as implausible as Marty killing himself. The Maniac feared no man. He didn't run away. He didn't give up. And he certainly wasn't the type to blow his own brains out.

"You buyin' something?" the guy at the register asked.

Tequila bought two candy bars and ate one, thinking.

Perhaps Marty was dead after all, but not by suicide. Maybe someone killed him. Someone high up in the family. Someone who was mad that Marty lost all that money. Someone who didn't want to be known, thus the suicide story.

But isn't the point of mob revenge to be obvious, to make sure a message is sent?

Tequila decided it didn't matter. Who knew why the Outfit did certain things? If Marty was dead, he was dead.

So what was next?

With Marty out of the picture for the moment, the only two left on Tequila's hit list were Slake and Terco. Daniels had said Terco was in police custody, and Tequila didn't want to mess with that. Jack was right, let the bastard rot in prison.

But Slake...

The man who raped Sally. The man who started it all.

Hector Slake had a date with a body bag, and Tequila was going to chaperon.

He left the gas station and wandered the cold city streets until he found a tended parking lot.

The same trick worked just as well as it had yesterday.

After getting the keys to a black Corvette from the frightened parking lot attendant, Tequila set a course for the suburb of Palatine for the second time in two days.

He wouldn't be going back a third. This trip out, Slake was going to die.

And die bloody.

CHAPTER 36

When Jack Daniels arrived at Marty Martelli's house via Checker Cab, she hadn't expected to see that many people.

It was a beehive of activity, cars parked helter-skelter all over the lawn with a line of them waiting to get in. Something big was happening. Either there was a major meeting taking place, or someone important died.

The latter proved to be correct.

Jack passed up the house in favor of a phone at a nearby Dunkin Donuts. She called up the 7th Precinct and asked for either Detective Pierce or Rowan, the cops working on the Martelli case. She got connected to Pierce.

"We just got the word confirmed, Detective. Martelli is dead."

Jack's legs began to give out. She was too late. Tequila had murdered another man.

"How?" she asked.

"Seems like the guy ate his gun."

"That doesn't sound like the Maniac."

"Who gives a shit? Ding, dong, the witch is dead. Case closed. Rowan and I are going out and getting butt-drunk. Wanna come?"

Jack was moved by the gesture. Maybe they considered her one of the boys after all.

"Not tonight, raincheck me. Thanks, Pierce."

"No prob."

Daniels hung-up, puzzled. She was sure Tequila would go for Marty. But with Marty dead, where would Tequila go next?

Slake. He'd go for the guy who started it all.

Jack picked up the phone. She needed to get some cars over to Slake's place to stop Tequila. It was doubtful the mob had a hold over any law enforcement officers in Palatine.

After dialing 9 and 1 Daniels put the phone back down. If Tequila saw squad cars, he wouldn't make a move. If he didn't make a move, Jack wouldn't be able to find him. No Tequila, no way to nail the dirty cops.

Jack considered the risk. If she used Slake as bait, and Slake died, it was no big loss to humanity. Slake was a scumbag.

But killing Slake would be Murder One. Jack would have no choice. Everything else Tequila had done could be called self-defense. This was premeditated. She'd have to arrest him, and he'd do time.

Daniels had to stop him.

She went back to the Checker Cab, which was waiting for her in the parking lot.

"You know where Palatine is?" Jack asked the cabbie.

"Yes, ma'am."

"Move it. And don't worry about any traffic tickets."

"Yes, ma'am. Are you sure you don't want to grab any donuts while we're here, officer?"

Jack stared at the man.

"No problem, officer. I don't like donuts myself. Buckle up."

Daniels snapped on her seatbelt as the taxi squealed tires, pulling out into the street.

She hoped she was figuring Tequila correctly.

She hoped she wasn't making a mistake in not calling the cops.

Most of all, she hoped no more people were going to die.

On that last count, she was dead wrong.

CHAPTER 37

Slake had the guns in a footlocker under his bed. He had several other anti-personnel goodies as well, including grenades, two claymore mines, and a Russian made RPO-A single shot rocket infantry flame thrower which was capable of bringing down a wall. The footlocker also contained a pair of NVG-500 Starlight goggles, which allowed for a person to see in the dark, and a Kevlar bullet proof vest with side panels and a chest trauma plate. If Palatine was ever invaded by a hostile country, Slake would be able to hold them off for a while.

But a hostile country wasn't invading.

Tequila was.

Slake strapped on the vest and removed a Thompson sub-machine gun from his cache, complete with the fifty round pancake magazine. A Tommy gun, made famous by Chicago gangsters. That's the reason Slake had bought it in the first place, because he liked to look at himself holding it in front of a mirror, pretending to be Dillinger. Of course, being able to fire two-hundred rounds a minute was a reason as well.

He also took his tazer stun gun, his night vision goggles, and, what the hell, a grenade. Thusly equipped, he headed for the kitchen and opened the fuse box, hitting the circuit-breaker and turning out all the electricity in the house

Then the spider hid under the kitchen table and waited for the fly to come.

The trick was not to kill him. He had to shoot to wound, lest Tequila die without revealing the location of the money. It was a sticky proposition, because Tequila wasn't treating him with the same consideration.

His best chance was to clip him in the knees, and hopefully the little shit would faint from the pain. Slake had shot people in knees before, and they usually weren't conscious for more than a minute or two.

If he didn't faint, Slake could always sneak up on him in the dark and taze his ass. Then it was into the basement, for the pain game.

He'd just gotten a new book through a mail order company called *Interrogation Techniques of the South Vietnamese*. Slake was anxious to try out a few things on Tequila once he had him. It was possible, according to the book, to extract any and all information from the most stubborn prisoner by simply using a hammer and a well placed pair of pliers. Slake smiled in the darkness. He'd get the money all right, and he might just keep Tequila around for a week or two, for shits and grins. There were a lot of things in that book he wanted to try, more than he could use in the few hours it would take for Tequila to give up the cash.

He shivered, partly in delight and partly because it was becoming cold in his house. Slake had shut off the heat along with everything else. He thought about playing with the breaker, seeing which switch was attached to the thermostat, but decided to stay put.

And so he waited, his mind wandering over the events of the last few days. He'd planned to rob Marty for almost six months before the event, but never in his wildest fancy did he think things would turn out this way. Tequila getting away, and stealing the money. Leman and Matisse dead. Killing Terco, and then killing Marty himself.

Slake had often fantasized about murdering his boss, but his fantasies always took place in his basement, with Marty strapped to the chair and pleading for his life. Slake had enjoyed killing that insufferable asshole, but not as much as if he could have dragged it out a little.

Well, there would be plenty of people to quench Slake's need to hurt. In Mexico. And these would be beautiful, innocent children, not disgusting, ugly old men.

A tinkling of glass. Coming from down the hall.

Slake turned to look, his Starlight goggles illuminating the darkness with a greenish haze.

He waited, Thompson pointed at knee level, ready to cut down anything that showed itself in the hallway.

But nothing came.

More glass breaking. This time in the dining room. Slake swung the gun around in the opposite direction, wondering what the hell Tequila was doing.

Minutes passed, with nothing happening. Slake was beginning to hate this idea. Instead of feeling like a spider in a web, he was feeling like a rat in a trap. And because he could see everything so clearly, he had the absurd notion that Tequila could see as well. Slake felt exposed, out in plain sight, without room to move quickly if he needed to.

A window broke in the garage, and Slake started to sweat despite the temperature. Where the hell was Tequila? Why didn't he show himself? What kind of game was he playing?

Silence again. The sweat crawled down Slake's back like a prickly grasshopper. Slake looked left, then right, then left again, chewing his lower lip, hands beginning to shake.

Time slowly ticked away, falling into the past like feathers being dropped from a cliff. Every second lasted a dozen heartbeats, every minute a hundred breaths.

Then the window above the kitchen sink shattered, showering the linoleum floor with glass.

Slake couldn't help himself. The anticipation had been too much. He fired twice in the direction of the breaking glass, cursing himself as he did. What if he'd killed Tequila? What if Tequila was lying out on the backyard lawn, bleeding to death?

He held his breath, listening, caught between going to check and staying put.

There was a groan.

Slake wasn't sure he'd heard it, wasn't sure it was simply his imagination, or some sound caused by the wind.

Another groan. Soft, but definitely a groan.

Slake's fear had been realized. He'd shot the little bastard and there was a good chance he was dying.

He had to go check.

Moving cautiously, Slake got out from under the kitchen table and crawled over to the door leading into the garage. Carefully, so carefully, he opened the door in a crouching position, gun aimed at knee level.

The garage was empty.

He went in low, seeing that the door leading into the backyard had its upper pane broken. Slake was tempted to peer through it outside, but that would simply frame his head as an easy target. He gripped the knob tight and took a breath.

Then he swung it open and ran out fast...

...tripping over Tequila and falling flat onto his face.

Tequila was on him in a heartbeat, knee in the small of his back, gun to Slake's exposed neck.

"Hi there, asshole," Tequila whispered.

"Fuck you, Tequila," Slake mumbled into the frozen ground.

"No Slake, that's where you're wrong. Fuck you."

Tequila hit him in the temple with the butt of his gun, knocking Slake out. Then he dragged him back into the house by his feet.

Slake would die, but not by a gunshot to the head. That wasn't fitting for the man who raped his sister.

The punishment had to fit the crime.

Tequila   got   to   work.

CHAPTER 38

Tequila found the circuit breaker in the kitchen, and after switching the power back on he went to Slake's bedroom and took some rope out of one of his drawers.

When Slake was suitably trussed up in the living room, expertly bound to a kitchen chair, Tequila poured lighter fluid in the man's lap and lit a match. Like most sadists, Slake was terrified of pain, and no pain matched the pain of being burned.

"You're going to speak into the mike and answer my questions," Tequila said, pointing to the microphone on Slake's computer. "Or I'm going to light your little dick up like a candle. Got it?"

Slake nodded, staring at the flickering match with eyes as big as golf balls.

Tequila selected the Record option on Slake's *Voice Generator* Program, and the computer took down everything the two men said. When Tequila was finished, he hit *Pause* and gave Slake a piece of paper to read. Unpausing, he asked, "So where is the money you stole?"

"In a safe deposit box," Slake read. "Only I can get it out. You have to keep me alive, if you want the money."

"I don't want the money," Tequila answered. "It's Outfit money. I'm going to let them take care of you. I'm sure they'll be more persuasive than I am."

Tequila paused the recording again. Slake's entire confession was on the floppy disk, including his admission to killing Marty. There was only one thing left to do, and with some simple direction from Slake, Tequila figured it out without difficulty.

Tequila played what he'd just synthesized, adding it on to the tail end of what he'd recorded.

"You bastard Tequila!" Slake's computerized voice came from the speaker. It sounded exactly like his real voice. "I'll kill you! I swear I'll... uhhh... uhhhggg."

Synthesized Slake began to pant and gurgle, and then he let out one last, droning breath and was silent.

Tequila ended the recording and then played it back, to make sure everything was saved.

Not only was it saved, but it was seamless. The real Slake and the digitized Slake sounded exactly the same.

"No one even knew you had a heart condition," Tequila said. "But here we are, listening to you have a fatal heart attack. It's a shame, because now you'll never be able to tell us where the money is hidden. How could I have known?"

"You lousy shit."

Tequila took the Demerol syringe from his pocket. He drew back the plunger, sucking in air.

"I hear an embolism is one of the worst ways to die, Slake. Painful as hell. I'm going to inject ten cubic centimeters of air into your vein. That will cause your blood to foam. Your heart isn't equipped for pumping foam—it can only pump fluid. So the air in your veins will cause your heart to skip, and then eventually fail."

Tequila got close to Slake, pressing his face next to the man who had ripped his life apart.

"I want you to do my one favor, Slake. I want you to scream while it's happening. I want you to scream as loud as my sister screamed when you were raping her. Do that for me."

Tequila hadn't needed to ask. As he brought the syringe to Slake's arm, the man began to wail like a fog horn.

"Hold it, Tequila!"

Tequila spun around, a .45 appearing in his hand.

Standing there in the hallway, her .38 Detective Special pointed unwaveringly at Tequila's chest, was Jack Daniels.

"Drop the gun. The syringe too."

Tequila did neither.

"Sorry, Jack. No can do."

Slake looked over at Jack, his eyes pleading for help.

"He's scum, Tequila. Not worth going to jail for. Let's put him away, in a cell with some hardcore bodybuilding lifer who will do to him what he did to Sally."

Tequila shook his head.

"He set me up, raped my sister, and caused her death. Plus he's killed others. China. My doorman and his wife. He has to die, Jack."

"In cold blood?"

"That's the only way a reptile can die."

Tequila holstered his .45 and turned back to face Slake. Slake howled, his entire body shaking the chair in spasms.

"Do something!" Slake yelled. "You're a cop!"

"Drop it!" Jack screamed. "I swear, I'll shoot you, Tequila!"

"Sorry, Jack. We all have to do what we have to do."

Tequila jammed the needle into Slake's arm.

Jack fired.

The bullet sailed over Tequila's head and buried itself into a wall. A warning.

Tequila didn't flinch.

Jack didn't have a clear shot at Tequila's legs with Slake in the way, and she didn't want to try a body shot because it might kill him. The only option was overpower him. Daniels burst into a sprint and dove at the small man, aiming high.

She caught him in a clothesline across the neck and they tumbled to the floor. Jack wound up on top and hit Tequila with a serious right cross.

Tequila's head reeled back from the punch, but he was able to get a leg up onto Jack's chest and kick her off. The cop suddenly found herself airborne for the second time that day, and she pin-wheeled her arms to try and get her feet under her. As luck would have it, Jack landed ass-first on the living room couch, bouncing back to her feet.

Tequila assumed a fighting stance, feet a shoulder-width apart and hands clenched to hit. But his face was peaceful. He felt no anger towards Jack, and didn't want to hurt her. But Slake had to die, and Tequila wasn't about to be stopped by Daniels or anyone else.

Jack clenched her fists as well, feeling weak, sick, and wondering why she was bothering to try and save a dickhead like Slake anyway. Slake was no better than Royce, and Jack had no problem killing Royce.

In self-defense.

This wasn't self-defense. It was execution. Jack had to try and stop it. It was her job.

Tequila advanced, pivoting on his hips and whipping around his right leg, sending a reverse kick at Jack's shoulder.

Daniels wasn't a stranger to the fighting arts. Raising up an arm to block a kick was a natural motion for Jack. So was stepping into the kicker and swinging at his unprotected body.

The block surprised Tequila, but even more of a shock was the pop Daniels delivered to his ribs. Tequila staggered back, hurt by the blow, and Jack followed up the punch with an opened handed slap across the face that spun Tequila to the ground.

Daniels moved on him, taking out her handcuffs. Her shoulder began to ache—the anesthetic was wearing off.

Tequila decided that enough was enough. He kipped-up to his feet, kicked the cuffs out of Jack's hand, and whipped his foot around again and smacked her across the face. Jack twirled, and Tequila twirled, and after they'd both made a complete turn around and were facing each other once again, Tequila repeated the kick.

The Homicide Detective went down.

Tequila moved on Slake, intending to press down the plunger on the syringe, which was sticking straight out of Slake's shoulder like a dart.

Daniels was as dizzy as she was hurt, but she opened her eyes to the spinning room and took Terco's .38 from her belt, her own gun having been lost in the scuffle.

Squeezing one eye shut, Jack fired twice at the space between Tequila and Slake, trying to scare the gymnast off.

Tequila didn't scare. Jack was going to have to shoot him.

"Help me!" Slake cried.

Jack took aim on Tequila's right leg, hoping the wound wouldn't kill from this close a range.

Slake tried to scoot away from Tequila's advancing form. He rocked back on the chair, pushing with his toes, becoming frantic.

Tequila was two steps away when Slake, with energy brought about by sheer terror, tipped his chair over on its side.

The side with the syringe in his arm.

He balanced there for a moment on two chair legs, realizing what was happening, eyes wide and seeking some other reality.

Then he went over, landing hard on his shoulder, an entire syringe full of air being forced into his veins before the needle snapped off from his falling weight.

Jack held her fire.

Tequila looked down on Slake as the man began to convulse. The shaking became so palsied that he twisted out of his ropes, his arms flailing around like unheld fire houses, flapping through the air at invisible bugs.

He screamed a lot.

Tequila and Jack watched as the convulsions became faster and faster until Slake's body went rigid with one spastic jerk, breaking off the back on the wooden chair.

Then he was still.

Tequila went over to the computer and popped out the disk. He put it in his pocket.

Jack felt for a pulse on Slake that she knew wasn't there. She turned to Tequila, her gun raised.

"Tequila Abernathy, you're under arrest. You have the right to remain silent. Anything you say—hold it!"

Tequila walked past Jack and into the kitchen. Daniels grabbed the short man by the shoulder and spun him around.

"I've got to take you in," Jack said.

"Later. I've got one thing left to do."

"You killed a man in front of me. I can't cover that up. You're under arrest."

"You said that already."

Tequila broke Jack's grip and walked through the kitchen, over to the garage.

"Freeze!" Jack yelled. "Hands in the air, turn around, now! "

Tequila froze, but didn't turn around.

"You were right," Tequila said.

"Turn around!"

Tequila turned, his face wet with tears.

"About the hurt," Tequila whispered. "You were right. It didn't go away. Slake's dead, but it didn't go away."

Tequila smiled sadly, a short, broken, bleeding man, looking more alone than anyone Jack had ever seen.

"And now there's nothing left."

"Hands on your head!" Jack commanded.

Tequila shook his head slowly and drew one of his .45s, pointing it at Daniels.

"I'm going to count to three," Tequila said. "When I reach three, I'm going to shoot you. Shoot me first, Jack."

"Tequila, don't..."

"One..."

"Tequila, don't make me..."

"Two..."

"Tequila!"

"Three!"

CHAPTER 39

The videotape of the robbery, the gun barrels from the Dumpster, the computer disk, and the severed hand of Slake's partner, all went into a cardboard box.

Then came the phone call.

"Put Fonti on."

"Who shall I say is calling?"

"Tequila."

"Hold on a minute."

Tequila sat on Marty's desk, waiting.

"A lot of people are looking for you," Fonti's low voice came on the line.

"I know. I want that to stop."

"Are you giving yourself up?"

"No. Because I didn't do it. A man in Marty's employ named Hector Slake did the honors."

"He did, did he?"

"He set me up. Had a partner with a tattoo on his hand to match mine. Used a voice synthesizer program on his computer to give himself an alibi and send me off on a wild goose chase. Then he killed his partner and tried to grind him up to feed his dogs. I saved the guy's hand for you. I also saved the Voice Generator program, and I've got his entire confession recorded as well. Incidentally, he's the one who killed Marty. If that isn't enough to clear me, I'm also leaving you two .45s—mine, registered in my name, used to kill Billy Chico in the Binkowski Liquor Store the night I was supposed to be robbing Marty. You've got friends in the Department. Have Ballistics match the slugs at the scene with my guns. I couldn't have been robbing him while I was killing Chico."

"Assuming I believe you, where's Slake?"

"While I was getting his confession, he had some sort of heart attack. It's on the recording. When the cops find the body, an autopsy will back that up."

"Where's the money?"

"He died before he could tell me."

"So why are you bothering me, Tequila, if you can't bargain from a position of power?"

"I'm going to jail, Fonti. I know you can get to me in jail. I don't want you after me, because we aren't enemies. I didn't do anything, other than try to stay alive. I know you're a man of honor and respect, and you wouldn't kill a person loyal to the Outfit. I know your men look upon you as a fair boss, which is why I'm calling. Slake's dead, Marty's dead, the money is gone, it's over."

"It isn't over until I say it is."

"Which is why I'm leaving you all of this, in a box in Marty's office at *Spill*. To prove to you I'm telling the truth, and to prove to you it is over. You've even come out ahead in the game."

"How do you figure? You killed Royce. He was my best man. "

"Consider it a trade. Royce, for a lucrative bookmaking enterprise, already established. Plus a dance club to boot. Marty's gone, so they're yours now."

Tequila listened to the silence, knowing Fonti was thinking it over.

"Supposing everything you said is true," Fonti finally said, "all you want is my guarantee I won't try to kill you?"

"Yeah."

"Something isn't right here. I think that something is the stolen Super Bowl money."

"Forget the money, Fonti. Forget everything."

"That's sounds vaguely like a threat, Tequila."

"Look at it this way. I go to jail for a while, and when I get out I go work for you. Or you try to kill me, fail, and when I get out I wipe out you and your family."

"You're joking, threatening me."

"Joking, Fonti? Ask your golden boy Royce how much I'm joking."

Another stretch of silence. Tequila figured it could go either way. Might as well flip a coin.

"Fine," Fonti finally agreed. "If I look at everything and decide you're telling the truth, I'll leave you alone. But if you're lying, you're dead."

"I wouldn't expect any less," Tequila said, hanging up the phone.

Then he left Marty's office, left *Spill*, and took a cab over to the *Blues Note*.

Bones noticed his entrance and segued into *Dead Shrimp Blues*. Tequila walked up to him and dropped eight hundred dollars into the bowl on the ancient black man's piano.

He sat at his usual stool, staring at the stuffed catfish on the wall that looked like a boot.

"The usual?" The fat bartender asked him.

He shook his head. "I'm waiting for someone."

"Guy came by the other day, asking after you. Big guy, muscles. Me and Bones played stupid."

Probably Matisse or Terco. It didn't matter now.

"Thanks... what's your name?"

"LaLinda."

"Thanks, LaLinda. All these years I've been coming in, I never knew you had such a pretty name."

Tequila dug into his pocket and gave her all the cash he had left on him, almost a thousand dollars.

He didn't see LaLainda's eyes bug out, because he had turned to see Homicide Detective Jack Daniels walk into the bar.

Jack sat down next to Tequila while LaLinda ran to the phone to tell her husband of her recent windfall.

"You made good on your word," Daniels said. "You said you'd be here, and here you are."

"I always keep my word."

"Then why didn't you shoot me when you counted to three?"

"The same reason you didn't shoot me, I guess."

After that tense moment passed and neither killed the other, Tequila had walked into the garage and out the door. Jack followed, and Tequila told her he'd be at the *Blues Note* later that night, if Daniels wanted to arrest him.

And here they were.

"Technically, you never finished reading me my rights," Tequila said. "You'd better finish, or I'll get off on a Miranda violation."

Daniels didn't respond for almost a whole minute. When she finally did, her voice was pitched quietly.

"After you left Slake's, I got to thinking. I'm sworn to uphold the law. But sometimes the law, and justice, aren't the same thing. They should be. But they're not. And maybe that's not right."

Tequila blinked. "You're not arresting me."

"I don't even know you." Jack winked. "Besides, I'm on vacation."

"Have a pleasant vacation, Detective."

"I will. But I do have a favor to ask."

"Name it."

"When you have a chance, I would like to talk to you about those dirty cops."

Tequila dug into his pocket and pulled out a piece of paper. He handed it to Daniels.

"That's everyone I know of on Marty's payroll. I'm sure the Feds can figure out the rest."

Jack gave the list a quick glance, recognizing the names of an alderman, a captain, the assistant super, and several cops she knew. Herb wasn't on there, but she wasn't surprised. That guy was naturally honest.

She tucked the paper into her back pocket and followed Tequila's gaze. He was looking at something behind the bar.

"What the hell is that?" Jack asked.

"Catfish."

"It looks like a boot."

Tequila stared at it, memorizing every detail, because he knew he'd be seeing it for the last time.

Since he wasn't being arrested, Tequila decided to leave Chicago. After all, he had money to do whatever he wanted. And Tequila knew what he wanted.

He was going to buy a lighthouse, somewhere out on some ocean. The only catfish he'd see were the ones he caught to eat. No more Outfit. No more killing. Just endless days of staring out over the infinite sea, like he did when he was young.

"This is yours."

Jack handed Tequila the paper shopping bag she'd brought in with her. Tequila opened it and saw pictures.

All the pictures Sally had made for him, dating back to when they were children.

"Thanks," Tequila said, feeling a knot in his throat.

"Say, what does a girl have to do to get a drink in this place?" Daniels asked. "I've been sitting here so long my ass is flat."

Tequila signaled to LaLinda on the phone, and she came running over.

"Yes sir, the usual?"

Tequila shook his head. "Not today, LaLinda. Give me two fingers of whiskey."

"Yes sir, and this is on me. Any preference today?"

"Jack Daniels," Tequila said. "Straight up."

"And for you, Miss?"

Jack was feeling pretty good, about herself, and the state of the world in general. And she still had another eight days vacation coming. Hell, she might even be able to work things out with her husband.

"I don't have a choice," said Homicide Detective Jack Daniels. She turned to Tequila and grinned. He grinned back, knowing what was coming.

"I'll have a shot of tequila."

BIO

J.A. Konrath is the author of seven novels in the Jack Daniels series, along with dozens of short stories. The eighth, STIRRED, will be available in 2011.

Under the name Jack Kilborn, he wrote the horror novels AFRAID, ENDURANCE, TRAPPED, SERIAL UNCUT (written with Blake Crouch) and DRACULAS (written with Blake Crouch, Jeff Strand, and F. Paul Wilson.)

Under the name Joe Kimball, he wrote two novels in the TIMECASTER sci-fi series which feature Jack Daniels's grandson as the hero, and Harry McGlade III.

Visit Joe at www.JAKonrath.com.

BIBLIOGRAPHY

The Jack Daniels Novels

Shot of Tequila
Whiskey Sour
Bloody Mary
Rusty Nail
Dirty Martini
Fuzzy Navel
Cherry Bomb
Shaken
Stirred

In the Jack Daniels Universe

Jack Daniels Stories (Collected Stories)
Truck Stop
Suckers by JA Konrath and Jeff Strand
Planter's Punch by JA Konrath and Tom Schreck
Serial Uncut by Blake Crouch and JA Konrath
Floaters by JA Konrath and Henry Perez
Killers Uncut by Blake Crouch and JA Konrath
Banana Hammock - A Harry McGlade Adventure

As Jack Kilborn

Afraid
Trapped
Endurance
Draculas by J.A. Konrath, Blake Crouch, Jeff Strand, and F. Paul Wilson
Horror Stories (Collected Stories)

Other Work

Origin
The List
Disturb
55 Proof (Short Story Omnibus)
Crime Stories (Collected Stories)
Dumb Jokes & Vulgar Poems

As Joe Kimball

Timecaster
Timecaster Supersymmetry

Made in the USA
Lexington, KY
15 July 2012